BLUEBIRD

MICHAEL SMITH

ANAPHORA LITERARY PRESS

QUANAH, TEXAS

ANAPHORA LITERARY PRESS
1108 W 3rd Street
Quanah, TX 79252
https://anaphoraliterary.com

Book design by Anna Faktorovich, Ph.D.

Printed in the United States of America, United Kingdom and in Australia on acid-free paper.

Edited by Kristen Cole

Published in 2018 by Anaphora Literary Press

Bluebird
Michael Smith—1st edition.

Library of Congress Control Number: 2018907159

Library Cataloging Information
Smith, Michael, 1971-, author.
    Bluebird / Michael Smith
    190 p. ; 9 in.
    ISBN 978-1-68114-445-0 (softcover : alk. paper)
    ISBN 978-1-68114-446-7 (hardcover : alk. paper)
    ISBN 978-1-68114-447-4 (e-book)
1. Fiction—Literary. 2. Fiction—Psychological.
3. Family & Relationships—Death, Grief, Bereavement.
PN3311-3503: Literature: Prose fiction
813: American fiction in English

BLUEBIRD

Michael Smith

CHAPTER ONE
A SHIFT

[AUGUST 14, 2015]

Henry Dunstan squatted and touched his hand to the boulder at his feet. The stone was dusty and warm and silvery in color. He lifted it, stood up, carried it in his arms some hundred yards, and dropped it upon a pile of boulders that together formed a wall, not yet complete. He turned, walked back up the slight incline to the field of boulders, knelt, and rested his hand upon another boulder. He imagined himself as the rock. Solid. Unmovable. Insentient.

He fell asleep squatting there. When he awoke, the sky was getting dark and it was time for him to get back to town. He looked over his property. Light brown hillocks rolling down into dry prairie dotted with a few trees and bushes here and there. There, dead center in the middle of his land, was his workshop. His heart swelled to look upon it. It existed only for him. He had finished building the interior of the workshop just four months ago. To add to the sense of sanctuary provided by the structure, Henry had begun building a wall of rocks around the perimeter of his land. This wall consisted of boulders piled upon each other by hand, to which he had added today.

His descent by motorcycle to home in Bluebird took ten minutes. The dirt road, suitable for motorcycles and four-wheel drive trucks, was surrounded by fields of alfalfa and corn once he drew closer to town. Once in Bluebird itself, there were a few people still about town or in their yards. Henry did not nod or give a peace sign to these, nor did they greet him, but they all paused to regard him in a way that suggested they had taken his measure.

Home was a two-story, white, Victorian build, set back on a large lot some thirty yards off the gravel road that made up the eastern edge of Bluebird. The surrounding properties were a mixture of weeds and farmland. A long highway drive east of Bluebird was Belleflower, a larger town with a high school; further still was St. Louis, Henry's birthplace.

The light that emanated from the many windows of his home did not provide Henry any particular comfort, but rather seemed to demand something from him. He stationed his motorcycle next to the shed just west of the house. In the shed, he washed his face, hands, and arms in a utility sink. He removed from the back pocket of his jeans a small triangular piece of flint he had found near his workshop today. The flint was cut into a short, fat triangle, less than an inch in length, of a light salmon-purplish color, with two notches on the bottom so that the overall shape was that of a tiny, fat, Christmas tree. An arrowhead, likely Osage, Henry thought. He deposited the arrowhead into an empty coffee tin perched on one of the shed's many shelves. He exited the shed and walked a few paces east on the asphalt driveway and up a few steps onto the covered front porch of the home.

Music radiated from inside. Henry looked into the kitchen through the open porch window. His twelve-year-old daughter and her flute sat at the table. Fluttering euphonious air. Henry's chubby eight-year-old son, Charlie, was also at the kitchen table, flipping through a magazine. Henry's wife sat there between the two children with her eyes shut. Henry approached and tapped the window with a fingernail. His wife, his daughter, and his son looked outwards. Henry went in. He patted his daughter's hair, he patted his son on the back, and he placed his hand awkwardly on his wife Melissa's shoulder. Melissa shrugged Henry's hand away.

With his father seated at the table, Charlie hurried to the fridge and brought his father's dinner on a plate and then microwaved it so that it was steaming from the crease in the saran wrap when Charlie served his father. The meat was too hot, and Henry blew on it for a while. Henry and his wife watched their daughter, Ginny, play her flute until her concentration broke and she put her music away, then Henry took up his fork and knife and cut into the meat.

"How was work?" Henry's wife asked—her standard interrogation, Henry thought. She had not always called it work what he did up in the hills every day. The question hung in the air.

Henry stared vacantly at the thundercloud his wife had seemingly just formed, trying to understand its dimensions. Why did she ask him the same question day after day? How to tell his wife and children that he envied rock and marble for being inanimate? There was nothing he could say.

"How was work?" Melissa asked again. She looked at Henry expectantly.

The meat had cooled, and Henry took a bite. He chewed on it without apparent delight, as if the meat were a mouthful of putty. Charlie and Ginny stared at their hands for a while and then escaped upstairs to their rooms. Henry turned towards the television. He had not answered his wife's question.

Melissa stood now and slammed her hand on the table. Her wedding band on the metal tabletop provoked a metallic thunderclap. "Don't you ignore me. Starting tomorrow, things better goddamn change around here. Look at me!"

Henry continued staring at the television, which was off.

Melissa struck Henry across his face with her fist, jarring him from his trance and knocking spit from his lips. Henry stood now, his black-gray hair hanging in his face. He seized Melissa's wrists in one hand and slowly turned towards her. She desperately screamed at him and tried to pull away as he held her wrists together. "Talk to me! Please talk to me!" she begged.

Henry nodded as if in agreement and released her.

Melissa shook her arms to get her circulation moving. Her face looked ragged and wild.

They had acted out this same scene more or less, a couple three times per month over the past two years. Their disputes always ended with some type of violence and with Henry agreeing to he wasn't sure what.

Melissa retrieved a pot from the cupboard, filled it with water, placed it upon the stovetop, and turned on the gas. When the water boiled for sanitizing the dishes, she called the children down from their rooms. Henry exited out the front door, walked to the shed, and smashed his boot through a cardboard box full of containers of oil for his motorcycle. He took a flashlight from the shed and returned to the front porch. Through the window, Henry watched his family, and they could not see him whatsoever now because it was darker outside which he verified by doing a little dance to which no one reacted. Now Henry stepped down from the porch, turned on the flashlight, and walked several paces towards the southwest corner of the lot. He found the little cairn of limonite there in the corner of the yard that marked the place where the family had buried two years ago their little son and brother, Albert. Henry pulled up some weeds creeping up on the rocks and with his boot flattened a spider that had made it up to the part where the family had carved the letters *Our Cherub, H.A.D.* into one of the rocks making up the cairn.

***

Dawn was the best time of day for Melissa Mallory Dunstan. When she got herself ready first thing in the morning and straightened her short hair off to the side in a little wave, she thought she had to be one of the prettier women who had ever graced Bluebird. Melissa had grown up in Bluebird in the old bungalow where her folks still lived about a ten-minute walk southwest of home down the gravel road past the little bridge. The thought entered her mind today that she was the Homecoming Queen come home. Melissa had been a real Homecoming Queen in high school, and she wanted to become popular in Bluebird again. Of course, after her long absence from town, it would take some work to again become the center of attention. Especially with Henry acting like a child.

Sitting on the front porch chair now with her eyes shut and her coffee, Melissa recalled that morning a few years ago when she had learned that God really did answer prayers. That morning, three weeks to the day after her son Albert's death, she had felt a warm wind and looked up and asked, *God, does this wind have the power to change us?* and He answered *Yes* the next day and the next and the next. There had been, ever since, winds in the mornings in Bluebird.

By dawn Melissa would submit her anxieties to the waking sky, offering them out from her mind to a space there above the swaying dallisgrass like cloud strings where she'd name them and number them.

One: Henry is distant and cold. Albert's death has been hard on all of us. The rest of us are moving forward, but Henry is stuck.

Two: I lived with Henry in St. Louis for ten years. I did my best. Henry doesn't even try here.

Three: Do Ginny and Charlie like it here?

Four: How long can I hold on like this?

Then the familiar wind would creep up, mellow and true, and drive the anxieties away, and Melissa would stare into the new vacancy. A knot of gratitude would form in her throat, and she'd touch her knee to the front porch wood in prayer and vow to be better and stronger and to do more to reclaim her place in Bluebird.

Just let my children learn from me and my family as long as they can, Melissa prayed, *and no matter what befalls us, at least Ginny and Charlie will have my strength and that of my family members and this town around them.*

And like memories of heaven, her tranquility wore off trace by trace once the sun was full up, and there was nothing she could do about it.

Melissa went back inside to make sure Ginny and Charlie were on track to make the school bus on time. Once the kids boarded the bus, which stopped on the gravel road east of the house, Melissa made the short drive from home over to Campbell's Dry Goods on Main Street in Bluebird.

Joe Campbell was inside his store as usual. Melissa told Joe she wanted to purchase a compact printer. She thought to herself that it might help their marriage if Henry could do some writing in the hills. Henry hadn't written a word to her knowledge since arriving in Bluebird.

"Thought y'all already had one of these?" Big Joe asked as he leaned his hulking frame over to make entries in a yellowed ledger. Melissa had purchased a printer from Big Joe for home a while back. Big Joe had deep glassy eyes and a baritone voice. He chewed slowly on some licorice.

Melissa looked at him sideways, and Big Joe said, "I don't see too many of these printers go through here. What is there, four hundred of us now?" He looked at Melissa fixedly as if trying to figure out if she were playing a trick on him.

She nodded in agreement and then explained, "The other printer I bought a while back was for home. This one is for Henry's workshop."

Big Joe chuckled richly at the word "workshop."

"You heard me." Melissa met Big Joe's gaze. Melissa was tired of being spoken down to for Henry's behavior. Melissa had nothing to do with Henry's workshop. It was situated in the hills east and south of Bluebird—it was made of steel and glass, and as best as she could tell, was of one level. It had a doorway on the east side and vast western-facing windows, all-in-all a farcical creation, as Melissa had heard many locals say. From whichever direction one approached the Dunstan property in the hills, the workshop shimmered in the sun like a sharpened blade. And during the past couple of years, locals had seen trucks and workmen of all kinds, always from out of town, driving up to the hills and back, spitting up dust and noise as they wove through

Bluebird. Henry had told Melissa a few months ago that the workshop had been completed, inside and out. Perhaps he would now give her a tour. To Melissa's knowledge, no one in town but Henry had been inside. Melissa had heard townsfolk calling it the "Dunstan Hotel" or "Henry's Day Spa"; such pronouncements were typically accompanied by laughter.

Big Joe handed Melissa a receipt. "If Henry wants us to like him, he's got to pretend like he likes us first."

Melissa held up a hand. She told Joe she'd be back in a few days for her order.

Over at her folks' haphazard house not far north and west of Campbell's store, Melissa helped her mom clean up the house while Melissa's father napped. Melissa felt grateful that Henry had given her this—moving from his hometown of St. Louis to Bluebird with the kids so Melissa could be there for her parents in their infirmities and could pay for their medical interventions and such. Melissa's parents were still young—not even retirement age—but their incessant smoking had caused all sorts of health problems. On top of everything else, her mom had recently developed high blood pressure and had started taking a new investigational blood pressure medication called DuCorps, manufactured by Maddux Brothers. Melissa straightened things up and took out trash and put together a couple of simple meals. What Mom said she wanted was for Melissa to just sit there, but Melissa needed to move on to other errands.

Later that day when the kids got home after school, Melissa helped Charlie with his homework. By the time Charlie's assignments were done, Melissa needed to find out which friend's place Ginny had ended up at and get dinner going.

Once Melissa put dinner on the table, the kids knew not to await their father. It was late, and the children were hungry. Empty plates around the table. Finally, Melissa could relax. Ginny went upstairs and returned with her flute. Ginny was getting better and could just play her instrument; sometimes, it wasn't so much clumsy note after note. Ginny finished a number. Melissa and Charlie clapped. Ginny smiled timidly. Charlie, proud of himself for being finished with his homework, looked at pictures of the new Corvette in his father's sports car magazine. Melissa let her eyelids flutter and come to a stop, and she could hear her own breathing and was in that place when she was aware she was falling asleep but could no longer pull it back.

A tapping on the window stirred her, and Melissa, along with Ginny and Charlie, looked towards the porch in the direction of the sound and beheld the sketch of their tenebrous husband and father peering inside at them from beyond the glass veil.

CHAPTER TWO
ROAD

[AUGUST 20, 2015]

A few days later, Melissa tiptoed into the kitchen at home, holding a large box wrapped in navy blue paper with a bow on top. Henry was in the kitchen, standing near the dining table, looking out the window to the east. Standing behind Henry now, Melissa looked out the window, too. The tall grass in the field on the other side of the road would sit down or stand up depending on what the wind gusts were doing. The kitchen was more or less the original kitchen from 1910 with painted white cabinets, light green painted walls, and a wall fireplace that had been covered over decades ago. Red and white gingham curtains, a foot long, framed both the larger window facing east and the smaller window above the sink, facing south. The same style of curtain in a longer cut hung down below the kitchen sink to cover the utility area underneath. The oven and refrigerator were freestanding, and there was no dishwasher. Little hooks for coffee cups were screwed into the bottom of the white cabinets. Five mugs, each a different color, hung from the hooks.

Henry turned around and faced Melissa now. He looked at the wrapped box she was holding.

"Surprise," Melissa said, in a modest voice. She handed Henry the gift.

He put the gift on the kitchen table, unwrapped it, and opened the box inside, removing a computer printer. He looked at Melissa curiously.

Melissa explained, "For the expression of the ideas inside of you, like you used to do. Remember?"

"Yeah."

The idea of the printer had come to Melissa recently in response to her prayers. Several evenings ago, she had asked God to help her communicate better with Henry. That night, in bed, Melissa's mind had miraculously reordered itself to perceive that Henry still had a burning hot flame inside of him but that this fire didn't translate into spoken language. However, if Henry were to write again as he had done in St. Louis, Melissa could perhaps comprehend him as she had once comprehended him. Henry's interior world had always been difficult to discern, but Henry's writing had been, for Melissa, a window into that world.

While basking in the serenity that had been given her in response to her prayer, Melissa had recalled one of her first dates with Henry in St. Louis. He had taken her to dinner at Circus Lights, still the fanciest restaurant she'd ever been inside. After dessert, she had teased Henry to recite one of his poems.

Don't tell me you're the first English professor in the history of history who doesn't like to toot his own horn, she had joked.

He had relented and put down his drink and recited to her a poem called *I Answer My Prayer*. This moment at the restaurant had been important to their romance. Here was Henry: smart, privileged, and resolute, and he could, in Melissa's mind, rescue her from poverty, and in return, she was humble and hard-working and she could save him from arrogance. Together, they could make a powerful marriage that others would envy.

The computer printer was off-white in color and eighteen by eighteen inches wide and ten inches high. Henry looked at it like he was inspecting a show dog, turning it around and looking at the underneath and patting it to sense its heft. Henry tugged on the electric cord a few times and noticed it with was already loaded with paper and ink. His right eyelid raised. He seemed pleased.

"I bought a compact one. Easier to throw in your bag to take up to your workshop," Melissa offered.

Henry nodded. "Handy."

"Do you remember that poem *I Answer My Prayer*?" she asked somewhat suddenly. This had not been part of her plan to ask him this question, but she wanted to remember the words.

"Which one?" he murmured. He looked at his feet.

"The one you recited to me at that expensive restaurant where we ate the snails."

"Les Escargots?" he corrected her.

"Whatever. You remember it?"

"Of course."

"And?"

"You want me to recite it?"

"I'm asking you to." Years ago, they had decided as a couple to use the term *ask* or its variations when husband or wife really wanted something from the other.

"Very good," he said easily enough. Perhaps he had feigned his earlier reluctance, but had in fact wanted her to press him to recite the poem. He put the printer on the table and looked again out the window to the east so that Melissa now faced him at a ninety-degree angle.

Henry began speaking in a melancholy voice.

I asked God
to remove the tiger
who had kept me
in a dark alley
from the start.
Those seasons
he taunted me
and stripped away
my freedom
and my dignity.
But he was after all
a tiger and it was
not his fault.

All God said was:
*There is a knife
and there is a tiger.*

I found in the alleyway
under a mound of trash
a box cutter.
And a lost lifetime later
after many hesitations
I threw a canister of screws
wet with restaurant grease
burning flame at his sleeping body—
he howled devastatingly
and crawled towards me

to rise up on hind quarters
and in familiar prose he mocked:
You wouldn't hurt a blameless friend
who was born to a wild end.

Then I plunged the razor in
and then I plunged the razor in
and then I plunged the razor in
and unzipped a scarlet N
where his throat had been.

When he was done, he walked out of the kitchen quickly into the master bedroom, and returned to the kitchen with his backpack. He loaded the printer inside.

"What does it mean?" she asked.

He told her the poem meant that everyone is unaccompanied in this world. That whatever you seek—fairness or justice or love or comradery or food or a pair of shoes—you have to steal from another. That you have to use your power and that there's no sense in waiting for God or the law to provide for you.

Melissa thanked him. She felt stupid for being grateful, but this had been one of the longer conversations they had had in some time without getting into an argument. For that, she was indeed grateful. Regarding the poem itself, she recollected its meaning differently.

He told her he needed to head out.

The agreeable moment was over. Henry took his backpack and exited the house through the front door.

Then I plunged the razor in and unzipped a scarlet N where his throat had been, Melissa thought. The words of the poem were more violent than she had remembered them to be. Of course, Henry had from time to time said and written some extreme words in those days. He had even gotten in verbal fights with some of his colleagues. Then again, he had been an English professor at Washington University, and sometimes, to her way of thinking, professors in their academic fervor could say things they did not mean, or at least never intended to act upon.

Melissa heard Henry's motorcycle start and then a moment later he drove by the front window. When he would be home again was anyone's guess. He had never been a person to come home at a set time every evening. But in happier times, he would at least call to say what his plans were and would take Melissa to movies or shows or dinner on the weekends. Now he did not even carry a phone with him.

Melissa was blameworthy, too, she knew. They had both been cold to each other since Albert's death. Although she had, to be fair to herself, become more emotionally available the past six months. *Why couldn't Henry just do like the man in the poem and shake himself and face his tiger and come back to reality?*

***

Henry drove his Yamaha motorcycle north from home down the gravel road to the highway, where he turned west and then reached the two-pump Amoco shortly. While refueling, Henry overheard David Campbell, a car mechanic and identical twin of Big Joe Campbell, buying a chocolate bar and a pack of Marlboro Reds, talking with the gas station cashier about a water dispute. David Campbell's auto repair shop was adjacent to the Amoco.

"With all the water Maddux Brothers is stealing away, all the corn around here will be goddamn drier than a Mexican spider's web," David Campbell was saying as he blew out a breath of smoke. Henry had heard from Melissa that David Campbell liked to talk about Mexico on account of a prior Mexican lady he had dated.

"I can't say I'm surprised," the gas man replied. "Money is king. Heard they have a new blood pressure medication that will probably soon grow into a money tree for them. DeCorpse or something with a funny name."

"Dee-Corpse? What a name for a drug," Campbell laughed.

A wind gust touched down near the gas station door and blew the door open part way.

"Goddamn wind," said David Campbell.

"And a hot one," the gas man said.

David Campbell, who could have been called Big David had the name been more catchy, was to be sure less massive than his brother Big Joe, in relative terms, but otherwise they were much the same, at least to the exterior world. David Campbell's hands, like Joe's, were massive but were grimy from his auto repair work. Due to his own work with his hands, Henry had recently become more observant of how big men were, and how big of hands they had. Henry could tell from David's hands that David had moved a lot of tires and auto parts over his lifetime.

The Amoco featured the standard gas station fare of potato skins, corn dogs, French fries, and chicken fingers, each laid forth in its own shallow pan, the whole assembly covered by a heat lamp. Henry stood next to the chicken fingers, close to the conversation between David Campbell and the gas man. The two men seemed surprised at Henry's interest and each looked over at him once or twice to see if Henry was still listening. After a time, the two men, each more substantial yet than Henry Dunstan, opened up their circle to allow him room. Henry asked a few questions to learn more about the nature of the water dispute. The two men explained to Henry that the principal river on which the town of Bluebird was dependent had been depleted more than usual by commercial concerns upstream. Upstream near Calypso, Missouri, about twenty minutes northwest by car on a road that split off from the main highway to Belleflower, a pharmaceutical plant belonging to the Fortune 500 enterprise Maddux Brothers had increased its water usage to a point that was detrimental to the local farmers of Bluebird, who needed water for their corn and alfalfa crops. Almost all the families in Bluebird depended on the sale of corn or cattle as an important source of income, if not the primary source.

David Campbell put out his cigarette in an ashtray on the counter near the cash register. He joked to Henry and the gas man that he could hardly turn on the television without seeing an ad for one of the drugs being pumped by Maddux Brothers.

"Sore? Buy this. Tired? Buy that. Insufficient blood flow for your erection? Buy the other. Whatever your problem, they have a fix."

The gas man chuckled.

The gas man said he had heard from some of the local farmers earlier in the day that in order to deal with the water shortage caused by Maddux Brothers, the Bluebird farmers would have to irrigate their fields less frequently. This close in the season to the corn harvest the Bluebird farmers could probably get by, but if Maddux Brothers kept up their thievery, next summer would be another story.

David Campbell said that there was a rising interest among townsfolk in banding together to find a lawyer to take on Maddux Brothers.

Henry Dunstan was intrigued by the conversation between David Campbell and the gas man. In the months since the completion of his glass and steel workshop in the hills, Henry's mind had been churning. The thoughts coming into his attention were not new. In his academic writing at Washington University, Henry had argued that power (that is, violence) in all its forms, was the primary currency in human affairs, the lowest common denominator that explained all human behavior. But now each strand of thought shouted at Henry loudly and directly, like the clash of thunder—the ideas presented themselves to Henry not as possibilities or arguments, but as truths to be implemented in the real world—truths as hard and solid as the rocks Henry used to build his wall in the hills. The water dispute could be a test care for Henry to test his theory of power in the real world.

David Campbell returned to his repair shop next door. Henry Dunstan loitered while flipping through an automobile magazine, and heard more of the same talk between the gas man and other customers, who were also worried about the economic impact of the water shortage. After a while, Henry purchased some snacks, placed them in his backpack with his new printer, and rode off on his motorcycle.

Arriving in the hills of Bluebird, Henry dismounted and entered his workshop and deliberately laid out the materials from his backpack: computer printer, gloves, and snacks and drinks from the filling station. Henry studied again the interior of his workshop.

***

The project had started two-and-a-half years ago, a few weeks after Henry and Melissa had settled in Bluebird. Originally, the edifice in the hills was to have had a dark wood floor and white walls with built-in bookshelves, furnished with artwork, rugs, sofa, and an antique escritoire from a shop in St. Louis that Henry had visited several times over the years. An architect had drawn out the space to that end. Construction had begun. The full exterior and some sections of the interior had been completed. Once the workshop was complete, Henry planned to write a novel there. He had had some notion of writing a story about a Medieval aristocrat. An aristocrat who, facing his own mortality, gives all his worldly possessions to an alchemist in exchange for a promise that the alchemist will turn him to gold.

Then, six months into construction of the workshop, Henry and Melissa's son Albert drowned in the irrigation ditch near their home. For a time thereafter, all construction on the workshop ceased. Henry was in agony. He barely left the house. The idea of writing a novel became foolish, impossible. Months passed.

When Henry was ready to continue construction of the workshop, he fired the original architect and hired a new one. He hired new craftpersons to completely gut and rebuild the interior of the workshop. Each new craftsperson who built out the interior, at Henry's insistence, worked in secrecy on only one small portion of the project, so that no one person who labored would see the completed project or know the identity of any other worker. At times, Henry even attached tarps to the ceiling to prevent a craftsperson from seeing beyond his assigned work space. And Henry required the architect to return to Henry all plans and blueprints when the project was completed. These Henry burned in a small fire outside the workshop. The interior of the workshop was a private matter for Henry and Henry alone.

***

Inside the workshop now, there was no desk or sofa or rug or artwork or television or even a bathroom anymore. The workshop interior was a large, single, dark, oval room. The floor and walls of the room were made of marble. Each of the two longer sides of the room contained a fireplace, also made of marble. The marble throughout the space was negro marquina, black with streaks of white throughout. The west end of the room was all glass. In the center of the room was a large altar, also made of marble. In one corner of the room, Henry kept a laptop with a wi-fi connection. All in all, as Henry looked around the interior of the workshop, he could not find any fault with it. He rubbed his finger across the marble surfaces. They were smooth and without blemish.

To the exterior Henry Dunstan now turned. Circumscribing the workshop lay the beginnings of a boundary of rocks Henry had been building for several months. Henry's vision was to build the wall alone, by hand, stone by stone. He had made significant progress to this end. On the eastern portion of the wall was an open slot for Henry to access his workshop. At some later date, he would build a secure gate into this opening. The rock wall had not been part of the original vision for the property, but he had decided upon it as a source of additional physical and spiritual security. Henry cherished the tangible permanence of the wall. He found a kinship in the boulders, and he considered the world from their point of view. The rocks emanated implacability and serenity simultaneously. They wanted nothing, they needed nothing, they demanded nothing, but if a person happened to cut himself and bleed to death in front of a heap of rocks they would do nothing to help.

As he studied the wall, Henry thought of the local farmers, their water, and the drug company. The farmers had little money or leverage of any kind compared to the drug company. He put the case to his wall. *What would you do, if you were human, and someone stole your water? Would you start a lawsuit? Would you petition your elected representatives? Would you write letters of protest?*

Henry leaned close to the wall to hear what it had to say. It spoke to him.

The sturdy rock wall, in its current unfinished state, reached the height of Henry's chest and extended at its base one-and-one-half times the length of his body lying down. He had located limestone, quartz, and rhyolite deposits along the foothills nearby in every direction. He would collect one or two large stones, carry them to his wall, deposit them, return, and repeat. From time to time while working, Henry would find pieces of flint buried in the earth. In a coffee tin in the shed at home, he had a collection of a handful of arrowheads and a spear point and short knife. These ancient flint tools told Henry that he was the not first person who had spent time on the land.

The stones making up the wall were implacable but not devoid of personality. On a segment on the interior side of the rock wall, for instance, southwest of the workshop and obscured behind a clump of brush, was a combination of stacked stones colored with gray and brown and pink and orange washes that came together, as if intentionally, to depict a tall water bird in the act of juggling or fanning or attempting to extinguish flames. Henry pissed on it from time to time to suffocate, as it were, the pretend blaze. He called it the Flamingo Fire.

***

The momentary freedom Melissa enjoyed after shuffling Ginny and Charlie out the door and onto the school bus the next morning each bathed, rested, combed, clothed, fed, shouted at, and homeworked was interrupted by the loud arrival of her brother's green pick-up with a spraypainted royal blue Camaro trailing about fifty feet behind. Her brother Pastor Darren jumped out of the truck and waved at Melissa through the front window. Darren had a large belly and bowed legs so that he looked to be in a perpetual half squat. Pastor Darren led the local First Baptist congregation, the town's sole organized faith. Melissa went out onto the front porch. Darren wielded a paper in his hand and Melissa's sister-in-law Sabrina lagged a few steps behind before being crowded out by David Campbell who had exited his Camaro and caught up with the couple.

"Look here Melissa," her brother Darren said. "Sabrina brought this home from the post office this morning. Where's Henry?" Darren sounded more concerned than mad. He held the paper with two hands. The words BLUEBIRD SOUNDER were printed along the top.

"Where do you think?" Melissa had told Darren a dozen times about how Henry was always in the hills these days. Melissa scanned over the paper Darren was holding. She assumed it was the product of the new printer she had just given Henry. She was pleased Henry had put the printer to use already.

"I got one, too. There was a whole stack at the post office. Henry wrote this baloney," coughed David Campbell, blowing out a breath of smoke and waving a hand in front of his face. "Henry played me for a fool. Acted innocent over at the Amoco while gatherin' infomation for to stab me with later. He says farmers ain't got rights. I'd like a word."

"Would you let her read it for heaven's sakes?" squeaked Melissa's sister-in-law in an authoritarian voice. Sabrina was much taller than her husband Darren, with red corkscrew hair on her bird head. When she talked her head seemed to bounce. Melissa would just as soon fight an angry ostrich as Sabrina. If Darren was the compassion and brains of the local church, Sabrina was its brawn and its judgment.

Melissa read the paper:

BLUEBIRD SOUNDER
Newsletter of Historic Bluebird

WATER RIGHTS ISSUE

Point

Bluebird citizens are anxious about depletion of water supply due to increased upstream usage by Maddux Brothers, manufacturer of DuCorps 200 mg tablets for blood pressure and other medications. Citizens call for their so-called Property Rights to be protected from encroachment by Maddux Brothers and for the law to support their need for water for farming.

Counterpoint

Property belongs to no one but itself. You may hold it or borrow it, but it was never yours; you have no Right to it anymore than it has a Right to you. To own Property is not to merit Property; to own Property is to have stolen Property.

There are no Rights, there is only Power. Without Power a Right is a Want. If you want Water, steal it with your Power, it belongs to no one.

"Henry did this?" Melissa asked beleagueredly. She looked towards the hills. This newsletter was not at all the type of thing she had wanted him to use the printer for. *Why couldn't he just try to fit in? Just wake up and act like a goddamn normal person.*

"Property belongs to no one?" Campbell said, irritated. "It's pretty clear that river contains Bluebird water, not water for some rich drug company."

The newsletter was just one sheet with a few short pieces printed on both sides. It was formatted nicely and had an attractive font. David Campbell jabbed at the paper with his cigarette stuffed between dirty crooked fingers, but Melissa slapped his hand away and waited for an answer to her question.

"Looks like it is Henry's work," Melissa's sister-in-law finally said. "See he printed his name there on the back and called himself editor-in-chief." Melissa recalled that Henry had come home quite late last night. He must have stayed up at his workshop writing the articles.

"I'll talk to him," Melissa said protectively, not of her husband but of herself. "I said, I'll talk to him," she said louder, and she backed her visitors off the porch with a glare and slammed the door against the wind. She didn't know why everyone had to bring their complaints about Henry to her.

Throughout that morning, Melissa received additional visitors from across town, each referring to the newsletter they had picked up at the post office and demanding action as if Henry were a child she could control. The townspeople were upset that Henry talked down to them, many of them pointing out to Melissa that he stayed up in the hills in his workshop and then descended with the newsletter as if he thought he was a Moses or something coming down with the Ten Commandments. Melissa was determined to berate Henry for embarrassing her and putting her in the middle of his dispute with the people in town. True, she did like being in the middle of a problem, but only when that problem belonged to someone else and she was the one giving the advice.

As she considered how to counterbalance the negative impact of Henry's newsletter, Melissa felt a heavy and invisible machinery moving inside of her. Gears spun inside her brain, waiting for her to make a change so that the gears could work instead of spin. Two years ago, in response to Albert's death, Melissa had forsaken a peculiar type of vanity that had contributed to the tragedy. But now Melissa felt a need for immediate action to repair her family's image in Bluebird. She began to reason that doing something, however precarious, was better than doing nothing. As Melissa grew closer to abandoning her weighty promise of two years ago, she felt herself falling and falling and falling and did not realize she had not yet acted on her renunciation, but having felt the thrill and peril of her decision, she presumed she had already jumped. Melissa paced about the house restlessly, her skin tingling and her heart racing, trying to rid the thoughts from her head about what she had already decided, but she could not or would not undecide it. So it was settled then that she had changed courses and hopefully calamity would not strike her family a second time.

Just after the stock market's close in the afternoon, Melissa turned off her desktop computer in the master bedroom, took a pill to settle her mind, left a note for her kids in the kitchen, then drove from home to Main Street in Bluebird. There, she found the base of the double track road off of Main that led up to where the workshop was located. She parked the car and hurried the rest of the way by foot to confront her husband. The road was framed by corn, alfalfa, brush, and tall grass, and the wind gusted and blew cedar-colored dirt onto her clothing and into her eyes. This path Melissa knew well from when she and her brother had taken excursions from town in their youth, and if given enough time, she could probably find more Indian flint here, or identify the cave near where they had regrettably found and tormented and killed a porcupine. She remembered asking her parents where all the people were who had made the tools out of flint. She could not recall what her parents had told her in response.

When Melissa arrived in the hills, she was beaded in perspiration and had dust in her eyes. She prepared her lines and approached the workshop's door through the opening in the boulder wall to the east. Henry met Melissa just outside the door. He had a calm look on his face that turned sour as soon as he saw Melissa. Melissa assumed this change was because her own expression was one of anger.

"Inside," she demanded and didn't wait for an answer, taking several steps towards the door. She wanted to yell at him inside, even though the likelihood of anyone passing by outdoors was slim.

Henry danced out of Melissa's way, as if trying to read her purpose.

"It's finished inside, right? Open this damn door." She grabbed the handle and found it locked.

Henry moved further and further away from her. "No one goes inside but me. Not you. Not anyone. Some water?" he offered.

Henry and Melissa passed an interval with no words during which she pursued him and tried to grab his keys. She cursed at him. He found an escape and slipped back inside the workshop. He returned in a moment.

"Where's my water?"

Henry tossed her a bottle of water. Melissa caught it and dumped it across her forehead and wiped the back of her hand across her brow.

"Inside," she demanded again. She was furious that he had never let her inside. She suspected he was hiding something there.

"I'm right here, woman." Their communication was a zero sum game where the total number of decibels remained constant. The louder she spoke, the softer he replied.

"That workshop is half mine," she roared.

"We made rules when we moved back. You got something for you; I got something for me. You got to come back to your hometown and be with your family. I got the workshop."

"I'm changing the rules."

"Veto."

"Go to hell. If you have something going on in there, now is a good time. You know I will rip your head off if you got something going on in there that I need to know about."

Henry shot her a glance and said nothing. She hated when he responded to her threats with silence. Finally, she removed a paper from her bra. It was moist and dirty. She balled it up and threw a copy of the BLUEBIRD SOUNDER at him.

Her throw missed the target and Henry stepped on it so the wind wouldn't sweep it away. He unwrinkled the page confidently. "This is what we talked about," he explained in an agreeable tone. "You said you wanted me to talk to you. Well, something has clicked inside of me. The ideas are coming to me unhindered and stronger than ever. I won't hold back. I started a dialogue with the whole town! City boy talking to stupid folk. And BLUEBIRD SOUNDER, same name as the first newspaper from 1840."

"What's gotten into you? I didn't tell you to write a goddamn newspaper. Why would you talk to them?" Melissa was baffled by her husband's behavior.

He didn't say a word.

"Fine. It's better than nothing. At least you and I are talking at all. No one has rights? No one deserves water? You're going to piss everyone off."

Henry was now the one shouting. "These are the same ideas I've always had. But in St. Louis the ideas were printed in academic journals, and read by no one. Out here, I'm in the real world. I'm going to test out the ideas!"

"What ideas?"

"What I said in the paper. This world is all about power..."

"You picked a swell time to become a philosopher."

"These rocks around here give me confidence. The ideas are coming to me strong and dense."

"You are absurd. People need to raise corn to sell corn. They need that money for food and mortgages. And here comes Maddux Brothers and takes their water and these farmers are supposed to start a real war with the drug company? I think if they have rights, they should take them up peacefully in court. The judge will see it fairly."

"Look at that boulder there," Henry said, pointing to his wall. He walked closer to it and touched a limestone boulder. He waved to Melissa to come closer to the wall. She stayed put.

"Listen to what this rock says, Melissa. It says, *I am old. I was created by explosive heat, by the trembling of the earth itself. I was created when something else was ripped apart. I can only be moved by a greater force. Don't preach to me. If you want me to move, move me.*"

Melissa curled up her face. "That's gobbledygook." She wondered why they just couldn't have a normal conversation anymore.

"There it is," Henry replied with contempt. "I try to tell you and you won't listen. But maybe someone in Bluebird will."

She tried to reason with her husband. She told him he could not possibly be correct, that there were no human rights such as property, because if he were correct, then there were no protections. She said that if there were no protections, then what was to stop someone from throwing rocks through Henry's workshop windows, or tearing down his rock walls with a bulldozer. Further, she pointed out that his philosophy did not account for the need to protect the children, and that if someone were to hurt one of their children, he surely would call upon the law to intervene.

Henry looked straight at Melissa's chest, and he kept his eyes focused there for a while.

"Don't stare at my tits that way when I'm talking to you," she roared. When he looked away, she shoved him and caught him off balance. He fell to the ground.

He stood up and shouted into her face. "Go home."

Now Melissa roared like a banshee, perplexed and shaking and hysterical. Maybe if talking could not bridge the gap between herself and Henry, then screaming and yelling and stomping and trembling could. Maybe if she were hiking on rock, and she came to a huge chasm and boards and ropes were not long enough to span the two sides, maybe if she just yelled and yelled and yelled she could create enough force to close the gap? To propel herself across? Or was she screaming because she had fallen through?

There was quiet now and the surrounding hills were unmoved by her shrieks. Bush and rock and hill and grass and a solitary pine tree all staring back at her, with nothing to say. And Henry too, as still as nature, as he retreated from Melissa back to his work of building the rock wall. She had been talking to the wind.

CHAPTER THREE
SIN

[AUGUST 24, 2015]

"**W**hy do you go up there all day?" Ginny had a featherlight voice like her flute, and her whole persona was tender and lenient, and even at age twelve with the sassiness of school halls she was incapable of guile. The tone of her question suggested pure curiosity, as if she wondered who had invented the telephone.

Henry was driving Ginny over to Dickey's Diner, Bluebird's lone restaurant, located a few miles up the highway east towards Belleflower. Henry thought the time had come for a frank conversation with his daughter. He did not know exactly how the conversation would go, but as Ginny's father his most sacred duty was to reveal the truth inside of himself, even if that truth caused her pain, or separated him from her.

"You go to school every day, right?" Henry asked. Ginny nodded without thinking.

"And other folks go to work every day?" She thought a bit and agreed.

"That's what I do, too. I go to work." He liked to say that what he did in the hills was work.

"But you don't work up there," she declared.

"Sure I do."

"But it's different. Jasmine's mom works at the airport. Kayla's dad works at the post office, ya' know?"

"Because I don't get paid?"

"Kind of." She paused and added. "It's not really normal. You know, in a building, where other people are working. On TV you see a bunch of people in a meeting or having lunch together when they're at work. And then they come home. You don't work with anyone else."

"Everyone has to be somewhere. You kids are at school, Mom's at the house, airplane lady's at the airport, postman's at the post office, farmers on the farms, bankers at the banks, Pastor Darren's at church, babies are asleep, I'm up there. It's my place to go, a place I can't let anyone inside."

"Not even me?"

"I'm sorry. I made the whole workshop based on a vision—or an awake dream—I had a long time ago. It's a private place, only for me."

"You had an awake dream?"

"One of a place where I was safe."

"You're up there a lot."

"It's quiet. And now that the building is done, I feel more brave."

"No one can hurt you?"

"More like I don't care if someone tries to hurt me. More like maybe I am the one who will do the hurting, if needs be."

Ginny laughed. He could tell she didn't believe him.

They arrived at the diner, and Henry pulled into the gravel parking lot and parked the car. Henry and Ginny took a seat at a round metal table outside. The weather was perfect. No menus were needed. In fact, Henry wasn't sure if Dickey's even had menus. Both father and daughter ordered the burger, fries, and chocolate shake. The owner Dickey was inside shaking hands with customers. Dickey's body was shaped like a person who ran a diner and ate too much of his own food. Dickey had a balding head that he attempted to cover with hair from the sides of his head. Henry wondered how many boxes of beef patties Dickey had moved over the years, and how many tons of meat it would all add up to. Henry imagined a big wall of meat around the diner consisting of every hamburger patty Dickey had ever cooked.

Henry didn't know how many times he and Ginny had gone out to eat before just the two of them. Not as often lately, but before that it had been routine, especially back in St. Louis. Here at Dickey's, they could sit inside or outside, and outside they could see, past the blotch of sycamores, the highway. When a car went by, Henry would speculate where it was headed and for what purpose, and though he couldn't prove it he'd guess most of the cars were going from Lampersville, west of Bluebird, to Belleflower, east of Bluebird, for groceries. Henry had joked to his daughter a time or two when they had seen one of those old vans driving along the highway with the porthole windows that the van was carrying a load of stolen kangaroos. Ginny laughed a lot harder at his jokes than his wife Melissa did. Ginny for her part would say that the cars carried bowling balls or flyswatters or something equally strange.

One evening last summer Henry and Ginny had come here and sat at this same table watching the road and seen a flock of bluebirds descend down onto the highway as if there were bags of raisins and mealworms piled there by an unknown hand. And then a semi-tractor trailer had come into view going highway speed and the birds had reacted too late maybe blinded by the western sun and a bunch of them had been scattered scarlet and rust and royal blue and feathers by the diesel's front grill: meat in a blender. The messy scene had upset his daughter but, in Henry's mind as he reflected upon it now, it had been a good lesson for her to see firsthand that life could end at any time and in any way.

As Henry and Ginny sat and awaited their order, the smell of grease and meat wafted about. The smell reminded Henry of a place he had taken Ginny to eat as a toddler: a barbeque joint not far from the condo down the street in St. Louis. Ginny would take these silly, tiny bites of her meat leaving her with more sauce on her face and fingers than in her belly. Henry would wipe off her face and hands. He had found it strange to watch his little daughter eating beef. On a farm a cow would have had nothing to fear from a little girl. But someone had raised and killed the animal and chopped up the meat so that the tiniest of humans could eat it.

Put the cow and the toddler in a barn and leave them there alone for a week—the toddler dies first every time, Henry had thought. *But when the toddler grows up, she can take a bolt gun and press it to the cow's head then slit the cow's throat. The child soon attains more power than the cow. Humans use tools to act upon the violence in their hearts.*

He thought about how when the kids were younger, everything had centered around them by necessity. When had they last eaten? When had they last shit the diaper? Had they gotten enough sleep? Why did Charlie cry at bedtime? When one had a fever how did you know when the threshold was crossed to go to the doctor? Is Ginny on track in school? What were they naturally good at? How would they make a living when they grew up? Would the world run out of oil by then?

Here's an interval, he used to think, *when I'll play toys with my daughter, and it's what I should be doing and it's what I am doing but I would not be doing this if it were just me. I am doing this for her. If it were just me I'd read or write or catch a film or eat or sleep or pump iron or anything but this, anything but make stuffed animals interact and fart. This daughter makes me more of myself, into a protector, the friend who makes her laugh until she pees, teaches her to be brave and walk on walls and pet dogs instead of running from them, and what was going on was that I giving her everything and the power of myself was all about her and all around her. And yet because of her I became less of what I used to be—no longer free as a bird in the wild. Restrained and practical. I made a choice to give up one thing for another, freedom for family, and it was a fair bargain I know it, it was more than fair and it was me and no one else who made the choice, it wasn't coerced, and it was a good choice, but it wasn't easy. And what would it have been like to have made such a monumental decision from some place other than pure freedom? Such was unimaginable.*

In those days, especially after his namesake Henry Albert had arrived, and Charlie and Ginny remained quite dependent, he had for a time lost himself where he was a moon to a planet of light of mother and children and his estimation of himself was a derivative of their estimation of him. It was a time of pleasant lightness when the demands of the day, of getting kids ready and putting kids to bed and feeding kids and cleaning up after kids to say nothing of his teaching position were greater than the time allotted. There was no room for pondering, and his function as a human seemed to be defined for him, and there was a healthy sense of exhaustion climbing into bed each night while pictures of the future were founded on Ginny and Charlie and Albert and different milestones they might reach whether in sports or academics or arts or professions or eventually themselves marrying and having children.

Then suddenly and without warning, a few months after the family uprooted and moved to Bluebird, Albert disappeared forever and irretrievably, like the light going out on a cathode ray tube. Henry experienced an awakening borne from this loss, a sense of a massive house curtain in his mind having been ripped up at the wrong moment so that he could see all the actors on stage behind the curtain practicing their lines without costumes or makeup or lighting or props so that the illusion of the play, once it had started again, could no longer hold power over him. He could no longer suspend his disbelief and lose himself in the costumes and the lines and the staging and the acting and the moment, so where others saw reckless Prince Hamlet making oaths to the heavens or wielding a sword, he saw a thin pockmarked man in a burgundy golf shirt and cargo shorts without eye makeup working a name brand bottled water while he took direction on improving his fake English accent and where to stand during the performance for superior effect and practicing swordplay with a stick. Where others found meaning in rearing children or donating to charity or improving the planet or learning a new skill or traveling to new places, Henry saw that the play ended the same for everyone—in a coffin or urn or ditch; all the beautiful prose uttered by every child and woman and man in the end reduced to the same pablum—*the rest is silence*—and maybe, maybe one in a billion chance there was a second and more beautiful play yet to come, for there was proof in nature that energy was never lost but rather changed forms. But that was at best a different show with different lines and plots and staging and actors, and it had nothing to do with the current spectacle, and in any event, there was no way to know anything about any sort of next.

Despite having been born to a dear mother and wise father and two steadfast older siblings, the toddler Albert had spent his final moments entirely alone and fearful, gasping and choking face down in rust-colored ditchwater, and wherever Albert was now, he was powerless to reveal, and how Albert had traveled there, he could not say for Albert could not transmit any information outside of himself into the natural world; such were the statutes of Albert's new province. Albert had been Henry's son and more than a son—a smaller reflection of his father's best self—and Henry had been Albert's father and more than a father—a god and a hero and a playmate, but whatever that connection had meant to either of them was dead, and the same would happen to every other bond and couples and families and parents and children and friends and cousins and lovers and strangers and grandparents and presidents and thieves and priestesses and brick masons and loners and celebrities and even dogs and cats were all castles of sand of various sizes and shapes awaiting the ocean's tide to wash them away. And anyone who could not see behind the curtain was a fool, and Henry himself had been a fool, but no longer. He had then and there solemnly dedicated himself to living in a manner where a future loss could not shake him. Better to harden himself and subsist than to stand unarmed and wait for another sword to pierce his heart of flesh. And with this shift in perspective, many other shifts had followed suit each in turn.

Perhaps the smooth and hard interior of my workshop is so comforting, Henry thought, *because it is like me; or I am like it.*

A young man wearing a brown *Dickey's* apron brought over a tray holding hamburgers and fries and shakes and Henry's reverie ceased.

Henry was starving and at the same time was overcome with an awareness that his dependence upon food rendered him pathetic. He wished some day to live on water alone.

Food makes me vulnerable. Food summons me to the Amoco and the diner and even to home at night for dinner. Rocks don't need food. But I do.

"How's school going?" he asked his daughter nonchalantly while he chewed without pleasure as if eating a mouthful of tissue paper.

"Oh fine, oh fine, oh fine, oh fine, times four," she said laughing. No doubt something she picked up from school, Henry thought. Lincoln Elementary was in Belleflower. Ginny was in sixth grade, and her brother, Charlie, was in second grade in the same building. Back in the day, Bluebird had its own school, but beginning in the Sixties, the Bluebird kids were all bussed over to Belleflower and back.

"At school most of your friends, are they from here or from Belleflower? Belleflower right?"

"The ones I talk to the most are from the city. Those kids there are cool." She bent a fry in two and dipped it in ketchup.

"The larger town you mean? Belleflower?" Henry liked to remind people that Belleflower itself was also a town and not a city.

"Not that again. I like the girls from Bluebird, too, but it's hard around here after school. Some of these girls here are mean."

"Oh?" He feigned surprise.

"You know. People say things."

"They tell you ancient riddles?"

She laughed. "Well, no matter what they say, I don't believe them."

"Tell me."

"Kids call your place up there "Dunstan Hotel". "Henry's Day Spa". And they always laugh when they say it. They ask me why my dad doesn't want anyone to see inside. They say you are hiding something weird in there. Like a terrible secret. They call our family the outsiders. Like I'm the weird one."

"You mean I'm the weird one, right? That's what you mean."

"I didn't say that."

"I know but you can if you want. You can never hurt me." In saying this he lied, for he knew she could, in fact, hurt him profoundly, if she were to die before him.

She shrugged.

Henry continued. "Odd people are the power for change. We weirdos have powerful ideas and visions that make the world explode and regular people can't bear it because they are afraid they will lose their own power so they have to kill the weirdos."

"Kill them?" Ginny asked incredulously.

"Sure, sometimes," Henry said. "Easier than listening to them. Sometimes the true weirdos kill themselves." Henry put four or five fries in his mouth and then suddenly spat them out on the ground.

Ginny laughed to see her father spit out his fries. Then she looked at him. "Are they going to kill you?"

He told his daughter that if he were killed, that it wouldn't matter because he would die eventually one way or another. And that regardless of when he were to die, no one would remember him in any event after his death.

As soon as he had spoken, Ginny's face dropped. "I remember Albert and he's dead."

"Of course you do. But after you die?"

"I'll tell my children about him."

"And after they die?"

"Grandkids."

"And after them?"

"Great-grandkids."

"And after them?"

"Great-great."

"How much do you know about your great-great-grandparents?"

Ginny looked down again and Henry could have comforted her with a joke, but his mind was elsewhere, and he lacked the energy to turn the conversation around and replenish his daughter's heart with cheer despite his desire to do so.

Ginny and Henry finished their shakes and stood up from the table. Henry dropped his trash in the parking lot. Another customer, seeing this, yelled out.

"Hey, your trash!"

Henry turned and looked in the direction of the customer.

"Keep America beautiful, right?" the customer said.

"This whole earth is a goddamn trash barrel," Henry muttered. He walked to the car, followed by Ginny.

Henry took the long way back home over west in the direction of Lampersville, driving slowly near the new landfill, which was just a dry river bed full of garbage. Henry had seen plenty of rodents over here before.

"Have you ever watched something die?" Henry asked his daughter.

"Last summer we saw that truck drive over all those birds."

"Close up I mean."

"Kayla's dog, Gravy, bit another dog. So her parents gave it a shot, to make it die."

"What color was Gravy?"

"I didn't watch him die. She told me about it."

"I want you to know what it means. Like how there's something and then there's nothing. And I mean *nothing*. It's important that you understand how final it is."

"Dad, no."

"It's not all bad. When you understand how life can all stop in an instant, then your life becomes free."

"Let's go home."

"I promise in thirty years you'll thank me," Henry replied.

"No, please."

He drove around the dump for a bit looking this way and that, keeping the car's headlights aimed towards the ditch as much as possible. There was some movement now and he stopped the car and a prairie dog stood there frozen in the headlights. Henry accelerated and the engine roared and his daughter yelled, "Daddy!" and then there was a faint thump. Henry backed the car up until the lights were aimed at the prairie dog again and then, without saying anything, Henry and Ginny both got out to look. The prairie dog was laying on its side with some quiver in it with wet crimson on its fur. Ginny began to sniffle and sob. She piled up a few pebbles as if for a headstone and got back in the car before her father could say anything. Henry found a stick and flicked the prairie dog into the ditch. Driving home, Henry turned the interior car light on and watched his daughter through the rearview mirror wrestle with the type of thing that knew no explanation. He had wished his own father had given him this lesson early in life, and maybe had Henry himself had enough of these lessons, he would have somehow built up a wall around his heart strong enough to protect him from the loss of a loved one. But now, on second thought, as he watched his daughter, he suspected she was not old enough to understand the lesson.

This whole world is a goddamn paradox. The lessons we need the most are the ones we'll never understand.

***

As the car approached the house, Melissa Dunstan was standing on the lit front porch with a broom sweeping up something vigorously. Henry rolled his window down, and as the car came to a stop, it was apparent from the sound that Melissa was sweeping up glass. Ginny ran up the steps to the porch and danced around the glass and went in the house.

"Congratulations," Melissa said bitterly when Henry got out of the car. "Told you your stupid newsletter wouldn't go over well."

"Someone came by here and threw a rock through the window," she added.

"I can see that," he muttered.

"Try to show some empathy," Melissa said.

"Everyone okay inside?" Henry asked absently.

"Yeah, everyone but the window. Luckily me and Charlie were out, too, to grab some milk." She kneeled down and brushed the broken pieces of glass into a dustbin.

Eventually, Melissa came inside and called the police to report the incident.

Sheriff Amos Haggerty arrived and Henry went out to greet him.

"I'll be damned. I saw your newsletter the other day. Fancy piece of work. Whatever you need you have to steal? Or something like that? No such thing as property rights? What do you expect me to do if your property don't mean a thing at'all to anybody? Why did you call me for help if you are not entitled to it?" The sheriff's tone suggested he had talked to people in town who were upset about the newsletter.

"I didn't call; my wife did."

"I've stopped a lot of bad from happening in my time," the sheriff said, "including things of this sort. You leave this to me." The sheriff rubbed the back of his own neck apparently in an uninterested manner. He looked around for clues.

Henry spoke.

"You have no power. Nature has power. She'll outlast us all."

"What'ch you propose I do?" asked the sheriff. The sheriff wore a beige police suit and on his belt he carried a service revolver and police baton.

Henry considered the question for a moment. "Just admit that when someone says they have the right to something, what they really mean is that they *want* something. The word *right* is a trick, to convert a want into some type of divine mandate."

"Good luck with your messages for the people. You'll be the goddamn pied piper in this town." The sheriff kicked a little rock down the asphalt driveway and chuckled again.

"I intend to speak out more."

"You ain't the first town crier," the sheriff said, his voice louder. "'Course God didn't hand no one their rights, or whatever it is you're so hot about. After Jefferson penned them famous words, I'll bet he full on busted out laughin' when he penned *the pursuit of happiness* then got hungry and called for supper from his slave. Declaration didn't give nothin' to nobody. Words on a page."

"Couldn't have said it better myself," Henry said.

"Here's your problem, now," the sheriff spoke over Henry.

The sheriff took a step closer to Henry Dunstan. Henry could smell the sheriff's sorghum moonshine breath as the sheriff spoke.

"Maybe some of what you say makes sense to some of us. Not all, not many, but a few of us. I've studied nature's ways. I know she's in charge, and not us. This whole swath of land all the way up to Canada is explained by glacial meltoff. Our whole continent is on a tectonic plate—and all the continents could be put back together again like a Pangea. If you made a line to show the age of the universe, and that line were a mile long, the human story would be no more than a scratch on that line. But no one cares what a person says when they don't care about the person sayin' it. Here you are, Mr. Aloof, tellin' us how to think in your fancy paper. Fact is no one likes you around here. I certainly don't. And because I don't like you I don't intend to listen."

"I'm past caring about the notions of stupid people."

The sheriff stood there chest to chest with Henry. The two men stared at each other for a minute. Then the sheriff leaned forward abruptly, causing Henry to step back a pace. The sheriff said, "Attaboy. How do you like my power?" The sheriff smiled, presumably because he had taken Henry's word *power* and used it against Henry.

The sheriff made a few notes, and there being no suspects he folded the notes and put them in his shirt pocket and drove away.

CHAPTER FOUR
KINGDOMS

[SEPTEMBER 24, 2015]

Henry arrived home long after darkness had fallen in its silent manner, and with its fall a drapery of immoderate celestial lights had been synchronously raised by an invisible hand over the countryside so that the atmosphere above shimmered through many layers of silver and gold. Henry had been up late preparing another edition of his newsletter. The newsletter was a single sheet of paper, a few paragraphs on each side, and he had typed up the new edition on the laptop at the workshop and then printed a bunch of them with the new printer there. On the way home, he had left the stack of newsletters outside the post office with a rock on top. He had made an arrangement with a post office employee to take them inside when she arrived in the morning. Bluebird homes did not have mailboxes so every citizen had to go to the post office regularly and it was an efficient way for Henry to get the word out.

BLUEBIRD SOUNDER
Newsletter of Historic Bluebird

WATER RIGHTS ISSUE II

Point

Bluebird citizens remain up-in-arms about depletion of water supply by Maddux Brothers. Citizens continue to call for recognition of their so-called Rights as if some Chicxulub will come down to crush their enemies.

Nature does not recognize Rights. Only Power. Which is to say Violence. The sun controls the solar system not through consent or rule but by the Power of gravity. The earth is a creation of brute force, not love. Humans are the same—what can you compel another to do? What forces can you bring to bear upon another to mold their behavior? You have the Right to nothing. You don't deserve a name or a home or food or love. You deserve nothing. Whatever you have, you have stolen through Violence, you have kept through Violence.

Inside the Dunstan home, the kitchen sink was full of hot soapy water and dishes not likely to clean themselves, and bills not likely to recede without intervention were lined up on the table. Henry's automobile magazine was open on the table to a page showing the new Corvette. Bold, blue, and sexy like a painted racehorse. Charlie had apparently left the magazine open to this page. Henry had told Charlie he would some day take Charlie to St. Louis and they'd test drive a Corvette from an auto dealership for a few minutes. Henry doubted now that this would ever happen. At some point soon, he needed to have the same frank conversation with Charlie that he had had with Ginny recently.

Henry removed his blue mug from the hook screwed into the white kitchen cabinet and made himself a hot cup of coffee and sat down at the kitchen table, clearing a place for himself by pushing papers to the side.

All was quiet upstairs where the children slept, but Henry could hear Melissa toiling in the master bedroom on the main floor. Melissa shortly came into the kitchen now her hair shambolic and pinned and she offered to cook him some eggs.

"I did another newsletter," Henry said. "It'll go out tomorrow morning."

"Thanks for letting me know," she said sarcastically. "I'll be on my guard." Melissa got out a frying pan and broke two eggs into it with one motion and then repeated this so that there were four eggs in the pan.

"I talk about how no one has the right to anything, not even a name. Not fairness. Certainly not love."

"You should have printed extras, going to be popular," Melissa said in a mocking tone. "Can't wait for Ginny to tell me she's being teased again by the girls around here."

"I think my message is empowering rather than cynical, if people would take the time to consider it."

"Oh." Melissa did not sound convinced. She got a plate out of the cupboard along with salt and pepper shakers. The plate was blue to match the mug Henry was using. She removed a bottle of catsup from the refrigerator and put it on the table, near Henry. She sat down at the chair across from him and sorted through a stack of papers frantically.

"If you have a right to a name and to love and fairness, then when you find love or fairness, or when someone calls you respectfully by your own name, you have not earned anything. In such a case, you are given something too easily, something that you cannot understand or appreciate. Like a teenage boy in private high school portraying King Lear on stage. No experience to bring to the part. He does not merit the role."

Melissa stood up and returned to the stove and used a spatula to fold over the eggs.

Henry could see his wife was frustrated. *Stone does not apologize*, he reminded himself and then carried on.

"If there's no such thing as inherent human rights—then when you find love or fairness or when someone calls you by your own name, in a dignified manner, you have earned the gift, you have extracted it from the other person, you have forced them through power to deal with you in that particular manner. In that respect you deserve the gift because you have used violence, your power, your status, your leverage to bring it about."

Melissa still stood over the stove. She went to the fridge, removed a bag of pre-grated cheddar cheese, opened it, returned to the stove, and sprinkled some cheese on top of the eggs in the pan. Henry began speaking again but Melissa interrupted him.

"Shut up!" she groaned.

There was silence for a minute or two as Melissa used the spatula to place the eggs on the plate and then serve the plate of eggs to Henry, bringing with her the salt and pepper shakers as well as a fork from the drawer. He put salt and pepper and a great deal of catsup on his eggs.

She watched him for a moment as he ate. She appeared to be thinking of what to say.

"You weren't nearly this talkative when Albert drowned," Melissa said matter-of-factly. Her words hung in the air.

"I was in the Hadalpelagic Zone," Henry replied, annunciating each syllable slowly. They had had this same conversation before.

"Me, too. But at some point life moves forward. You still have two living children who need you."

They need my honesty, Henry thought, *more than my love. Long after love dies there will still be the truth of this world.*

"When Albert left the world, I felt like I was orbiting the earth without a helmet. I couldn't take in enough air to even breathe." He spoke like a record being played at a slow speed.

"You just went away. Period. And you never came back."

"I loved Albert. He was everything good and carefree: a pure receptacle for love and a pure reflector and refractor of love. To him I gave everything of myself, and I withheld nothing from him."

"He was my son, too. But I've got my feet back on the ground. Just help me out once in a while with the kids and the house for God's sake."

Henry thought his wife had a point. When they had moved from St. Louis to Bluebird, he had indeed told her he would help with the kids. He had inherited enough money at the death of his parents that neither he nor Melissa needed to work.

"I'd be more likely to come home if you seemed happy to see me," Henry said.

"It's not my job to be happy for you," Melissa said angrily. Henry ate his eggs in silence while Melissa rifled through papers on the table. Eventually, Melissa stood up without saying more and went into the master bedroom.

Henry finished his eggs and put his dishes in the dishwater in the sink. He went into the bedroom. Melissa was shutting down the computer. She looked furtively back at him. She straightened a stack of papers on the desk. Now she went to the dresser and removed her pajamas. With her back to him, Melissa changed her clothes for bed. He watched her. Her waist hourglassed into fleshy hips. Her skin was vaguely rippled like the top of shiny hot loaf of bread. He wanted to put one hand on each flank and spread her open before him and consume her. That is what her body was for after all. It was a creation of nature, an animal with two legs connecting into a hairy, smooth pleasure orifice. He wanted her to turn around with her top off and let him have what he wanted.

She twisted around with her pajama top on her breasts poking out like little tents.

He continuing ogling her. She appeared to be tired.

He asked, "Why are you still up anyway? I got home late."

"Listening to your garbage," she said a bit more cheerily. "I've just been busy. Busy, a lot to do. Here and there. This and that. Errands. Housework. The kids. Email. Facebook. Stuff." She avoided eye contact with him.

Melissa changed the subject as she got into bed and pulled the sheets over herself. "Have you come across any products lately that really stand out to you?"

"Now what?" Henry was confused.

"Food, gloves, a certain brand of clothing—anything that jumps out at you that you encounter in your daily life. Anything where you think—this company really has its act together. Like when Apple started iTunes and you were telling me how everyone at Washington University was buying an iPod? Or Amazon. One day you've never heard of it. The next day you are buying everything there."

Henry thought about this.

"There's Tesla. That's a company no one was talking about five years ago. Maddux Brothers is another one. I never heard a thing about them six months ago. Now that everyone is talking about them, I see they have pills for erections, blood pressure, depression. Seems like everyone in the country needs one of their drugs or another."

"I don't want to hear it," Melissa said in a startlingly angry tone. "Sounds like you are taking their side again. Like in your damn newspaper."

"You asked me a goddamn question, and I answered." *Jesus*, he thought, *just when we are having a normal conversation.*

He moved back to his side of the bed. They both lay there in bed as far apart as the bed would allow, each staring up at the ceiling and saying nothing. Finally, Melissa spoke.

"Heard they're having a meeting tomorrow to discuss the water dispute."

"Oh?"

"Over at Tom and Shirlene Mack's place out back. Tom Mack told Darren they could use his yard if there's not enough room at the church, and Tom Mack and Darren are expecting a big turnout."

"I'm going over," Henry said suddenly.

"You shouldn't."

"My theory is in motion, and I can't go back."

She rolled over and faced away from Henry. After fifteen minutes or so, her breathing slowed down and grew heavy. He went into the bathroom in the hallway between the kitchen and the master bedroom and removed his briefs to relieve his pressures, but his lube was in the nightstand in the bedroom, so he used some spit to wet his hand. He envisioned Melissa bare and spread before him, and in his mind, he slid himself up her body and penetrated her from behind over and over until he was finished.

***

The next day Henry and Melissa walked south and then west from home along the gravel road until it turned to asphalt closer to Main Street. Once on Main, they walked a few hundred yards further south until they reached the small road leading to the Mack residence, a squatty rust-brick rambler with a metal carport. Melissa and Henry followed the arriving crowd into the large rectangular backyard of cracked patio and scattered grass and dilapidated fence and spare parts, where folks were standing around holding lemonade in paper cups. Henry took one for himself and one for Melissa. Henry stood away from the group while Melissa exchanged greetings with her friends and acquaintances.

Pastor Darren and Tom Mack eventually moved to the front of the group, and Mack whistled to get everyone's attention. Henry studied them. What Henry noticed most in other men was how tall or strong they were. Men had historically dominated women not because men had better ideas or had received any special authority from God, but simply because men were bigger and stronger and could more easily inflict their will upon women. Henry wondered how history would read if women had been physically stronger than men. Perhaps the planet would have been a planet of peace, perhaps not.

Both Darren and Mack were slender in the shoulders but round in the middle, something like bowling pins. Mack's head and face were covered in wild tufts of hair. Pastor Darren, who used the words *brother* and *sister* for the townsfolk, thanked Sister Shirlene Mack for the lemonade and greeted everyone by name. Pastor Darren deferred now to Brother Tom Mack who explained that a smaller vanguard of the larger group had already met with an attorney, a Rob Beverly from Belleflower, to assess whether the Bluebird farmers should sue Maddux Brothers about the water shortage.

According to Tom Mack's report, Rob Beverly had explained that if twenty or more farmers would pool their money together, they would probably have enough resources to get the attention of Maddux Brothers. If twenty families contributed twenty-five hundred dollars each, Rob Beverly had explained, they could start with a war chest of fifty thousand dollars. With that amount of money, Rob Beverly could file a formal legal complaint against Maddux Brothers and begin the document exchange phase of discovery. Maddux Brothers would be legally obligated to disclose to the farmers copies of all paperwork related to the company's use of water from the river. Hopefully, the farmers would find a smoking gun in the documents, perhaps an email or other paperwork proving the Maddux Brothers knew it was taking more than its share of the river water. Perhaps this could lead to a quick and favorable settlement of the case for the farmers.

"What do you make of the attorney?" someone asked from the crowd.

"He's as sharp as the last-standing needle of the spruce," said Tom Mack, who alternated between poetry and platitudes. "I'll tell you what, he looked us in the eye, he did, talked to us man to man. Plenty of books on his shelves, big ones, the kind that you are supposed to read. I dare say he's a human encyclopedia. He lives here in the county. Latter-day Saints fellow. He's helped an awful lot of people with their legal troubles, dare I say."

"Isn't Jeff Sands over there?" another voice asked.

"Glad you asked, I wanted to bring up that piece, too," Tom Mack said. Chatter broke out among the crowd.

"Quiet," Pastor Darren said in an unconvincing tone, "we want everyone to hear." Although the warning had been timid, it was sufficient for the crowd to silence itself again.

Tom Mack explained to the group that a fellow named Jeffrey Sands was the Chief Operating Officer of Maddux Brothers. Sands had grown up in Bluebird, moved away to go to college, and spent most of his career working for Maddux Brothers back east. Jeffrey Sands and his wife had recently moved to Belleflower, not far from Calypso, Missouri, at the time that Jeffrey Sands had been named the Chief Operating Officer of the Maddux Brothers plant in Calypso. COO was the top of the ladder at the Calypso plant, and his ties to Bluebird would probably make him an ally.

Pastor Darren added that the strategy was to use the lawsuit to put pressure on the COO Sands to reach a favorable deal with the farmers of Bluebird.

Tom Mack took over again. He held up his long hands. "We already got ten families committed. That's twenty-five thousand dollars in our war chest. Now then ten is twice five and two less than a dozen. Three less than the baker's dozen. Ten in totality who signed on the dotted line. We just need twice again as many."

Mack flashed his hands to signify the numbers he was using. "And if we surpass twenty, so to speak, all the better to make a sudden impact, like a stack of hay bales thundering to ground."

A bunch of hands shot up in the crowd, and Tom Mack took care to write down all the names in a spiral notebook. Mack explained how at first he and David Campbell would go into Belleflower periodically to meet with counsel, and Mack would keep everyone up-to-speed.

"What do you think, Pastor Darren?" another voice from the crowed asked.

Pastor Darren straightened his tie and tucked in his bright teal button-up. He had a resonant but sometimes wheezy voice. He seemed like a reluctant preacher who had to remind himself of his duties from time to time. "Well, we've got earthly tools, and heavenly tools, and I pray that we use both sets of tools. It sounds like Mack has scoped out the earthly options for the group. I'd like to suggest that we pray, together and individually, for the Lord's help. Shall we pray?"

Everyone bowed but Henry. Henry believed if there was a God that God had plenty to do without people whining about their problems or making up systems of laws that God supposedly favored.

"God our Heavenly Father, God who made the water and the land that needs the water, and God who made the xylem, that magical riverway of the plant kingdom, and God who knows that with sunshine and Time, the plants of the land will convert themselves into worthy fruits for men and women and children, hear us now, oh, Lord."

Pastor Darren paced back and forth with his words. Henry, the only person present with his eyes open, enjoyed watching Darren move about. Pastor Darren wasn't always this outgoing, but when he got into a rhythm he was fun to watch.

"Now God our Father, Thou knowest how to construct a pharmaceutical and how to heal the body and when Jesus thy Holy Son was upon the earth there was no need for pharmaceuticals he was the Prozac and the Oxycontin and the Extra Strength Tylenol and the Clonazepam and the Humira. He was the drug of choice and the drug of lowest cost, too, and he was covered by all the prescription plans, and since His Holy Death and Resurrection, there have been no drugs as powerful as Him to command the body to heal. Dear Lord, hear us pray."

Several in the crowd uttered, "amen."

"Thou knowest what they need, and what we need, and God our Father, the Father of Jesus who made a few fish and loaves into many, we ask thee to multiply the water upon the lands so that all men have what they need!"

"Amen." A few others in the group joined in energetically.

"And if it be not possible to multiply the water upon the land, make Maddux Brothers a more efficient operation that plenty of water remains for our corn, and if this be not possible, oh Lord, we humbly submit to thy judgment whether they or we are more worthy of water, whether it is preferable that they further enrich their corporation and their shareholders, or whether we be worthy of mere survival upon our land in our little Bluebird Jerusalem founded by our forbearers, and we will await thy judgment, rain or shine."

"Amen," shouted nearly everyone and they broke into clapping.

"In Jesus name, amen." Pastor Darren was finished, and he nodded a toothy smile to honor the rhythmic inspiration the Lord had given him on this night.

Collective enthusiasm from the crowd. David Campbell stomped out his cigarette on the dirt and lumbered up to the front and easily put one long arm around Tom Mack and the other around Pastor Darren and proposed a lemonade toast to Tom Mack and his wife for the hospitality and to Pastor Darren and his wife for their sacrifices for the community.

Henry interrupted the jubilee with a severe tone: "How much power do you have?"

Those closest to Henry were quiet, but the noise of backslapping and congratulations drowned out Henry's voice so he spoke louder and asked again, "How much power do you have?"

Tom Mack motioned for Henry to come to the front. This took a moment. Melissa Dunstan retreated to the rear of the crowd and stared at her feet.

"How much power do you have?" Henry let the question hang over his audience.

"You say you have the right to that water—whatever that means—and the lawyer seems to agree. I want to know how much power you have on your side, total, how much power?"

"Shut up!" shouted Sabrina, Pastor Darren's wife.

"Anyone here related to a judge or someone in the legislature?" Henry spoke over Sabrina's objection.

Nobody moved.

"Well, how much money do you have, after you burn through the fifty thousand? Can you get up to half a million? Can you go up to a million dollars?"

"Ain't going to take no million," David Campbell said angrily.

Henry waited for a moment and started again, "Goddamn fools. Wake up! Anyone here have a kindergartener? What about you Rich Burke? Rich, how do you get your boy into his pajamas at bedtime? Your boy listens to you because of your parental rights under the law? Is that why he obeys you, he's aware of the statutes of Missouri and the common law? Or is it because you are twenty times his size, and he doesn't want a beating?"

Henry spied a cup of lemonade on the nearby card table. "Let me show you a lesson about how Maddux Brothers sees the situation. See this card table here? It belongs to me and Melissa. We loaned it to the Macks, bought it with our own money over in Belleflower."

Henry showed them a piece of tape on the side with the name *Dunstan* printed on it.

"That cup of lemonade is on my property. God says that's my property! Because I bought it. Has my name on it. Bill of Rights says no one puts anything on my property without my permission. I command you to move, lemonade!" he yelled.

"Get off of my table! You are standing on my property, I demand that you move!" Henry yelled louder. "Will someone tell this goddamn cup of lemonade to get off my property! It's my right!" he roared. "I'm going to sue that cup of lemonade. Ask the judge to order it to move. What about my rights?" he roared again. Silence.

Finally, Henry grabbed the cup of lemonade and threw it as hard as he could across the yard the lemonade fanning through the air and the cup lightly striking the fence.

"Why'd that lemonade move? Because of my rights? Or because of my power?"

Henry now removed some folded-up papers from his pocket and held them up. "Here are the financial statements of Maddux Brothers. But you might call the whole thing their statement of power. They make pharmaceuticals for arthritis, depression, blood pressure, and a million other maladies. If you add all up all their assets, they have thirty-six billion dollars. Billion with a B. Your fifty thousand is a nickel to them."

"Five cents worth of power," Henry reiterated. "You come up with a million, that's only a dollar, one single dollar, to Maddux. Now who do you think is going to win the fight? And for every sad story you put out there about running out of water, they can put out a hundred as many about an old lady in pain who needs their pills. You publish an article in the paper up in Belleflower, they publish three in the WALL STREET JOURNAL. You call a city councilman to plead your story, they call the White House."

A few looked at Henry as if they followed him, but most of the group was visibly ready for him to finish.

Pastor Darren put his arm around Henry. "This is my brother-in-law. God loves him. He married my sister, Melissa. That doesn't mean I agree with him, but everyone is entitled to an opinion."

Henry lowered his head.

Pastor Darren gently stepped in front of Henry and finished his lines. "Henry and I are saying two kinds of the same thing to a point. We can't do this on our own folks. We know this. This is why we pray folks. God wants us to use the peaceful methods at our disposal. So we will use the legal system and we'll rely on it do right, but we'll also ask God for His help. God is mightier than us all."

A few shouted amen, and Tom Mack reasserted himself anticlimactically and stood in front of Henry and Pastor Darren. "As far as the lawsuit goes now, show of hands, who stands shoulder-to-shoulder and arm-in-arm with me and David Campbell?"

All the same hands as those who had already committed shot up as Tom Mack checked the hands against those already in his notebook.

More congratulations and it was time for small talk now and catching up on herds and corn and kids. Melissa and Henry slipped out without ado and walked towards home.

The night sky was immense and cloudless and black-blue, and the stars so thick it was as if they had been brought in taped to a curtain at the school play. Henry thought if you could pull back that curtain you could see forever-wide and forever-long and forever-deep in every direction and dimension without any ending or explanation or rest stop even, like falling down a gaping hole for infinity, and to Henry the shadowy outline of homes and corn and irrigation wheels and weeds and trees and fence posts and bushes and tractors and barns and stables, as he walked side-by-side but not hand-in-hand with his wife, down the old road and under the foot bridge supported by pipe culvert, looked inconsequential against the vastness of the heavens.

CHAPTER FIVE
THE MERCHANT

[OCTOBER 12, 2015]

The leaves of the couple hundred oak, walnut, and sycamore trees in Bluebird were turning gold and auburn in preparation for winter. Beneath the trees that stood as tired sentinels, cornfields had turned yellow-brown and dry; the fields were ready for harvesting. The sounds and movements and dust from the corn combines filled the air. A combine would move through a field of corn, fell the stocks, collect the cobs of corn, remove the kernels of corn from the cobs, then transfer the golden kernels to a large farm truck, which in turn took its load to a corn elevator in Belleflower. Cattle would then be moved to the empty field to graze on the fallen stalks and cobs. Everywhere there was talk of a subpar corn yield.

Amidst this season of harvest, Melissa moved about Bluebird like a ballet dancer. It was one of those Monday holidays late in the year when the banks and stock markets are closed, and Melissa had a free day. She felt generous and jittery and wanted to surprise as many people as she could today with her charity. Even so, remembering that tomorrow she would be stuck at her desk all day staring at the computer, she felt a wave of nausea inside of her. Melissa had figured out a way to earn extra income that Henry did not know about, and she intended to spend some of this money today to offset the negative feelings aimed at her family because of Henry's words in the SOUNDER. Her first stop was at her parents' bungalow. There, her parents were camped in the living room as usual, watching television. Her father complained of having nothing to watch. Melissa called the cable company and upgraded the cable package to one with dozens of extra sports and movie channels. Her parents reported that the new DuCorps medication Melissa's mother was taking, still in investigational studies, seemed to be a miracle drug. Melissa's mother's blood pressure was staying under control without all the swelling or excess urination caused by other blood pressure medications.

Over at Rich and Trina Burke's home, Melissa asked Trina what their young boy's favorite color was. Learning it was blue, Melissa called Wal-Mart and paid for a blue bicycle to be shipped to the boy in a few days. Next, Melissa went by Big Joe Campbell's store, and she gave him some cash and told him the cash was to replace the store window at the rear of his shop. The window had been taped up for a few months now. Big Joe was eating slices of cheddar cheese out of a paper bowl. He asked Melissa if she wanted a taste but she declined. Melissa asked Joe if any products had sold particularly well lately, or if he himself were especially impressed by any company's product offerings. After a moment, he said he did not know, off the top of his head, but would think on it and let her know if anything came to mind. Afterwards, Melissa visited David Campbell at his auto repair shop. She gave David two pounds of chocolate bars and a carton of Marlboro Reds that Melissa had just purchased from David's brother Joe.

She left David Campbell's auto repair shop and hurried over to Shirlene Mack's home for a meeting of the Bluebird Society. Beyond the goodwill Melissa could generate from her individual acts of generosity, Melissa believed the best way to elevate her status in Bluebird was through participation in the Bluebird Society. The Bluebird Society was an informal group of ladies, chaired by Shirlene Mack, who were dedicated to rebuilding the town and increasing tourism to Bluebird. Shirlene, past retirement age, was a frenetic wigged mother-hen figure with smiling disposition and waving directing arms who somehow knew the lineage of everyone who had lived in Bluebird for more than a generation. At home she kept little black and white pictures of all the early inhabitants of Bluebird. Shirlene excitedly welcomed Melissa into the group.

Shirlene and the other ladies told Melissa that the Society had decided on the old schoolhouse as the building they'd like to renovate first. This original Bluebird schoolhouse, opened in 1845, seven years after the town's foundation, had started with only one teacher and had four teachers at its height in the late 1800s, but had closed in the 1960s at the time that the school system began to bus children from Bluebird to the schools in Belleflower. After generations of vacancy the old schoolhouse, in its present state, was nothing more than a stump of red bricks with a brass historical marker. The Society's idea was to put out collections jars at Campbell's Dry Goods, the Amoco, the car repair shop, and Dickey's Diner, and ask people to donate spare change. Eventually the Society would travel up to Belleflower and try to find empathetic business owners there who would be willing to donate a little money towards Bluebird renovation or if not, would be at least willing to leave out collections jars. Once the schoolhouse was completed, the Society intended to renovate Campbell's Dry Goods and the First Baptist Church.

A few minutes into the meeting, Melissa began to assert herself. The ladies were talking about making more copies of the visitor's brochures that were given to tourists who came to Bluebird. The brochures were available at the Amoco and at Campbell's Dry Goods.

"These handouts are too plain," Melissa explained, "even ugly girls dress up for the dance." Melissa offered to prepare a more colorful trifold brochure.

A bit later in the meeting, discussion turned towards whether the Society should create a website or to otherwise be more aggressive in trying to collect funds for renovation projects. Most of the ladies were in favor of moving at a comfortable pace so as not to overtax any one Society member or offend locals by asking them too aggressively for money.

Again, Melissa spoke up.

"Ladies, success isn't inevitable here. It's we who control it. Why wait any longer than we have to to transform Bluebird?"

"Let's let folks be folks," Shirlene said. Shirlene looked to the veterans of the Society who all appeared to be in agreement with Shirlene.

"Our kids deserve a better Bluebird," Melissa replied. "Imagine if we had a cupcake shop and a ladies' clothing boutique and a real sit-down restaurant. Imagine how that would feel."

In this regard, Melissa was acting on a weakness in her own character—her own embarrassment at having grown up poor and rural in comparison to the life Henry had led and the opportunities he had enjoyed. At the time Melissa had met Henry in St. Louis, for instance, Henry had just returned from a six-month Spanish language program in Madrid. By contrast, Melissa had learned Spanish in college and had never so much as traveled to a Spanish-speaking country, not even Mexico. Henry had been to every big city in the world Melissa could name; Melissa had been outside of Missouri only a handful of occasions.

The ladies seemed reluctant to commit themselves to anything beyond a few limited renovation projects. Bluebird was a poor farming community, and it was not realistic to dream of too much more.

Melissa stood in front of the group and called upon something she had learned in one of her business management classes in college. She recalled the notion of creating an image of what needed to be accomplished before bludgeoning people with all the operational details.

"Here's my vision. Close your eyes and tell me if you can see what I see. I want Bluebird to be the most famous of all the old Missouri historic towns, more than Fillmore or Washington or Ezra. And forget Yellowbird. Imagine Bluebird Main Street renovated and featured in travel magazines so that tourists and money will flow in. It'll be what they call symbiosis. Think: Sedona, Arizona. Think: Golden, Colorado. Now think: Bluebird, Missouri. And folks will move here and our population will increase. And those who come will make new jobs, and more people will stay here and come here on account of those jobs. And our kids and their kids will stay and grow three- and four- generation families here."

There followed a heavy silence. Finally, Shirlene straightened her wig and spoke up. "Melissa hon', we all want Bluebird to be strong, it's just that we got different ways of going about it." The meeting concluded without the Society being persuaded to adopt Melissa's more aggressive tactics.

Fortunately, I have a much better way to raise the money we need, Melissa told herself as she walked home from the meeting. Melissa had learned how to day-trade in the stock market from a neighbor in St. Louis, and she had a real knack for it. There were plenty of books about day-trading strategy but Melissa's mantra was this: *I have to be greedy; I have to want the money more than the person I am taking it from. There is only so much to go around in this world and too many people to share it. If I don't seize my share, no one will save it for me. Money is like water or air—it belongs to no one.*

About halfway home, Melissa walked past a small field where the corn harvest was underway. She decided to watch for a time. Looking at the dry fallen corn stalks, one of the lines from one of Henry's SOUNDER articles circulated through Melissa's mind. *Steal the water! Or someone else will.* Henry's point seemed to be that property could not be owned, so any claim of ownership was by definition an act of theft. Melissa wondered if Henry was by extension accusing her of being a thief, someone who made money day-trading the stock market not because it was fair or right but simply because she was willing to take something from another and keep it for herself. She decided Henry's polemic was inapplicable to her own situation because her motivations for raising money were altruistic and designed to improve the town.

Standing there near a barbwire fence watching the combine move back and forth in the field, it occurred to Melissa that all of the farm equipment she had seen today was John Deere brand. Perhaps she should look at John Deere's financial statements and decide if there were any good day-trading strategies involving this company.

With the New York markets opening at eight thirty in the morning and closing at three in the afternoon, Missouri time, Melissa had lately been trapped in front of her computer monitor most days. Her ears and eyes had stood constant vigil for market news that might shift prices up or down, and she had not slept well lately. Melissa would recite her methods and principles in her head again and again, and sometimes when Ginny and Charlie returned from school, Melissa was just emerging from the bedroom for the first time since she had seen them off to the school bus.

Without informing Henry, Melissa had annexed thirty thousand dollars from their shared bank account to get her trading started. There was nothing wrong with this—it was her money, too, but she feared that if Henry knew about her day-trading habit that he would start asking too many questions and would find out that her day-trading had been directly linked to Albert's drowning. This would be catastrophic to her reputation if word got out.

Soon after Henry and Melissa had moved from St. Louis to Bluebird, Melissa had been monitoring one morning the rapid depletion of her trading account on a day when all her trades were going poorly. The market paused briefly during New York lunch. Right before the end of the lunch hour, anxious, she pumped ten thousand dollars into a tip she had suitably investigated and held for just this moment. While she watched her account balance fluctuate on her computer screen, she heard the creaking of the front door. More likely than not it was Albert, up from his nap. Albert was two years old and could get out of his crib on his own and could walk pretty well. He had soft charcoal kinked hair and a plump belly usually not completely covered by his t-shirt. He liked to go into the front yard to push around his plastic lawn mower on the asphalt sidewalk. And, Melissa assumed, Albert was probably fine, but ideally she would count to ten and if she didn't hear his sing-songy voice through the window she would peer out or go stand on the porch until he came to her. But the stock price was rising sharply, and she could not walk away from the computer. Her ten thousand became fourteen thousand, and the stock price was still rising. Five more minutes and her holding was worth seventeen thousand. The price kept rising. She watched her investment climb to nineteen thousand before she sold her position and then walked briskly to the front door. Nine thousand dollars profit in one-half hour. Not bad.

Out in the yard Melissa had called to Albert loudly but calmly. She walked around to the north of the house where Albert usually wound up in the pile of dirt with his toys. He was not there. She walked down a few steps and opened the cellar door. No sign of Albert. Now Melissa started running, uttering prayers and sweating heavily, for he was not in the places where he usually played. Albert was not in the shed west of the house and not behind the shed. She ran through the tall weeds on the south side of the house. No Albert. She looked to the east of the house—it was just lawn, nowhere for Albert to hide. He could not have gone as far as the rail fence by the irrigation canal—he had never shown an interest. The fence was out on the eastern edge of the yard, but it was only to mark the territory; it couldn't actually keep someone in or out. There was a flash of red just beyond the fence, and she yelled out again and ran to the spot and she found him face down his red t-shirt undulating in rust-colored ditchwater; when she turned him over he was long gone on his angel flight: there was no Albert in there and no trace of him either even when she begged God and the heavens to put him back while she attempted to resuscitate him for a time.

But Albert did not respond at all, and later at the hospital after it all ended and she let herself fall apart, when she accounted wildly for the event to Henry and the doctors she was humiliated about her day-trading so she made up an alternate account. Melissa told Henry and the doctors that she and Albert had been taking a nap together and that Albert must have awakened and left the house without her noticing.

The months after Albert's drowning were a blur of hysterics and despondency as Melissa drowned in a sea of ink murky from the absence of Albert's presence, a black lightless sea of surprising depth and dimension, as if each water molecule were a portal to a new dimension of greater darkness and profundity within which new molecules revealed further portals deeper yet, such that she could never hope to reach the bottom. It was an awesome sense of interior movement, so powerful that Melissa could only surrender to the undertow; the slightest resistance or withholding would have crushed her. And yet the blessing of the inevitable passage of time and the structure of a household and two other dependents to care for including, in direct response to Albert's accident, driving Charlie and Ginny to Belleflower often to learn to swim, kept Melissa from completely going to pieces. And sensing God's presence in the wind had helped her feel that someone was there looking out for her.

As for Henry, to Melissa's way of thinking, he had abandoned Melissa psychologically after Albert's demise. At home, Henry would stare out the windows—as if shifting from one window to another would make any difference. East in the mornings and west in the evenings and north at night. Henry had started spending more and more time in the hills. Henry would return from the hills dirty and tired with preoccupied eyes. Certainly, Henry had had nothing to say to make Melissa feel better.

If anyone should have been crushed by Albert's death, Melissa had thought more than once, *it was me, and not Henry. I am the boy's mother. I carried him and gave birth to him and breastfed him. I found him in the ditch. Henry needs to shake himself of his self-pity and participate in the family again.*

Immediately after Albert had drowned, Melissa had abandoned her day-trading obsession and never returned to it—obvious enough after the tragedy. She had promised herself she would never do something so stupid and reckless again.

But now, after more than two years, Melissa felt that circumstances warranted a change. Just as she had abandoned the day-trading to be a better mother and to better protect her family, she now needed to return to it, in order to protect her family. Her children were being teased in town on account of Henry's aloof and arrogant behavior—the least Melissa could do is earn extra money to cause people in Bluebird to think positively of the Dunstan family. And more than that, if Melissa were successful in her plans and could raise money to rebuild the town, she could not only protect her children in the short term but make Bluebird more appealing and charming so that her children might stay in Bluebird as adults.

What good is it being the Queen of Bluebird, Melissa thought, *if I have no subjects?*

The combine came to a halt and Melissa ceased her reverie. She was still holding the large fountain soda she had purchased that morning at the Amoco after she had visited David Campbell's auto repair shop. She had drunk half of the soda and the rest was now watered down. She walked the remainder of the distance towards home. When she arrived near the house, the front yard was full of men at work. Some men were digging holes, some were pouring cement into holes, and others were standing around. Henry directed traffic and he approached Melissa excitedly and informed her how he had decided to install a tall chain link fence with barbed wire all around to protect the family. Multiple times now a window on the home had been broken by a thrown stone. The breaking of the windows coincided more or less with Henry's publications of the SOUNDER. Henry had stayed up late a couple of times in the shed peeking out at the house to try to catch the vandal, but so far his timing had been off. In response to Henry's news about the fence, Melissa told Henry the same thing she had told him before.

"Why don't you stop agitating people with your stupid newsletter? Let Sheriff Haggerty do his job. This place looks like a jail. One more reason for our kids to get bullied at school."

Infuriated that he had ignored her wishes, Melissa entered the house and slammed the door. Moments later she emerged and launched her vertical tub of cola onto Henry's shirt and then went back inside. Seeing this, two men on the fence crew laughed out loud.

***

Around dusk, the crew finished placing the fence posts, and the crew leader informed Henry that the fence posts were deeper than for a typical enclosure and closer together and the chain link itself would be buried in dirt at the base to avoid the problem with vandals or critters slipping in underneath. The men departed until tomorrow. Henry entered the house to take a long nap.

Hours later, after dark, Henry emerged from the home dressed in dark clothing. After a quick visit by flashlight to Albert's marker of stones in the corner of the yard, Henry laid himself face up under the cloudy starless sky on the front grass out by the old post and rail fence where Albert had filled up his lungs with irrigation water. With the new chain link fence to be completed tomorrow, perhaps the vandal would come one final time to try to break another window. Henry lay there on the grass and waited for any sound at all. Initially, the weight of nature's endlessness set in and toyed with his brain. The stars in the sky above his head were after all giant, dense stones without feeling. They had witnessed the drowning of his son and had not intervened. He knew it was pointless to be angry at the stars. Perhaps it was not anger but jealousy. They were independent, free, beautiful, and full of light. They were also beyond caring or sorrow.

Henry regained control of his thoughts. He needed most of all to listen. The more he listened, the less room there was for considering. Several hours in according to the placement of the Big Dipper, and in any event well into the darkness, there was a new sound—the scuffling of feet on gravel. Henry grew more attentive as the sound grew nearer, signaling that someone was walking from town northward on the gravel road towards the Dunstan residence. Henry suspected that if this person were the intruder, the intruder would turn at the asphalt driveway to walk closer to the home. Henry, situated about twenty-five yards north of the driveway, was safe so long as the intruder didn't look directly at him. When the feet-on-gravel sound turned definitively to feet-on-asphalt, Henry knew the person was now closing in on his home. Henry finally allowed himself to sit up. The intruder was a tall boy, teenager in size, whom Henry believed was the sheriff's son, based on the boy's gait and shaggy hair. Henry moved his body into a slow crawl and then a low squat and shuffled sideways as the boy reached into his pocket and hurtled a rock into one of the higher windows where the kids' bedrooms were, the sound of glass shattering the air.

When the boy turned around to run off, Henry was right there upon him and slammed him to the ground with a forearm to the neck and pinned him easily and roughly, holding the boy's face down in the grass and dirt while the boy gasped for air. The lights in the house came on. Henry yelled at Melissa through the broken window to check on the kids. Melissa screamed that Charlie had been hit by the falling glass on his leg and was bleeding. Henry slammed the boy's head into the ground repeatedly until he was sure he had broken the boy's nose, then ran inside as the boy scurried off. And though no one would ever notice, the soil turned to rich rubicund in the spot where blood from the boy's nostrils had mixed with earth.

CHAPTER SIX
SKELETON

[OCTOBER 13, 2015]

Charlie's leg wound was not dire but was deep enough to require a good irrigation and stitches, so Melissa drove Charlie in the middle of the night into Belleflower to the closest hospital, with a handtowel wrapped compact around the thigh where the glass shard had fallen just so upon the exposed flesh of the sleeping boy. At birth, Charlie, who was named after his paternal grandfather Charles Edward Dunstan, had straw coloration which had reminded Melissa of the straw pony Charley that Melissa had sometimes ridden as a girl at a hobby farm outside of town, and she was glad about that now because Charley the pony had survived a grim leg infection which she took as a sign that Charlie the boy would be fine.

"Why don't we have a hospital?" Charlie asked as they came to the crest of one of many hills on the undulant highway along the way to Belleflower.

"It's too small," Melissa replied. She liked that Charlie was talkative, even moreso when he was anxious. She wished Henry and Ginny would talk as much as Charlie did. It was easier to understand a talkative person.

"Will we get one?"

"Probably not."

"Why?"

"We need more people."

"Why?"

"To stay busy."

"Why?"

"To make money."

"Oh."

"If we had a hospital it would be empty most of the time and there wouldn't be enough to do, and they'd have to close it, and everyone would lose their jobs."

"Like that Blue Bear ice cream store?" the boy asked. Blue Bear was a little parlor with self-serve ice cream, frozen yogurt, and TVs that played only cartoons. Blue Bear had opened in Bluebird the prior summer but had closed for good once the weather changed.

"Yeah," Melissa said.

"The old man was nice."

"The one who worked there?"

"Is he sad?"

"I think so."

"Maybe he could go to the sad hospital."

"They do have hospitals for sad people."

"What do they do there?"

"They take medicine."

"Did Albert go to the hospital?"

"You are a smart boy. Do you remember little Albert?"

"No. But you showed me pictures."

"Do you worry about him?"

"Who?"

"Albert."

"He's with Jesus."

"That's right, my Charlie. Don't ever forget that."

"Okay."

You will forget, she thought, you will, but then you'll remember again if you forget. The impossible balancing act in life was that to have peace you had to forget certain things and remember others, but sometimes the things you remembered for good were laced with pain, and some of the things you forgot for pain were mixed with heaven, and impossible to keep the accounts wholly clean. Melissa's sister-in-law Sabrina, linear in all matters religious, had told Melissa that she, Melissa, needed to read the Bible more to make sure she remembered Jesus. Melissa didn't think remembering and forgetting had much to do with intention. She would forget Jesus sometimes, that's all, for no reason, and then just as unexpectedly would remember Jesus at other times. And in any event, forgetting was a prerequisite to remembering, and forgetting was dependent upon remembering so that each was the condition precedent and subsequent of the other.

Charlie, whom she could see in the rearview mirror if she turned on the interior light, had nodded off. This brought her relief. She recalled that somewhere out here in the bumpy country between Blue-bird and Belleflower was the spot where, years ago, Melissa's father had pulled off to assist a stranded Indian lady whose VW Golf had broken down—the lid up with engine hissing steam. Melissa's father had offered to give the woman a ride, and Melissa had moved from the front seat of the car to the rear to allow the woman to sit in front. It was one of those things Melissa would never have believed if it had not happened to her, and in any event, she had thought about it so many times the memory had become true even if her recollection was not entirely factual.

Once inside her father's car, the woman had introduced herself:

My name is Debbie Black. I am from the Osage. My Indian name is Wa-Tse-Mon-In. Or Star that Travels. This is fitting as I was reared in a trailer park in Arkansas and after the divorce of my folks, I went to Arizona with my mom who found work at First Security in computers. Later, I had a baby and followed a cousin to Oklahoma. And now that baby, my baby, is all grown up. She has just received a scholarship to go to law school at Mizzou. She wants to be a tax lawyer! My daughter! Not only that but she is pregnant and will make me a grandma soon. So I am going there to help my daughter and to be a grandma.

Debbie Black had recited her life story to Melissa and Melissa's father matter-of-factly as if interpreting ancient glyphs inside her mind. From the backseat of her father's car, Melissa watched Debbie, and unlike other adults, Debbie when she looked at you never looked away. Debbie's eyes were flat and not lively and not preoccupied—the eyes of a person who was witnessing everything around her without apprehension or judgment, like the eyes of the land.

Melissa recalled Debbie and her narrative like it was yesterday because when her father had pulled off the highway, Debbie who was reaching under the hood of her automobile awkwardly and then turned around to see her visitors, was tall and naked head to toe—no shoes even—and had scratches about her back and upper arms, and she had thick straight hair in every direction between her legs and going up her lower belly like a Persian cat. Debbie's spoke to Melissa's father once he had pulled over and rolled down the passenger side window.

Hello sir. Can you help? I went to a party in Lampersville, and a man forced me into a backroom and violated me. He was threatening to kill me after. I escaped with my just my car, and now it is broken. Can you take me to Belleflower?

Melissa's father had quickly given Debbie the knitted blanket from the trunk—*nah, you go on, you just keep it now, it's yours*, he had said when they had dropped her off at a motel in Belleflower with twenty dollars cash and Debbie had assured them her daughter would drive down from Columbia and meet her at the motel—and in the car she had laid the blanket across herself loosely but had not bundled herself up inside it or tucked it in or acted embarrassed in the least so that Melissa could still see the rug between Debbie's legs through the openings in the blanket in broad daylight, and now dwelling on the encounter Melissa wondered if it hadn't have been chilly out if Debbie would have used the blanket at all.

Debbie had talked the whole ride into Belleflower. Looking back on the whole event now, Melissa was not sure why Debbie had talked so much. Perhaps Debbie thought that talking would put her hosts at ease given the unusual situation. Debbie had unfolded history in her manner:

The history of the world according to my people is like a play with curtains opening and closing. So first is Act One which is there was Grandmother Moon and Grandfather Sun. They were the beginning. They lived in the sky.

For Act Two, there was water which covered over all the earth. No land could be seen anywhere.

So for Act Three who could go below to the water and tame the water and make it into something for all the creations? It was the elk, the mighty elk—he was chosen to go below, and he got into the air and the water and bellowed and bellowed and this made the wind to blow away the water until there was some land.

Which is what we call Act Four, the time of just the land before the people. Beautiful sacred earth.

From here there were people, my ancestors, the Osage people, who lived upon the land, which is what I like to call Act Five. For thousands of years, my people, we dwelled all around this country. For fur and meat we hunted large animals. Would you believe there were mammoths and sloths and horses? We would use tools, beginner tools from stone or bone. But my people were very clever. We were not born yesterday! We made more interesting weapons as in taking stones, sharpening those stones, and attaching them to spears—these were excellent for hunting. Especially when a spear was carved to be more stable in the air. Fluted spears is how they are called.

As Melissa continued towards the hospital in Belleflower, she checked the rearview mirror again. Charlie remained asleep. She remembered it was maybe three years after her father had picked up Debbie that Melissa and her brother Darren had come across some flint in the hills near Bluebird. She had understood from Debbie's story exactly what she and Darren had found—decades or centuries ago, an Indian had carved the stone into a point, tied it to a spear, and used the tool for hunting mammals. Later, the Indian had died, and left the flint behind, and now Melissa had found it.

Later and later, many have come and gone—we are still in Act Five, the Act of my people—our people the Osage settled all around here in the Missouri area. All around there and there and there. We were living in long houses. By now some of the big game animals are gone. But I told you we were not born yesterday! We learned how to kill the smaller animals like rabbits, and we also learned what plants to gather and eat. Fishing was good here with so much water. And the water could be also used for irrigation such as for vegetables. My people loved the gourds. Who did you think started the Jack-o-Lantern?

Now comes Act Six of the play. This was the arrival of the white man and the white man stealing or claiming the land for himself. Stealing and claiming are for my people the same thing. My people made a bad mistake and closed the curtains too early on the Act of my people. My people they gave up big chunks of their land in Missouri to the white people in exchange for lands in Oklahoma. The big change was that the white God had told the whites in their Bible that their destiny was to take a space permanently and even to remove others from that space and divide it into private property for each white man and his family. Of course, this was not new, my people also lived on the land and they would fight against newcomers but for them what this was a question of use and not of ownership.

But what was impossible for my people was the white man said one could own the land which is like owning a chunk of time or a slice of history. Imagine saying you owned the year 1930 for example. And all the memories from the year 1930. Every song. Every smell. And of course, the white man made the rules, and also the white man was the police and the judge to punish the breaking of the rules, and whenever he needed he could also change the rules or even the history of the rules or the story of the source of the rules. And he had the guns and the people and most of all he carried with him the disease which could not be fought against even with great courage. And then the white man borrowed from my people many notions of liberty, which when they organized into a government, they turned these from protections into weapons, the sharp bloody spear of liberty.

After saying this, Debbie had guffawed deeply and showed a bit of sadness.

Melissa hadn't seen or heard of Debbie since then but had seen coverage on television that President George W. Bush had signed a law permitting the Osage tribe to form a new government whereby they themselves could determine who was in the tribe which, of course, was upside-down as if for example, Melissa had to petition the government for permission to call Ginny and Charlie her children.

I'm a lot like you Debbie. Something bad happened to me and I just have to keep moving forward.

And Melissa considered what Debbie had said about how for the Indian, to claim ownership of property was to claim ownership of a memory or a period of time. *What if some other person, some third party, owned all of my memories pertaining to Albert and I had to pay that other person to have permission to think of Albert? Is that what the white man did to the Indian? Stole all his memories?*

At the emergency room in Belleflower, the doctor stitched up Charlie. Charlie cried as they pried his skin open to clean the injury and sewed him up, and when it was over, he couldn't drag Melissa out of the soap-scented hospital fast enough; she knew he was old enough now to remember past trauma and never again would view the hospital as a fun dispensary of stuffed animals and suckers but only as a place of fear and harsh smells. By now, it was morning. Melissa took Charlie to a truck stop and let him order breakfast. Melissa watched him eat. He looked much like his father. His body was thicker than Ginny's. His eyes were spaced apart, and his nose was protruding and birdlike. Melissa wondered if Charlie would look as serious as his father when he grew up, like a president on a coin in profile. Probably not, if Charlie so much as smiled once in a great while. Charlie was too young for Melissa to know what he'd become, but he was good and eager to please and trusting and she had believed that moving home to Bluebird would prolong the innocence of her children. But what did it pay to be so careful and protective, a brief lapse and the worst could happen as it had with Albert. Maybe if Melissa were less vigilant her kids would learn how to navigate more on their own and would end up like Debbie Black, riding the waves of life without being crushed by them.

***

When Melissa arrived home with Charlie, Henry checked in on his son. Melissa said Charlie was doing fine—he was on antibiotics and in ten days would return to the doctor to have the stitches removed. Henry told his son how by the end of the day the big chain link fence would be finished and that would be the end of worrying about the windows and the flying glass ever again. Charlie seemed satisfied by this and was too tired to talk. Henry gave Charlie a couple of automobile magazines. Charlie smiled. Henry yelled to Melissa that he was going to go pick a fight, and he rode off on his motorcycle.

Henry Dunstan dismounted on a side street off of Main in Bluebird. He kicked loudly at the front door of Sheriff Amos Haggerty's residence. When the sheriff answered the door, Henry displayed a giftbox and said in a loud voice that the giftbox was a belated birthday surprise for the sheriff's son. The boy, apparently duped by the ruse, peeked his head out from the kitchen. His face was bruised, and he quickly disappeared.

"How'd Kevin bust his nose?" Henry demanded.

"What business brings you here?" asked the sheriff, looking curiously at the present Henry was holding. "My son's birthday was three months ago."

"Your boy has been busting out my windows with rocks. Last night he crossed the line and some of the glass cut up Charlie's leg." Henry talked loudly in hopes that the sheriff's son Kevin would overhear everything.

"Sounds as though you are callin' my boy a liar," said the sheriff, coming out of his morning stupor and widening his long stance in the doorframe. The sheriff wore his police uniform, but the top wasn't completely buttoned and his yellowed undershirt was visible. Around his neck was a chain with a circular onyx pendant with some type of inlay that glistened here and there. The sheriff stepped forward close to Henry.

"He told me he busted it playin' basketball last night out back here with his older brother who was home for a visit. Boys will be boys."

"That's something else," Henry said skeptically, "because I broke it last night when I stuffed his head into the dirt. I caught him breaking my window. Now why do you suppose he did a thing like that?"

"I imagin' whoever busted your window out speaks for all of us. Nobody around here likes you much."

The two men stood there close for a while, neither saying anything. The sheriff spoke again.

"You don't touch my boy, or anybody else around here."

"You tell Kevin not to touch my kids or my property. I'll give him a lot worse than what he already got."

"Who's defendin' his property again? Ain't got property rights? Or only you've got the rights? All these folk should let Maddux Brothers pharmacy traipse on through and steal the water, but don't anyone get near Dunstan's place or he'll take the law into his own hands."

"I never said I had the right to hurt your boy. I'm saying I did hurt your boy and I'll do it again if I need to. Whether or not I have the right. If he comes to my house again, I will hurt him. Not because it's right, but because I can. I'm stronger, I'm bigger. That's why, that's how I will hurt him."

The sheriff put his hand to his hip. "Then you'll deal with me."

Henry ripped open the box and the sheriff jerked and put his hand on his weapon and in so doing the sheriff's necklace with onyx pendant jumped and floated in the air for a moment. The giftbox was empty.

"This warning is for you too," Henry muttered. "You keep away from me. I've got nothing to lose."

"You watch yourself now. If the law bends your way, it bends mine as well. If I was you, I'd ask people around here about me before you get too far to come back safely. Now I'll give a guy an inch and I've given you more than that, but I ain't ever given a mile."

Saying this, the sheriff closed the door.

As Henry motorcycled home, he remembered a tale Melissa had told him about the sheriff. Some years ago, before the Dunstans had moved to Bluebird, the sheriff had caught a vagrant in town peeping into residential windows. When Sheriff Haggerty had called the county attorney, he had learned that voyeurism wasn't enough to put a man away unless the fellow had seen something he wasn't supposed to see or abused or exposed himself in the process. So the sheriff had driven the fellow over to Belleflower and dropped him off. Days later when the sheriff came home early for lunch, the same drifter was peeking in on the sheriff's wife—Toots, as the sheriff called her. So he handcuffed the drifter, drove him in the squad car over to the bathroom at the Amoco, and squirted toilet bowl cleaner into his eyes. With his hands cuffed behind his back, the vagrant's only possible relief from the poison in his eyes was to plunge his own head in the toilet bowl. An hour later when the fellow emerged from the bathroom with his sight partially restored, his hair, face, and shirt soaked in toilet water, his face red and burning from the toxins, the sheriff uncuffed him, pointed him to the road out of town and told him the next time he came to town there'd be shit in the toilet. There were plenty more anecdotes of this kind spotted through Bluebird lore, for those who cared to seek.

***

The fence crew had returned to the Dunstan property and was making a commotion, but upstairs inside Charlie slumbered. Ginny had gone over to a friend's. Melissa was lying down on the bed. Melissa still held the bloody hand towel and thought about Charlie's wound and the smell of the hospital and the infection of Charley the horse and the smell of Debbie when she had gotten into her father's car all those years ago on the highway. She heard the front door open. A moment later, Henry entered the bedroom. Henry told Melissa what he had done with breaking the boy's nose to be able to recognize him later and entrapping the boy by ruse and threatening the sheriff and his son with violence, and Melissa, hearing her husband speak of defending the family with force, suddenly had a desire to be taken by her husband, and she uncomplicatedly dropped the towel to the floor and slid off her pajamas and indigo panties while he stood at the end of the bed; she turned over on her stomach and raised up her hips high and splayed her legs wide so that he could see all the colors she knew he wanted—vermillion and salmon and coral and flamingo and rouge and gold—and she hadn't bathed or shaved and it had been a long worrisome night and what she wanted was biological and primitive like gasping for air, and she did it like she knew it was the last time she ever would.

CHAPTER SEVEN
SEED

[JANUARY 19, 2016]

Henry's stone fortification in the Bluebird hills was nearly complete. It was eight feet high all around and nine feet wide at its base.

Henry had named the wall Epoch One. He liked the word *epoch*; it suggested something geological and timeless. Having dedicated himself wholly to building the wall, Henry had, a few weeks ago, ceased publication of the SOUNDER, and most days anymore, he did not see his family at all. He would leave home before sunlight with his plastic travel mug of hot coffee and backpack of supplies before anyone else at home had awakened. After sundown, he would continue working by moonlight or starlight or no light, a relentless mover of rocks. He had taken to loading his backpack with stones too so that he was carrying even heavier loads, back and forth, forth and back.

Today, arriving at his sanctuary by four-wheeler, something inside his chest told him he would finish the wall before sundown. He parked the four-wheeler, put his mug of coffee on the cement pad adjacent to the workshop's door, and dumped the contents of his backpack there, too. He wore jeans, work boots, a parka, a black knit cap, and work gloves. He tightened the laces of his boots. Then, he walked up the slight incline east of his property to the boulder field. His breath turned to mist in the cold air. The earth was covered in a thin layer of frost that he knew would melt off within a few hours. Henry squatted and lifted up a sturdy chunk of limestone. When he lifted the limestone, he saw that the earth underneath was less compact than usual—perhaps there was gravel underneath, he thought. He set the boulder to the side and removed his gloves and used his hands to scoop up the loose dirt and rock. He let a handful of dirt sift through the cracks between his fingers until only small rocks remained. He ascertained that these were not rocks but pieces of flint.

Long ago an Indian hid his treasures here and then died and now I have found them. Long ago the Osage roamed around this area hunting game, fishing, and growing gourds, and all that's left are a few relics here and there. Perhaps the Indian intended to come back for the flint tools, but had died first. Or, perhaps the Indian knew he was going to die so he had hidden up his valuables to a later day.

Henry sorted through what he had found. There were ten flint arrowheads, three flint spear points, and one flint knife. Most were grayish in color but some had salmon or beige coloring. The flint knife was five inches long and of a dark color unlike any stone he had seen around Bluebird—a brown stone colored like petrified mahogany with hints of burnt orange. It was straight along one edge and triangular along the other edge, like a filet blade, and then notched at the bottom to form a small handle. He gripped the knife and the handle was big enough for only two fingers so that the way to hold the knife was to put his extended thumb against the straight part on the back of the knife and wrap his index and middle finger around the handle with the blade pointed away from him. Held as such, Henry could imagine either thrusting the point of the knife into a dead mammal or grabbing a man from behind, the blade pointed away from the person holding it, and slitting the man's throat with the very tip of the knife. He carried the flint tools with him to the workshop and set each piece on the ground on the cement pad adjacent to the workshop's door. He put his gloves back on.

As he continued building the rock wall, he pondered the Indian's buried flint. The Indian was a hunter who had used spears and arrows to kill mammals, and the knife to skin them. Such a person would have been patient and careful and able to walk softly and stand still for indefinite periods of time, and able to suddenly act decisively and mercilessly. The flint tools were an enduring obituary of the life of the hunter Indian. Henry imagined, by contrast, the futility of his future obituary—born in St. Louis to a lawyer and a neurologist, died in Bluebird of unnatural causes, husband, father, Ph.D., associate professor of English at Washington University in St. Louis & etc., all roles he had played but not reflective of his native power, like calling the Mississippi river *a body of flowing water that starts at Lake Itasca, Minnesota and empties into the Gulf of Mexico*, without describing how the river had gained strength, through the relentless upheaval and drainage of titanic glaciers increasing itself through violent persuasion over ages and ages, wearing and tearing itself through sandstone and dolomite and shale and bedrock and limestone, hacking narrow and deep incisions through obdurate material and wide easy swaths with floodplains through weak material, obstinately mixing and sifting and shifting and stirring and depositing and hauling plants and silt and muck and loam and clay and sand and pebbles and gravel and even larger stones such as boulders, the very boulders he used daily to build his secure perimeter, from, to, and along its banks down to the sea, down to the sea, down, down, down to the sea! Always towards the sea! Leaving behind slopes and cliffs and bluffs and gorges and plateaus and plains and valleys and levees and falls, and at the river's peak, driving and chasing and whipping into a frenzy water at the rate of nearly two million cubic feet per second, then in the end, altering and explaining in one way or another two-thirds of the land mass of the continental United States.

Henry would not risk dying and leaving behind a vacant obituary. Completing the rock barrier would tell people what he wished to become, what he had started to become. He increased his pace to a light jog. A boulder in each arm and one in his backpack. He pushed himself into a sweat. He removed his parka and continued at a brisk pace. Eating and drinking were silly—he could eat and drink later. The wall looked even now along its crest, but Henry told himself he would make fifty more trips and err on the side of the wall being too large rather than too small. Hours later, Henry counted only ten loads of stone remaining. Soon enough, he carried in his arms the final load of rocks. When he reached the wall, he collapsed in an exhausted raw heap. Then, rallying himself, he arose and one by one placed the final stones atop the wall.

Finished! Henry roared into the sky. The wall was tangible and substantial. It was mighty and unfeeling and merciless and true to itself. It occupied space in multiple dimensions. It completely encircled and protected the workshop. The only way into the workshop now was to enter through the three-foot opening in the rocks on the eastern edge of the boundary. Within twenty-four hours, a strong iron gate would be placed to guard the opening.

Henry experienced massive movement inside of his soul. He thought of the creation of the earth itself, mountains thrust up and the land cleaved into valleys by the pressures of heat underneath and the shifting of tectonic plates. He imagined neon, volcanic magma spilling forth in every direction. He pictured his body being cut open and covered in magma, and then the magma cooling into lava atop his tissues and organs to sheath them from intruders real and intangible. He imagined, long after his death, scores upon scores of people walking up towards the Bluebird hills to behold his work. They walked in awe, dressed in funeral garb, and gasped or wept when the fortress of rocks came into sight.

Who built this? one visitor would ask of another.
Someone who understood that a rock will always outlive a man, a second
    visitor would reply.
He must have had a heavy weight about him, a third visitor would say.
I have a heaviness in my chest just beholding his work, the first visitor
    would add.
It's like an enormous piece of flint, the second visitor would say, in
    reverence.
No, the whole thing is a gravestone, the third visitor would clarify.

Henry was now weary. His body felt shapeless and depleted, the way a piece of beef would feel after boiling in a stew kettle over a fire. He sat near the door of the workshop and used a bottle of water to wash his face, neck, and hands as best he could. He ate beef jerky and string cheese and chocolate and nuts and raisins, and he finished the remainder of his coffee, now tepid.

Next, Henry entered his workshop. The interior, twelve feet in height, was a singular spacious egg-shaped room. The structure's only door opened to the east, on the wide end of the oval-shaped room, and the more narrow west end of the oval featured floor-to-ceiling glass with no breaks or streaks or visual hindrances of any kind, so that by day the rolling prairie below was visible and by night the unsearchable darkness. The flooring of the workshop's solitary room was a flat polished surface of negro marquina marble which was black with white flashes of light through it like a constellation, with massive fireplaces of marble of the same color on both of the long ends of the egg built into marble walls floor to ceiling of the same color. And in the precise center of the room was a marble altar, again of the same color, rising like a gargantuan sleigh bed flying through space with sculpted scrolls falling delicately from altar to floor on the short ends of the room.

Henry decided to rest atop the altar. He gathered wood and dead brush and stuffed both fireplaces full. He lit two fires with the matches he always kept on his person. The room warmed rapidly on account of its shape and the conductivity of its materials. Henry removed all his clothing and laid himself flat upon the stone sleigh after lifting himself upon it. The sleigh was five feet off the ground. There, Henry allowed himself to sweat and sleep and sweat and sleep with eyes facing the mirrored ceiling. At night, the fire was the only light, and it flickered off the stellary ovoid: no end and no beginning. Other than water breaks and bathroom breaks and to stoke the fire, he was there supine through two nights, and when he had slept sufficiently, he felt strong.

He opened his eyes and looked about the space. He examined from his position on the altar the marble surrounding him in every direction. The marble surface was flat. The marble surface was singular rather than plural. The solid rock of the earth's mantle was one singular entity in nature. Slabs could be cut and removed from the mantle; or, with time and pressure the mantle could be thrust up and broken off from the whole, leaving boulders, rocks, stones, and pebbles. But still, no matter how depleted or scarred, the earth was always seen as a singular as was the earth's mantle. Perhaps this is why rocks were so serene and uncaring, Henry thought—because they were part of a massive whole, had always been, would always be.

Henry closed his eyes and relaxed and in his mind joined his body to the marble. His flesh hardened, his blood stopped, his mind emptied itself of all activity. After a time, a shadow-spirit entered the ovular room in his mind. It was the spirit of a gargantuan woman. She was dressed in soothsayer robes. He had met her before, a long time ago, at a carnival in St. Louis. He had been eighteen then. Those years ago, in the soothsayer's presence, and under her direction, he had had a vision of the marble altar and its surroundings.

The soothsayer looked upon him now as a mother looking over her baby in a crib, and wordlessly communicated to him.

I have been waiting for you to be ready. You have not been ready until now. Now you are a man and you are ready. I have come to deliver to you your fate. I bestow upon you the fate of rocks. Forever you shall be known as Henry Dunstan, king of the piled stones.

After this pronouncement, the shadow-spirit disappeared.

When Henry awakened, he stretched out his body, washed himself with what remaining water he had, and dressed. The laptop in the workshop indicated it was afternoon and that it would snow in Bluebird in the coming days. He was starving, and his body cried out to him for nourishment. He was ashamed at his dependency on food but the hunger was intolerable.

***

Henry stood in line at the Amoco in town to buy his food. An ugly middle-aged man approached Henry. The ugly man was accompanied by a striking teenage girl. Henry had noticed the girl from across the way. There seemed to be a beam of light shining down upon her or perhaps emanating from inside of her.

"I'd like to barge in upon your time," the ugly man said. "My name is Nathan Washington. I'm sure you know my name already. I am a great citizen of the great town of Bluebird. I believe we have seen each other about, but I have never had the great pleasure of meeting you."

Henry nodded.

"You received your college diplomas in the great city of St. Louis at the great institution bearing the name of this nation's first President?"

Henry nodded again.

"It is a marvelous institution of higher learning. Did you study journalism at all? I hear you are a man of letters?"

Henry nodded again and looked at the man's daughter. She smiled back at Henry, and they shared a moment of humor surrounding Nathan's manner of speaking.

"My lovely daughter here, if I may introduce her to you, Claire, is interested in pursuing this trade. She is one of the brightest and most beautiful persons upon this earth. Would you be willing to provide her with some type of internship as a favor to me?"

"I'm busy now but she can come by and we'll figure something out." Henry looked at Claire even as he referred to her in the third person. She looked admiringly upon Henry. Henry thought that having Claire Washington involved with the SOUNDER would allow him to keep up the newsletter with less work for himself.

Nathan and Claire excused themselves, and Henry completed his purchase. There was a small dining table inside the Amoco. Henry hurried there and sat his things down. He was ravenous. He ate potato logs, chicken breasts, pizza, and handfuls of candy, which he washed down with a large fountain soda.

Henry returned home. He parked his four-wheeler in the shed and removed from his backpack the flint arrowheads and spear points and the knife he had found in the hills recently. He placed all of these but the knife in the coffee tin where he kept his other discoveries of flint. He took the knife and put on some goggles and switched on the grinding tool and sharpened the blade of the flint knife until it was even and thin and satisfactory to him. He put the knife in the backpack and left the backpack in the shed near his four-wheeler.

He went inside the house and greeted his wife and children who were gathered in the front room listening to Ginny play her flute. He watched for a moment, then retired to the bathroom for a lengthy shower. He stood under the showerhead for an hour. He shaved his face and his armpits and his chest and the back of his neck. He shaved a second time. The cleansing of the exterior of his body brought attention to the interior of his body. He felt ashamed that he had eaten so much at the Amoco. He thought of the pizza and chicken sitting there lazily in his stomach. He plunged two fingers into his throat until he vomited there in the shower, the partially digested food particles swirling around the drain. He finished his shower, cleaned out the drain, and dressed himself in clean jeans, utility workshirt, socks, and underwear. He used a rag to wash the dirt and mud off his parka and boots. Once the parka was clean, he draped it over his arm and went into the kitchen where his family was seated at the table, eating lasagna with garlic bread and mixed vegetables.

Melissa stared at him as if waiting for him to say something. Henry hung his coat over the empty chair at the table. He brewed a pot of coffee. He removed a pot from the drawer under the stove, poured milk into it from the refrigerator, put the pot on the stove, and turned on the burner. He removed the yellow mug from its hook below the white cabinetry, filled it with coffee, and placed it in front of Melissa. When the milk in the pot was warm, he turned off the burner, added cocoa powder to it, stirred, and poured some of the hot chocolate into the purple mug, which he placed in front of Ginny. He repeated this, pouring hot chocolate into a light blue mug, which he placed in front of Charlie. Henry filled his own indigo blue mug with coffee and sat down at the metal table at the chair that held his parka. He took a sip of the coffee from his own mug. It was very hot and very strong. Melissa pushed her coffee cup away from herself. Ginny sat at Henry's left taking small bites of her garlic bread. Now she took a sip of her hot chocolate. She glanced at her father and smiled. Henry reached over towards her and gently stroked her hair and scratched her back. Charlie sat at Henry's right. Charlie took a sip of his hot cocoa and nodded in delight. Henry reached over and pulled Charlie's chair closer until it was touching Henry's chair. Henry extended his right arm around Charlie's shoulder and pulled Charlie towards him. Charlie leaned to his left and hugged his father tightly, both of his arms around his father's mid-section as if holding a life preserver in a raging river. Melissa looked on in the curious and protective way a female dog watches a child play with her pups. They all sat there like that for over an hour, no one speaking, with Henry rubbing his daughter's back with one hand and hugging his son with the other.

The phone rang. Ginny hesitated, then stood and answered it. By the way she was talking, Henry assumed it was one of her girlfriends from school. Ginny said she needed to go over and work on a project with her friend for the world history fair. They were doing a report on the Netherlands. The lowland empire that had ruled the world centuries ago. On a cold night such as this, Melissa said she would drive Ginny over, even though the friend was just in Bluebird. Melissa said Charlie would ride along, too, for something to do. Melissa and the children huddled by the front door and bundled up in coats, gloves, and scarves. Once she was dressed, Melissa opened the front door and exited without speaking.

Charlie and Ginny both paused and looked at their father. Henry kissed his own right thumb, pressed it to the center of Charlie's forehead, and held it there for a moment as if to leave a tactile memory and blessing that would last forever. Charlie rubbed his forehead and looked at his father in wonder. Henry motioned for Charlie to step back and for Ginny to step forward. Henry kissed his right thumb again, pressed it to the center of Ginny's forehead, and held it there for a moment as if to leave a tactile memory and blessing that would last forever. Ginny waited for some kind of explanation, which was not forthcoming. Henry opened the front door and motioned for the children to go with their mother. The children did not move away from him at first, but he motioned to them again, and they descended the porch. The children got into the car and something about the cold night and the light frost on the ground muffled the sound of the car door shutting so that it sounded like a rifle being shot in the distance.

As soon as the car drove out of sight, Henry put on his parka and went out to the shed. There he removed from his backpack one of the new blue St. Louis Rams knit caps he had just purchased at the Amoco and put it on his head. Rams' gear was on sale now that the team had moved to Los Angeles. He put on his new work gloves and made sure his flint knife was in his backpack.

He mounted his four-wheeler and drove to his workshop in the hills. The drive at night, in these conditions, took around fifteen minutes. The night was still and cold and his face smarted in the wind. Arriving at the workshop, he dismounted the four-wheeler, sat his backpack on the ground, removed a headlamp from his backpack, turned the light on, and affixed the lamp to his head. Then he commenced building Epoch Two. Epoch Two was a rock wall running parallel to and outside of the existing Epoch One; the same monumental effort he had completed a few days ago, all over again. And following Epoch Two there would be Epoch Three. And so on.

***

Winter persisted, each day colder and darker than the day prior. One day, a county utility truck with a hydraulic lift arrived in Bluebird in the afternoon and replaced the bulb on the solitary street lamp on Main Street. When the lamp illuminated that evening after dark, the hoary winter air was rendered an alien yellow and the few leafless trees were made into black profiles against the evening sky. Car windshields were covered in light blankets of snow. The few sets of tire marks on the snowy roads were not fresh. No humans or dogs or cats were visible, although lit interior windows of homes proved the town had not been vacated, but was rather in an embargo against the cold and moisture. The air smelled of smoke.

On Main Street across from Bluebird's new post office—four decades new—the screen door on a painted brick one-story creaked open. A young woman with shoulder-length ebony hair emerged from beneath a porch light. She placed her boot gingerly into the snowfall as a test and finding the snow shallow and dry she pressed on easily, the snowpack under her feet making muffled crunching sounds. She walked several paces in a northward direction now beyond the umbrella of hazy streetlamp light, and then turning east in darkness continued along then under the little bridge and onwards for a ways until after turning northward again briefly she arrived at the Dunstan residence. A chain-link fence completely surrounded the house. The young woman buzzed the intercom attached to the fence. Inside, someone pushed a button that allowed the driveway gate to swing open.

Inside the home, Melissa Dunstan had been reading the WALL STREET JOURNAL on the internet. Studying the financial markets made her queasy, and she had been sipping on an herbal tea to steady herself. When Melissa heard the knock at the door, she turned on the porch light and opened the door to Claire Washington. Melissa knew Claire to be a senior in high school. Claire was the daughter of Nathan Washington, a lifelong Bluebird resident. Nathan's wife had died of ovarian cancer soon after Claire's birth and never having remarried, Nathan's sole occupation other than his work at the electrical plant in Belleflower appeared to be doting on his daughter. Claire's boots were trendy and knee-high. She wore a short heather gray dress and a red wool trench coat. The trench coat opened like an upside down V around the navel, which made Claire's artificially bronzed legs, bare in the cold, look even longer. Claire had full cheeks that dimpled when she smiled and engaging acorn eyes with full lashes. Delicate flakes of snow had gathered in her hair and the soft waves of hair gathered along her coat collar. Claire looked more innocent cheerleader than exotic dancer; nevertheless, Claire made for an unusual visitor on this frosty night. Melissa scowled and waited for Claire to begin the conversation.

"Good evening Mrs. Dunstan, may I ask if Mr. Dunstan is at home?" Claire asked in polite twang.

Claire struck Melissa as someone who blinked and smiled a lot to get her way—the curse and gift of beauty.

"Evening is inconvenient, I suggest you try another time." Melissa didn't know why Claire was here, but she didn't like that Claire seemed to know Henry. And Melissa was tired and needed to get back to preparing for her trading the next day.

"I'm sure he would like to meet with me if he knew I were here."

"He's not."

"I'll come by tomorrow afternoon after school."

"That won't work." Melissa was being none too helpful. Her blood was racing.

"How about early morning?" Claire pressed undeterred. "I'm a morning person."

"Are you now?" Melissa snarled.

Knowing it was unlikely Claire would arrive at the house prior to Henry departing for his workshop, Melissa cheered up a bit and said, "Sure, sure, you come by in the morning, that'll be perfect. Now can I get you a hot drink before you get on your way?" This was spoken more with an emphasis on Claire being on her way than Melissa providing a hot drink.

But Claire was already down the steps, her hips swaying. Claire turned her head and neck around just so while her body pranced forward so that it looked like she was in a shampoo ad the way her glossy hair bounced.

Next morning, Henry exited the house early under the film of daybreak. He carried his plastic travel mug of coffee in one hand and keys to the four-wheeler in the other. Over one shoulder, he carried a backpack full of supplies. Melissa observed Henry through the kitchen window. Henry was dressed in heavy clothes and a blue St. Louis Rams knit cap that looked new to Melissa. Henry stopped by Albert's makeshift headstone in the corner of the lot and knelt there for a while. Then Henry stood, went out of view for a moment to retrieve the four-wheeler from the shed, and then returned into view as he drove back up the driveway, exited the lot, and waited for the gate to close behind him. When Henry turned to face the road, Claire Washington was standing there and waved meekly to Henry. Melissa, watching through binoculars, wondered how often this same encounter had occurred before without her witnessing it.

Melissa could see through the binoculars that Claire was wearing bluejeans tucked into tan suede cowboy boots with a skintight pink cable knit sweater on top. Claire's hair was pulled up into a knitted wool beanie with curls out of the hat perfectly to frame the face and sculpted neck. She looked like the rich kids at the movie house up in Belleflower on a date. Henry dismounted his four-wheeler, the engine still running. Melissa cracked the window an inch but could hear nothing from her location inside the house.

***

"Washington's daughter?" Henry said, his breath visible.

"Yessir."

"Claire?"

"I am me," she smiled politely, her face radiating uncomplicatedness. She reminded him of a puppy or a young child.

"So you are," Henry said.

An awkward moment passed between them.

"You still interested in helping me out?" Henry asked over the sound of the four-wheeler's engine.

"Of course."

"What are your reasons?" Henry asked, now that Claire's father was not around to answer for her.

"I'd like to get a scholarship to a good university. My dad thinks that getting a letter of recommendation from a former faculty member at Washington University will help me get a scholarship there. He thinks you're my golden ticket."

"So you're not interested in journalism?"

"I haven't made up my mind."

"But you're willing to try it at least," Henry said as a statement rather than a question.

"So what do you want me to do?" Claire asked Henry.

"Up to you."

Claire looked confused. "What did you and my Daddy decide I should do for your newspaper?"

"Doesn't matter. You figure out something to write about, if it's good I'll put it in the next edition. If it's no good, I'll tell you so and you can try again. We'll figure it out."

She stared at him blankly.

After a silence, he threw her a bone. "Ok, a couple ideas to get you started. One, overview of our town, who are we? Two, what do the farmers say about the water now that it's been a while since they kicked off their lawsuit?"

"Which one should I start with?"

He chuckled. It had been a while since anyone had listened to him.

"You're the student. I'm the teacher. Come up with something and we'll talk." He waved to her briefly and hopped on the four-wheeler and sped off.

***

To Melissa, Henry's interaction with Claire looked like a lover's quarrel as Henry drove off on his four-wheeler while Claire appeared to still be talking. Melissa returned to her station at the computer in the master bedroom. Papers were scattered about the desk and the bed. The papers were mostly notes she had scribbled. One note was a list of thirty companies she was following closely: John Deere; Tesla; Disney; Match. These were companies she had identified as being undervalued.

She had put John Deere on the list after she had noticed that nearly all the farm equipment in Bluebird was John Deere brand. Tesla was a new automobile manufacturing company Henry had told her about. She had written Disney on the list, because when she had called the cable company to upgrade her parents' cable package, the customer service representative had told Melissa that Disney owned several popular cable channels such as ESPN and Discovery. Match was an online dating service that Shirlene Mack had mentioned. Apparently Shirlene's daughter had met a few guys online using that particular service. Given the right set of circumstances, Melissa believed the share prices of these companies could escalate quickly. One of the other names on the list was Maddux Brothers. It seemed like all the pills her parents took were made by Maddux. The name had a question mark by it—Melissa needed to review their stock history more carefully. Plus, she didn't know how she felt about investing in the very company that was intent on destroying the farms of Bluebird.

Melissa was surprised at the fear she now felt that Henry might cheat on her with Claire. Jealousy had long been a struggle for Melissa in her marriage to Henry, so much so it had almost led to divorce in the early years in St. Louis. She had read all kinds of self-help books and had undergone therapy and even taken medications. Eventually her hard work in therapy and the birth of the three children, which in her mind had tied her more to Henry, had helped her manage her envy. But lately her sleep had been fitful and her thoughts manic from her constant attention to her trading portfolio. Moreover, there were hardly any attractive women in Bluebird to worry about, so Melissa allowed herself that perhaps she had had her guard down when Claire entered the picture.

Her mind was racing, and she began pacing about the bedroom. After fifteen minutes, she realized she would not be able to function logically today. She sold all of her open trading positions and turned off the computer. She began assembling different puzzle pieces in her mind to try to sort out whether she needed to worry about Henry being unfaithful.

Henry had not cheated on Melissa yet. That much was true; that Melissa knew; that Melissa needed to keep telling herself—because if he had done it she sure as hell would have caught him. But Melissa could not entirely trust Henry. Henry liked being alone, and he was non-communicative and cold, and such persons, in Melissa's mind, were the most likely to cheat. Melissa pictured the blue St. Louis Rams knit cap Melissa had seen Henry wearing that morning when he had driven off on his four-wheeler.

I've never seen Henry wear that before. Claire must have given it to him. Henry doesn't even like the Rams. He's a Steelers fan.

Melissa pictured the outfits Claire had worn lately. Hooker's clothes, Melissa thought. The prior evening, Claire had worn a narrow-cut bright red coat. This morning, Claire had worn a skin-tight sweater.

How handy for Henry that Claire is young and fresh and bubbly and spry and lithe and apple-chested and eager to please and doubtless fresh and snug and eager between her silky legs and likely wettens up real fast and tart for him like a swollen grapefruit.

As her thoughts spiraled away from her, Melissa pictured herself catching Henry in the act of kissing Claire on the marital bed, the head of which was opposite the master bedroom door, so that in her fantastical visualizations, after announcing she was taking the kids to Belleflower for dinner, and then coming home duplicitously early and entering the home quietly, the kids still waiting in the car, and suddenly opening the bedroom door, Melissa would surprise the illicit lovers and have all the incontrovertible eyewitness proof of betrayal she needed to justify divorce and would scream *keep your whore!* and then grab the banker's lamp from the table at her left and hurl it at her husband.

Melissa went to the bathroom and splashed water on her face and took a sedative from the medicine cabinet. She went outside into the morning air to slow down her thinking. Setting aside the setbacks of today caused by her jealousy, Melissa was in general achieving the goals she had set for herself. She was making good decisions in the stock market, and it was all for a good purpose. She felt like God was on her side, blowing a soft helping wind into the sails of her stock picks, whispering ideas to her by morning coffee on the porch, illuminating her mind to see the patterns of the future. Melissa had already donated ten thousand dollars cash to the Bluebird Society for the school renovation project, telling Shirlene Mack it was a gift from herself and Henry, but that Henry wanted it to be a secret. Melissa did not want Shirlene to thank Henry for his donation—this would cause Henry to become suspicious and learn of Melissa's clandestine day-trading, whereupon Melissa would no doubt feel guilty and confess to her husband her role in Albert's death.

The outside air was cold. Melissa returned indoors. She calculated how many more months it would take her to earn the extra one hundred thousand dollars for the school renovation. Once she had that money, Melissa imagined herself wrapping the cash loosely in white tissue paper and walking over and presenting it to Shirlene. In her fantasies, Melissa would say, *Here's your school!* No doubt, Shirlene would melt into tears of gratitude and call the other ladies in the Bluebird Society and tell them to come right over; they'd all stare at the money and count it and celebrate Melissa's goodness and generosity and hail her as the Queen of Bluebird and the Homecoming Queen Come Home.

Melissa imagined even a barbeque with pulled pork and sweet corn and biscuits and beans in honor of her achievements, and everyone in town would be invited and there would be balloons and clowns and a bounce house for the kids. Such a celebration would be an evening of demarcation—dusk for embarrassing old Bluebird and dawn for a new proud restored fashionable Bluebird with herself the queen at its center.

But the problem was that the target date for the hundred thousand dollars changed every day, depending on how her trades that day had fared. Some days Melissa made no money or lost money. It was impossible to predict the future. And there were dozens of permutations playing out in her mind at all hours like graphing algorithms in an exhausted software program. And her mind was frayed from overuse.

She looked down at her body seated there on the carpet of the front room. Her legs were extended in front of her in the shape of a V. She had been sitting in this spot for an hour and had not stretched a single limb. She laughed at her own inability to manage her jealousy. She swiveled her head ninety degrees in each direction and then back to center. She reached her right arm over the left side of her head and used her fingers to stretch the left side of her neck by pulling her head to the right.

She jumped when the phone rang—it was the sonorous ring of the Stromberg-Carlson black landphone in the kitchen. It sounded like someone clobbering a bell with a hammer. Melissa walked into the kitchen and picked up.

"Hello?"

"This is Claire Washington. May I speak to Henry? I've had trouble reaching him." Melissa thought Claire's voice had a sultry tone to it.

"You came by this morning. What's this about?"

"I would like to speak to Henry. I need to make an arrangement with him."

Melissa slammed the receiver down. *An arrangement? What kind of arrangement?* Melissa was stupefied. This was the third occasion now that Claire had tried to make contact with Henry. That Melissa knew of. Last night Claire had come by in the snow wearing the red topcoat, then this morning Claire was waiting for Henry outside the gate, and now Claire had asked for an arrangement with Henry.

The phone rang again. Melissa picked up the receiver and slammed it down again without answering. She noticed the time on the microwave clock. Ginny and Charlie would be home from school in a few hours. Melissa did not want to lose the whole day to her mental paralysis. She could exercise or read or run to the store or talk to a friend or cook dinner. Anything but stay trapped inside her mind. She stepped out onto the front porch again and looked for a sign. Something exterior to herself that would help her find her moorings. The sky was mostly drab but a cloud in the shape of an arrow seemed to point downwards. She walked to the southwest corner of the lot where the arrow-shaped cloud seemed to be pointing. The ground was hard and cold on her bare feet.

Our Cherub, H.A.D.

Albert's final resting place.

There was fresh dirt all around the base of the marker. She remembered that Henry lately had tended to this sacred spot more than ever, and that gave her some peace to be reminded of Henry's connection to Albert. Melissa breathed in deeply through her nostrils and tilted her head back to absorb the serene atmosphere as snow had started falling from the sky. She felt a wet drop on her nose, then her chin, and now one on her cheek. She told herself that Henry was loyal, and that she needed to reign in her jealousy or be destroyed by it. Envy had been a problem for her in St. Louis, one she had learned to handle, and acknowledging it was half the battle. Envy was not a new uncontrollable sensation, just new for Melissa's life in Bluebird with Claire coming around, but the same tools from St. Louis would work here too. She fell to her knees. "God please! God help!" Another deep breath in, and let it out. And again. In and out.

Just because I think it doesn't mean it's true. In. Out. Whatever I imagine will manifest itself as truth. In and out. Deep breaths. I am responsible for how much weight I give to my feelings. Take my medication when I need it. In and out. I am okay. In. Out. In. Out. I am okay. Okay. Okay.

She was softening and the land was softening, too, as the heavens gently unfolded their billowy generosity of snow wherever sky touched earth, purifying the terrain into a never-ending mantle of white.

CHAPTER EIGHT
HEARTH

[MARCH 18, 2016]

Between winter solstice and vernal equinox as the earth tilted its northern hemisphere gradually closer to the sun, the days grew longer, and Henry grew more productive on his land. In the evenings, as Henry toiled, the sun cast stretched shadows eastward across the pallid canvas, giving the appearance that two men and not one plodded back and forth burdened with stones.

One day during this season of shadows, Henry walked into town to purchase a new wheelbarrow from Big Joe. The only wheelbarrow Joe had for sale, outside of a special order, was yellow in color.

"What's it for?"

"That's for me to know," replied Henry, "tell me how much I owe."

Joe chuckled at Henry. Joe bit off a piece of the jerky he was holding and chewed while looking Henry over. Henry grew impatient and pulled out a stack of bills and left them on the counter. He pushed his wheelbarrow outside. Henry wore a dark parka and a knit Rams hat he had purchased for himself at the gas station a while back. The hats had been on sale given the football team's sudden departure from Missouri; Henry had purchased ten of them. Henry pushed the yellow wheelbarrow up the dirt road leading from Main in Bluebird to his property in the hills.

The wheelbarrow was contrary to Henry's original intentions of moving all the rocks by hand, but his desire to complete Epoch Two of the enclosure was so fervent that he allowed himself this luxury. In recent weeks, he had begun to experience pain in his wrists, shoulders, and neck. Without the wheelbarrow, Henry had been using his body purely as a force of nature—one unit of energy exerted to move one unit of rock. His body had eventually responded in kind by developing fissures, grindings, and erosions among the muscles and sinews.

Henry arrived at his property. He felt renewed looking upon it. Epoch Two, a second barrier of stacked rocks running outside of and parallel to Epoch One, was well underway. Epoch Two was two or three feet in height all around, and, like Epoch One, was nine to ten feet wide at its base. The work ahead of Henry was to add rocks to the existing foundation of Epoch Two until that wall achieved the same height as Epoch One. Henry stationed the wheelbarrow east of Epoch Two, passed through the three-foot opening he had created in this wall, and stood on the ground in between the two walls; five feet of flat, empty earth separated the two walls at their foundations. From this vantage point, he considered the magnitude of Epoch One. Collectively, the rocks imposed a sense of awesome power. Henry could almost hear the earth herself groaning underneath their mass. He leaned forward so that each hand touched a different stone. The stones were cool to the touch but the round stone under his right hand was cooler than the flat stone under his left hand.

To become insentient does not require abandoning my unique identity. I would still be myself. These thoughts gave him comfort, for he had begun to worry that his quest to become uncaring like stone would extinguish any sense of personal identity. He thought of the rocks making up the Flamingo Fire—they had maintained a sense of character despite being inanimate. He thought of how some rocks made up riverbeds and how some were buried deep in the earth and how some were made into walls. All had unique identities.

Henry now used his key to open the iron gate protecting the three-foot opening in Epoch One, which was aligned with the opening of similar width in Epoch Two, so that he was now completely inside the rock fortification. He walked over to the workshop. He removed another key from the pocket of his jeans, unlocked the workshop door, opened the door, took a few steps inside, removed the spare cash from his parka, and placed the cash on the marble floor inside the door. He picked up his backpack, brought it outside with him, locked the door with the key, returned the key to his jeans' pocket, and dumped the drinks and snacks from his backpack onto the concrete pad just outside the door. He drank a liter of water from a bottle and put a piece of beef jerky and a piece of string cheese in his mouth. He chewed these for a while, swallowed a few times, and then spat out the remainder onto the dirt. *Rocks don't eat, but I do.* He walked around quickly to the rear of the property, past the clump of brush standing as sentinel near the south face of the interior of Epoch One, and stood before the

Flamingo Fire. He unzipped his pants and urinated all about the wall, as if smothering a fire with a firehose.

He returned to the east side of the workshop, exited through both walls, and pushed the yellow wheelbarrow up the incline to the boulder field. Now, using his body as a tool with leverage, he could move three to four times as much weight per trip as he had done without the wheelbarrow. A few hours into the day's labors, as Henry unloaded rocks from the wheelbarrow by hand, onto the existing foundations of Epoch Two, Henry felt the presence of someone behind him. He turned to see Claire Washington. It had been some two months since his prior conversation with her, in which he had given her a few ideas to work on for the SOUNDER.

Today again, Claire looked like an image torn from a style magazine. She wore pinstriped blue slacks, a dark floral print on top with plunging neckline, a long tidewater blue wool coat, and suede blue boots. She smelled citrusy and fresh. Her eyes were shadowed in turquoise and gold and she had sprayed her bushy naturally curly hair to look wet.

"I like your hat," she said, "my daddy likes the Rams."

"It was on sale," Henry said, "my head gets cold."

"I want to show you something," she said pleasantly, reaching into her coat.

"What do you think of my walls?"

"I finished my research for the newsletter."

"How do you know about my workshop?"

"They call it the Dunstan Hotel. Or Henry's Day Spa. They make fun of you. They curse you. They don't know how nice and helpful you are." She blinked at him. Her mannerisms were not sensual but more those of a dog wanting a treat.

"What do you think of my walls?" he asked again.

"You must be strong," she said.

He nodded. He did feel strong. "Bring your articles to Dickey's later," he said.

Henry pushed the empty wheelbarrow back up the incline to gather another load. Claire followed him for a while and even dirtied herself when with some difficulty she placed a boulder in the wheelbarrow. Henry pressed on without speaking, and after a time, Claire returned down the way from which she had come.

In town, Melissa was running a few errands in the sedan. Melissa needed to mail a parcel at the post office and then pick up a notebook and pens over at Campbell's Dry Goods. Today, Melissa had watched the stock markets start into the red and bounce around fervently until nine o'clock local time when she had decided to take the day off from trading. It had been a pleasurable day. Melissa had napped some, started into a new book, painted her nails, and baked a beef roast with potatoes and carrots. The home had greeted her children after school all warm and comfortable. She had told her children that when she returned from errands they'd all sit down together and have a nice supper and maybe even watch a movie together on TV.

Having made her purchases at Campbell's Dry Goods, Melissa drove southward to the end of Main swaying her head and drumming her thumb on the steering wheel to the beat of the radio. As she made the slow three-point-turn to go back northward towards home there was a young girl descending the dirt road that connected the town of Bluebird to the hills of Bluebird. Melissa silenced the music and slowed the car. Sure enough, it was Claire swaggering home. Claire might have been on a nature walk, but she was dressed more for attention than exercise. Melissa's jealousy, like any vice, had a way of summarily accelerating to its prior maximum. *Mermaid whore just pleasured my husband,* Melissa imagined and she inspected Claire as best she could from a distance.

When Melissa arrived home, Charlie was chasing Ginny around the front room with a Nerf bat. Melissa slammed the door shut. She grabbed the bat from Charlie and threw it to the ground. She screamed that he would not get any dinner tonight. Charlie burst into tears and covered his face with his hands. Ginny ran upstairs and hid in her bedroom closet. Charlie joined his sister there. Melissa pulled at her own hair, then seized the kitchen curtains beneath the sink and tore them from their moorings, then threw the curtains across the room. She kicked at the dining table until her foot slipped and she rammed the table with her leg. This opened a gash in her shin. Melissa went to the bathroom, dabbed up the blood, put some gauze on the wound, and took three of what she normally took to settle herself. She filled the sink with cold water and soaked her hands there for a time. She splashed some water on her face. She eventually emerged from the bathroom, committed to reinstating her children's trust in her. It took her an hour to convince them she was sorry. Then, they all sat down to the beef roast dinner she had prepared earlier. The children grew more and more comfortable and talkative as they ate. Melissa learned a lot about their friends and school that she had missed in the past while.

After dinner, Melissa moved the dishes to the sink. She filled the sink with hot water, dish soap, and a small scoop of powdered cleaning tonic. She asked her kids if they would prefer to drive into Belleflower for a malt or watch a movie on TV. Both children voted for the drive and the malt. There was a new place in Belleflower that had gigantic malts of every variety.

Melissa and her children exited the home and got into the sedan. She pulled out of the driveway, turned north, drove a few hundred yards, and paused at the STOP sign that joined the Bluebird road to the highway leading to Belleflower. To the left was a superlative sunset—the sky was a rippled lake of magma with thin gray fingerprints smeared across it, and the sun itself a massive glowing ball of fire held up, it seemed, by a string just above the horizon.

"The sun is mad," Charlie said.

"Irate," Ginny added which drew a frown from Melissa. "We saw a movie in school about how it's a big ball of hot gas under constant pressure and it blows out heat to stay in balance."

"Sounds like me when I got home today," Melissa said jokingly and apologized again. The kids laughed as if relieved that the episode was behind them.

"What if that string got cut and the sun fell it would land in the ocean," Charlie said.

"And boil the water and the boiling rising waters would roast us all," Ginny agreed.

"It can't fall," Melissa corrected her children, "it's not like a base-ball."

"At school they said it would expand and explode and swallow everything we have ever known," Ginny said.

"That will be long, long after all of us are dead." Melissa thought the kids were referring to her earlier wrath by analogy.

A few miles up the highway towards Belleflower, the sign for Dickey's Diner became visible. Fat Dickey had purchased an old drive-through theater back in the late 1960s. He had knocked down the original ticket and snack bar building, and built his restaurant there. The massive open gravel area from the drive-through now formed a giant parking lot for the diner. More recently, as everyone in Bluebird had heard through gossip, Dickey had started slowing down on account of congestive heart disease. As such, he had turned over management of the diner to his son Rickey and daughter Nicki. Despite this, however, Dickey was almost always at the diner. Fat Dickey and his wife lived in unincorporated Lampersville, west of Bluebird. Rickey and Nicki and their families both lived in Belleflower. The word in Bluebird was that Dickey's children had never once condescended to set foot in Bluebird proper.

Before Melissa reached Dickey's, a four-wheeler coming from the other direction turned into the gravel lot. Melissa's heart started pounding. She slowed down and followed the four-wheeler into the diner's parking lot, keeping plenty of distance between the two vehicles so that she would not be detected.

"Why are you turning here?" Ginny queried.

"I need for both of you to be quiet. Don't worry, we're still going for treats." Melissa was trying to calm her racing thoughts. She made sure to take deep breaths. She remembered she had more sedatives in the glove box if necessary. She looked straight ahead to avoid betraying any emotions to her children.

The driver of the four-wheeler parked and dismounted. The driver wore a dark parka and blue knit hat and appeared to have the same body shape and gait as Henry, but Melissa was not positive it was him. The driver opened the double glass doors into a little vestibule that formed the main entrance to Dickey's. The driver's back to Melissa's car, Melissa now maneuvered immediately behind him. Melissa clearly identified the driver now as Henry, for he had removed his hat and she could see his face in profile.

Just inside the vestibule stood Claire, who greeted Henry with a smile. Claire was dressed as before when Melissa had seen her, except that Claire now wore a large gold watch on her right wrist, carried a gold clutch, and had substituted a small cloak for her wool coat so that the rippling shape of her body was even more evident than before. Melissa wondered if all these accoutrements were gifts from Henry.

"Who's that girl?" Ginny asked.

Using all of her focus Melissa said, "oh, that's a nice girl who wants to work on the newsletter with Daddy. He's helping her."

"Daddy!" Charlie yelled, unsuccessfully trying to get his father's attention.

"I'm sorry, guys," Melissa said suddenly, still looking straight ahead, her armpits torching her sweater with moisture and her stomach sinking, "I'm dizzy. I need to get back home to use the bathroom, how about that TV movie after all? I'll make you shakes and we'll go to Belleflower soon, I swear." The kids voiced their dissatisfaction. Melissa drove them home nonetheless.

Once inside the house, Charlie raced over, grabbed the remote, and turned on the TV. He flipped through the channels. Ginny joined him on the sofa. Charlie stopped changing the channels when he came to the original *Charlie and the Chocolate Factory*.

"I'm going to run to the bathroom," Melissa said. In the medicine cabinet she found a sedative and a painkiller and swallowed both just with the saliva in her mouth. She came back out and told the kids there was ice cream in the freezer in the shed she needed to fetch. Out in the shed, Melissa rummaged around manically until she found Henry's bottle of rum. She took six or eight swigs and grabbed the tub of starlight mint ice cream from the old chest freezer. She came back inside and made shakes in the kitchen with the ice cream, bananas, Oreos, and some milk. She brought the shakes into the front room, handed one to each child, and kept one for herself. The kids yelped with glee at the sight of the shakes. Melissa sat down on the sofa next to her children. She wolfed down her own shake, then fell asleep. Even though their mother was asleep, the kids enjoyed her calm company, and they put themselves to bed when the movie ended.

***

Inside Dickey's Diner, Henry sat facing inside the crowded restaurant. Claire faced the other direction towards the smudged humid glass. The air they breathed smelled of grease and char. Henry ordered the burger, fries, and chocolate shake and Claire asked for only a glass of water. Claire removed her cloak. Her black and teal floral print shirt was cut in a plunging U and her neck bones and sinews were delicate as if carved from amber above a spirited chest that pushed out like two ripe grapefruits. Her skin was supple and golden. Bright yellow-brown eyes on a face beaming with light framed by curly jazzy rich hair. Long expressive fingers and wrists. She was a specimen of magnificent splendor. As before, Claire gave off a light zesty scent, something like a strawberry lemonade. Henry admired her like a Vermeer or an ice sculpture or a fancy gadget at a science show such as a perpetual motion machine, something made to appreciate from a distance, not to own or consume or defile, and he studied her construction and formation to understand how the whole was made up of individual brushstrokes.

"What are we doing here?" he asked.

She looked flummoxed. "You said to meet here."

"I prefer being alone in the hills. Don't go there again for any reason. What I do there I do alone." Henry spoke in a grave tone.

She nodded. "Why do you need to be alone?"

Henry didn't want this chit-chat, but he needed to eat his burger to refuel, and there was no sense in sitting there silent while his food cooked. He took a big spoonful of his shake and ate it like medicine. Time spent buying food and time spent eating food was time wasted, time he could have spent working. But he needed the energy.

"Everyone is alone. Everyone is always alone. Few are honest about it. I don't surround myself with fixtures or screens to disguise my solitude."

Claire seemed curious rather than put off by his lugubriousness. "So what about now? Are you alone now?"

"Of course. You, too. You might say that we are not alone because we sit at the same table, that you are accompanied by me at this moment, that I am accompanied by you. And we are accompanied by all these other people eating and those people working." Henry waved his hand about to indicate the presence of other people.

"Yessir. I would say so." Claire looked about the restaurant and waved demurely to a family she recognized.

"No. You are alone. No one can help you. No one knows anything about you or your life or your experiences. Everything is entirely up to you. To you alone is the burden of you. Now, seated at this table, we're two trees in a forest. Each utterly alone. Those people eating and working, they are other trees also in proximity."

"Why get married? Why have kids then? Your wife is pretty. She has gorgeous eyes."

Henry looked at Claire suspiciously. "You don't know me. I'm talking to you because I need energy and my hamburger is cooking and I will eat it when it's ready." Henry used his hand to push his hair out of his face. He had not had a haircut in months.

"Sorry, sir. I'm used to saying nice things to people. I like to make people feel good. It's hard for me if someone doesn't like me."

"You might as well be nice to a rock."

Claire looked like she would contest what Henry had just said but instead repeated her earlier questions. "Why marry? Why have kids? Why do anything if it all just ends?" Her native positive temperament neither challenged nor negated his view but was borne of curiosity like a scientist studying a cell through a microscope. Henry surprised himself by continuing in the conversation rather than dismissing this girl without any life experience. Claire was more inquisitive and mentally formed than he had given her credit for. He cheered up a bit.

"To add to myself, to add to my story, to add to life. Why does a river grow? Why does it perpetuate itself unconsciously? It's the same for my wife as for me. I don't help Melissa; I don't make her happy. Each of us—me, Melissa—is an independent sovereign power of nature, expanding and colliding with other powers. If in the mountains there is a barren slope of slate with water running down its face, it would be absurd to suggest the river is helping or comforting the mountain. Each started there since forever, absent any choice, and remained there due to something more elementary than volition even, and each contributes to the larger makeup of nature, and yet each is alone: water is water, rock is rock. A rock with water on it is a rock with water on it, not some combination of rock and water, not a couple, not a marriage, not a partnership or a friendship, not some lovely pairing where water needed rock and rock needed water. There's no sentimentality in it."

Claire rolled her eyes a bit. "So that's how you approach your life, work, family, everything? Avoid feeling feelings?"

Henry spoke as if he were trying out some lines for the first time. "I'm not avoiding sentimentality or not avoiding sentimentality. I'm trying to learn from the rocks I use to build my walls. They don't get worked up one way or another. If you want to act sentimental, that's up to you. But it's a fiction. There's no sentimentality in nature."

She looked at him directly and smiled slightly to soften the blow of what she would say next. "You, sir, are what my Daddy would call a hypocrite. You want people to understand that you are like a rock or like water. But if I am nice or friendly, as part of my own personality, you would squash that. I will allow you to be a rock if you please. But you won't allow me to be human or a fragile girl, which I am. I am part of this planet too. Just like you. Just like everyone. Even if for now we talk about the world as we see it, not counting say an afterlife in some other place, you have to admit that there are many types of people in nature; you want everyone to think that nature is strong and hard and never smiles, but people are part of nature and so am I.I like to laugh and smile and there are plenty others like me, too. Your version of nature is pretty narrow."

This was all very interesting to Henry. Claire's inability to sympathize with his world weariness made her a powerful if unlikely sparring companion where she neither followed his patterns into a downward spiral, nor lost energy from his gloominess, nor reverted to personal attacks to gain the upper hand. It was as if darkness itself were in an argument with light and darkness said, *I am dark, therefore, all is darkness* and the light said, *I can see that you are dark and I can see darkness over yonder, but I am light.* And the darkness could see the lightness shining from the light. There was nothing for either to argue about. He chuckled at himself, bewildered that Claire was the first person in Bluebird he'd had any type of meaningful conversation with in some three years.

Henry shifted in his seat and looked over at the grill to see how his food was coming. Fat Dickey made a sign to indicate that Henry's burger was almost up. "After I refuel, I'm going back to work, so if you want to talk to me about something you should do that. Or we can keep talking about the other."

"Okay." She pulled a folded paper out of her clutch and handed it to him.

"What's this?"

"These are the notes I made for my part in the BLUEBIRD SOUNDER. That first part there on the light green sheet—those are some reports of who we are, racially—one of your suggestions. I talked to one hundred different people at the post office. Fifty-five where white. Thirty were Black. Five were Native American. Eight were Hispanic. Two said *Other.*"

"Other?"

"I guess they didn't know?"

"This is good, what are you going to do with it? What's your angle?"

"Angle?"

"What's your take? What's your spin? How do you explain the data?"

"I can't say. I thought we could just print the numbers, sir. I think folks will like that."

"No such thing as not having an opinion. That's why you collected it, because it told you something. What's it telling you?"

"Like I said, it seems interesting in its own way."

"This is the part where I am trying to teach you something. What surprised you about the numbers?"

"Well… I didn't realize there were so many Native Americans or Hispanics."

"And?"

"And… and so… maybe it would be interesting to find out if different groups of people feel differently about different issues?"

"OK. Good. That's a start. What else?"

"I talked to a bunch of the farmers, the ones you told me about. There were two I didn't talk to. The rest yes. They all had plenty of water last fall."

"They did?"

"Yessir, everyone I talked to said so."

"This is a big deal. You have to be one hundred percent if I'm going to print this."

"Positive."

"They shot themselves in the foot."

"Who?"

"The farmers. They are complaining in court that Maddux Brothers stole their water. Company uses a lot of water for manufacturing, and it's depleting the river. For the farmers in town, the plaintiffs in the case, those asking the court to intervene in their favor, they need to prove harm to their corn and other crops from insufficient water, and then prove they lost money from not having as much harvest to sell. It's not enough to prove their cornfields are damaged, without tying that to a water shortage, and at the same time it's not enough to show there's a water shortage without tying that to damaged cornfields. They have to be connected. If the farmers had plenty of water last fall, that means they were just speculating or guessing that they would be harmed, but really weren't harmed. Courts don't give out money for speculative damages, only for actual damages."

Claire nodded.

Fat Dickey brought over Henry's hamburger and said hello to both Henry and Claire.

"Heard you turned things over to your kids?" Henry asked.

"Yeah, I'm getting up there I'm afraid. I can't do this forever. I hurt everywhere. I'm an old hobble horse."

"You look great."

"Some days I feel great… I wanted to give Nicki and Rickey plenty of time to adjust and learn the ropes before I'm six feet under. I imagin' it won't be the same for them. Probably hire an on-site manager and run the thing from afar if they can get away with it. Not what I did but that's okay."

"You just keep working now, and the rest of us will never know the difference."

Dickey patted Henry's shoulder and walked off to chat with other guests.

Henry consumed his hamburger mechanically in silence and then stood up, taking Claire's notes with him. "This gives me some good ideas. Okay to use your name with this?"

"My Daddy said that was fine I think. I'll double check with him?" she said apologetically.

"He's not here. No time to double check. What do you think?"

"I think he'd say it's probably fine?"

"Look, we don't have to do this. You said you needed a recommendation when you apply to Washington University. I can't give you a recommendation if I don't see your work. Up to you to get dragged into the town drama or not."

"Okay?"

"Okay, as in I print your stuff?"

"Okay, sir."

Henry pushed his remaining fries over towards her and walked out of the diner.

Early next morning a new supply of SOUNDER newsletters was stacked outside the post office. Henry had reached an arrangement with one of the employees there that she would move the newsletters inside the post office once she unlocked the post office first thing in the morning. In return, Henry would slip a hundred dollar bill into the middle of the stack.

In this latest edition of the SOUNDER, Henry gave Claire credit as a reporter and published her demographic statistics on the makeup of the citizens in town. He also published a piece on how Claire had learned through interviews that the farmers, despite their claims to the contrary, had in fact had plenty of water the prior growing season, and Henry speculated that this would be the coffin nail for their lawsuit. For his editorial, Henry wrote his own piece in response to the enthusiasm he had witnessed at home and around Bluebird around the rebuilding of the monuments in town and the hope of attracting more tourists and their commerce:

BLUEBIRD SOUNDER
Newsletter of Historic Bluebird

ON PROGRESS IN BLUEBIRD

Point

Bluebird citizens are not immune from getting swept up by the energy of community ideals. Perform acts of charity. Buy local. Help the poor. Improve our schools. Rebuild our town. Develop sustainable energy. Save the environment. Such ideas are described with hopeful excitement as good and contributing to Progress and Civilization; the notion of continuous human improvement from generation to generation. A supposed explanation for all Life: the beginningless story of the wild pulsating Cosmos, all of Time, Space, Matter, and Light culminating at long last in smart refrigerators and wearable fitness devices!

Counterpoint

What you call Progress is the coincidental arrival during a portion of the Age of Man of certain discoveries such as tools and medicines and clocks and printing presses and semiconductors which have promoted life for humans collectively on earth. This is the sort of evidence of a thousand monkeys banging at a thousand typewriters and will not delay the human from soon joining the dinosaur in a footnote. Do you suppose any of your actions or inactions will be remembered by the universe after you are gone? What deed can you perform that will make the universe hesitate?

The history of the world is not a story of Progress but of Violence: of wind; rock; fire; water; Time. They forever shift and scrape and clash and collide and change but do not advance towards an end. These is greater Power in Nature than humanity and when Nature's Power rises up again that will be our finish. It will eradicate every whisper of connotation from the human experiment.

When the sun arose over Bluebird, it cast westward shades across the ashen land of ramshackle vehicles and fences and tractor parts and power poles and awakened its bleary-eyed citizens to Henry's latest diatribe. Henry was not there in town to see the smirks and laughs constituting the rejection of his editorial remarks. Nor was he there to notice the genuine interest many showed in the demographic snapshot that Claire had assembled regarding the racial makeup of the town citizens and what that might mean to Bluebird's future. Nor was he there to overhear the chatter about whether he had finally learned how to get along with at least one person in town and was genuinely helping the daughter of the widower Washington. Nor did he overhear those who had seen him and Claire at the diner, who conversed about whether he was sleeping with Claire. And he did not see and hear the plaintiff-farmers curse and shout and swear in God's holy name to slit his throat from ear to ear for printing the article about how the lawsuit could not be substantiated because the farmers' damages were only speculative as the water supply had remained sufficient during the autumn.

Henry Dunstan was that morning in his own shadowland of brush and grass constructing his fortress of rocks. There, his dawn drawn-out ghost with wheelbarrow looked like a titan pushing a plow except that where the shadow titan tilled no earth was turned so that it gave the impression of a Sisyphean plowman condemned to work the same plot of territory throughout a futile infinity.

CHAPTER NINE
THREE SHARDS OF FLINT

[APRIL 2, 2016]

It was the season of the opening of the buds. Easter had come and gone with a little excitement—an egg hunt on the grounds of First Baptist for the kids in town—and a larger-than-regular crowd had attended Pastor Darren's sermon on Easter morn entitled *Overcoming Our Fallen Nature*. This lecture had instructed Bluebirdians that humans were the Lord's most disappointing creations because they were the only form of matter He had created which were both animate and disobedient. All in all, Pastor Darren's sermon had been well received by Bluebirdians and well discussed throughout the day. In general, spring was a pleasant season in Bluebird for winter was falling and summer was rising.

But the farmers of Bluebird were worried and were not pleasant. Today, the earth was holding its temperature, which would elevate past ninety degrees within a few hours, the planting season was near, and water would soon be a problem. The latest edition of Henry's SOUNDER had infuriated the Bluebird farmers. This recent publication had alleged that, despite Maddux Brothers having drawn more than its share of water from the river, the farmers still somehow had had enough irrigation water. Already, word had gotten back to the lawyers for Maddux Brothers who were demanding surrender from the plaintiff-farmers who apparently had no valid legal claim. It would be easy enough for the farmers to clarify that they had been misquoted in the SOUNDER, but still this setback represented another hassle and expense—to have to pay a lawyer to clear up such needless confusion.

Just before noon, a group of men walked up the dirt road leading from town to Bluebird's eastern hills. The most noticeable noise they made was that of heavy, slow, rubbered or leathered soles clopping on dirt like a troop of lame horses. Second was the sound of men cursing and talking each in a native tongue peculiar to himself and his kin.

"Have you ever known such a rat in your entire? 'Tis a big rat that will require a big fire."

"The trouble with troublemakers is they're eager to give but reticent in the taking."

"He barks a lot. Now we get to bite."

"Four words is all you need to know to understand that woman of his: money and more money."

Tom Mack had approached Sheriff Haggerty about forming a posse to punish Henry Dunstan for printing his lies in the SOUNDER. Although Sheriff Haggerty had declined to join the posse, he hadn't discouraged Mack either, which was all the sanction Mack needed. Mack had in turn recruited the Campbell brothers and several other men to join the posse. Tom Mack had borrowed a rake from Big Joe Campbell's store. Big Joe himself carried a sack of coins from his store that he had been saving to take to the bank. David Campbell carried a tire wrench from his repair shop. These men and a few others ambled their way up to the Dunstan Hotel, weapons in hand, a malformed army with no particular plan about what to do when they arrived, and no particular training to that end either, except that they were all big men, older true, but still capable of violence.

As he had done daily for many months now, Henry today labored on Epoch Two, the second boundary of stones surrounding his workshop. He had arrived in the hills early and had already moved more than a hundred wheelbarrow loads of rock from the quarry to his property. He was tired and needed to rest. Henry laid down a blue plastic tarp on the ground in between the Flamingo Fire and its protective shrub three feet to the north, and lay himself down upon the tarp, his face towards the sky.

To Henry's left was the familiar water bird of the genus Phoenicopterus playing with fire at the base of the tall boundary. *Flamingo*, Henry knew, derived from the Old Provençal word meaning flame so that the bird's name was also its color, like an orange orange or a plum plum. *The Fire-Colored Fire*, Henry said aloud. He told her what he had achieved this morning and as always she listened to him without interruption for as long as he wanted to speak and he talked to her for a while. To Henry's right was the large unkempt meadow willow, wild and virile, which shrouded all view to the north. Above: the wan daydream sky.

When his parents had died together in a motor vehicle accident along highway 55, and he had as their sole child inherited their estate, and Melissa had approached him about moving from St. Louis to Bluebird, he hadn't said no, taking care of her aging parents was by nature necessary and expedient and inevitable and he was ready for a break from teaching, not just a break but a change—but he had foreseen in daymares the stagnation of his intellect in Bluebird leading to decay and ultimately to despondency—there wasn't a single museum or theater or movie house or library or important newspaper or bar or bookstore or coffee shop for Christ's sake—and so he had bargained with Melissa for the workshop as a place where he would he imagined install an escritoire and bookcases and warm rugs and the other necessary earth-toned implements of the western artist, and most certainly over the years, compose some supreme and exquisite novel contemporaneously with his descent into misery and pour unfairly into the novel's sheets every particle of his inevitable isolation and desolation—the thin worn signatures of the tome like the ratty teddy of a disturbed orphan boy, expected to play the role of father and mother and nurse and brother to the unquenchably needy child—so that the eventual reader apprehending all this wanton indigence erupting from the page would, though not being asleep, awaken to a feeling of utter helplessness; and the novel would be passed from hand to hand and parent to child and taught in the schools and reverenced by many thoughtful persons and; in this way, Henry would be judged by the sole judge whose opinion mattered—Time—as one who had traded his sanity for immortality like so many before him. But unexpectedly, once Melissa and Henry had arrived in town and he had wandered the hills and vales and acquainted himself somewhat with bush and tree and water and rock and had surveyed the destined plot for the workshop, he had been surprised to understand that the land supplied a parallel universe to the city with a physical counterpart to each and every variety of activity he had pursued in St. Louis: the winds were endless symphonies, and rock formations could be art galleries, and the night sky took the place of muses and movies and trees and brush played the role of friends and dirt roads through open scenes were trips to Rome or Jakarta or Tokyo. Even his writing had its perfect replacement in the countryside, obviating any plans to use the workshop as his writer's studio; he found that in the blank slate prairie of Bluebird a rock was a word and a cluster of stones a phrase and a section of wall a chapter and lining up stones was the bodily equivalent of the cerebral labor of writing—not a beggarly substitute but a rich and wonderful surrogate—triggering the same innovative neurons in his gray matter—and the project of rock boundaries surrounding the workshop a novel as it were within which the man building it formed the central conceit, to wit, the story of a dogged and ardent protagonist who had most of his adult life distracted himself with the pursuits and entertainments and intellectualizations of an urban center, believing that some great good in the world was possible through artistic expression or family or education or conservation or humanitarianism or medicine or politics or world travel. And all the while a tiny seed of renunciation had lain hidden inside his heart and from time to time had hissed, *you are not everlasting, you cannot outrun nature*. And so Henry, who, when thrust into a country of scarcity of corn and hay and fences and irrigation canals—a country where scarcity meant fewer hindrances to perceiving and understanding nature—and in light of the lifting of the artificial curtain when his son Albert had drunk the fatal waters—was impressed upon in all his free time by the secret rhymes and rhythms of nature. And he began to apprehend that what had started for him after his majority at a carnival in the city in response to an invitation initiated by a gargantuan soothsayer as a fantasy or meditation of a brief escape from the world to the haven of marble was not simply a token to be revisited once and again, but was a true vision of what he wanted to and would become—to someday himself resonate like the stone in his vision, to exist without zenith or nadir, to distill his character, to become indifferent and formidable and impervious to sorrow like marble itself. In other words, the gargantuan soothsayer of the carnival long ago had despite his intentions to thwart her in fact foreseen his future when in her presence he had retreated, in his mind, of his own accord to the cold altar marble sanctuary with razor sabre in hand and she had witnessed and seen it all.

And had she foreseen also that his parents would die suddenly and without warning and his wife would take him to Bluebird to care for her sick parents where the dormant vision would blossom? And had the soothsayer also envisioned Albert's death face down in the ditch, that the toddler would die for no particular reason and to no particular end; that this death would wound Henry so perfectly to his heart of flesh so much so it would trigger Henry's efforts to overcome sentiment for he wished to never again be vulnerable to such grief and so long as he remained emotional people and events would have power over him and as he examined nature about him he sensed only relentless placidity and power and no sorrow or longing, and he vowed to make every effort to become like nature even to the point of uncaring and indiscrimination. So much so that his routine visits to Albert's final resting place were not to shed tears but to test his progress with unfeelingness, like the heating and cooling of the blacksmith's fire against a tool, which progress was slow and worked in fits and starts; he loved his boy Albert even to the depth of the memory within his bones and he loved his other boy, too, and his girl, too, and his wife, too, in a different way. He would if he could take comfort from some type of proposed continuation beyond the grave such as his wife had consumed lock, stock, and barrel, but he could not see beyond the abundant stark evidence that the natural world was formed from power—not love—by explosions and expansions and the fight of matter to overwhelm antimatter and eventually the sun and stars rent the bright day from the bawling dark night and without will or intention power begat power and power begat power and power begat power and POWER BEGAT POWER and POWER BEGAT POWER, and the solar system combined as a disk and the planet formed as a sphere of metal and water and air and land from heat and time and pressures which tore mountains from hematic plains leaving open sores of valleys and raped gashes in the lands for the savage waters and even the few permanent creations of humans, such as the Great Wall or the Great Pyramid or even Notre-Dame, were themselves the result of sanguinary unfeeling exertions—the bloody blind toil of slaves and peasants—and not of tenderness. And with power as the governing force in the universe, Henry had come to view himself as a sort of earth as it were with his own gravity and his family were moons to his earth; they were no longer the cardinal reason for his existence, but they were still relevant although perhaps too a time would come when he needed to free himself of even these moons to further purify and concentrate himself. And in this vein where a man would become rock and shed himself of all frailty, we begin to understand why Henry Dunstan didn't have a use for the people of Bluebird, the goddamn stupid, uncertain, sentient, emotional, fallible, yielding people of Bluebird.

With all this in his mind, Henry fell asleep, the Flamingo Fire protecting him on his left side, the willow protecting him on his right side.

As Henry slept upon the earth, nothing came into his mind, not a white light increasing in intensity, not a distant but mild opening at the end of a narrow tunnel, nor a starry blissful sky, nor colorful or colorless visions; there were no kind or summoning voices or songs of birds or familiar chords or the pulsing of his own body; he was overcome by no anxieties or paralysis or sense of self-observation and given to see no shades of past or future endeavors; no fears from which to retreat or hopes to which to run were presented; no subconscious breakthroughs materialized; no clowns or priests or cherubs or chesty mermaids or angry pointy men appeared; no neurological activity was manifest but that needed for bodily maintenance such as breathing and blood flow.

Henry awoke when he heard the men's low voices. Henry had left open the man-door at the eastern edge of Epoch One during his nap— no one had visited him here since Claire's brief visit of a few weeks ago—and the posse of angry men from town had entered there. Not having discovered him yet, the men were walking closer to the bush that shrouded him from their view. Henry arose and moved himself into their pathway, fearful they would see and destroy the Flamingo Fire if they came past the willow. Tom Mack was there with the rake, while Big Joe Campbell held some kind of heavy tube-shaped canvas bag, and David Campbell wielded a long piece of iron, and there were other men with them too.

David Campbell was the first to step towards Henry Dunstan. As he did so, he swung the tire iron wildly at neck height but missed as Henry danced to his right, but Tom Mack was there holding the rake straight across with both hands in front of him to corral Henry from escaping, and the men closed in until they had formed a tight menacing circle around Henry.

Tom Mack spoke first. "You twisted tongue." Mack, his own hair and beard flailing thick and wild like a lion, kicked at Henry and landed a few blows to the legs.

"Send your bride to try to make nice with your gifts," Big Joe added slowly. "Did you think little Melissa could cover for you forever?"

"What's this about?" Henry yelled, trying to get his bearings.

Big Joe Campbell swung the sack of coins across Henry's right shoulder. It stunned Henry, knocking Henry to the ground. The men closed in further. David Campbell and Tom Mack kicked at Henry. It seemed they would soon render him senseless.

Henry suddenly shot up into a squat. He withstood a few blows as he wildly reached two arms out and ripped down the corduroy pants of David Campbell and his underwear with it. Then, Henry seized David Campbell's hairy scrotum in his right hand like a baseball and pulled down with his full weight until David Campbell fell to the ground beside Henry. Henry rolled over on top of David Campbell, which provided Tom Mack an easy target for the wood end of the rake—Mack now brought the rake down decisively on Henry's head. Henry began to bleed. Henry knew that another blow from the rake would render him unconscious—he pulled Campbell's scrotum harder until the skin in his hand ripped—Henry screamed, "I'll tear him apart! I will!" David Campbell wailed in pain as Henry now stuffed a finger into the tear Henry had created to get the required grip to rip off the sack entire. The circle of men backed off.

"I'll rip him fucking bare! Get out!" Henry commanded. David Campbell pled with his comrades to obey as Henry continued pressure on the tear when the men delayed their exit.

Tom Mack and Big Joe Campbell and the others turned and walked reluctantly single file out from the rear of the property to the front and one-by-one out the open gate in Epoch One. Henry, who had dragged David Campbell to his feet, followed behind David Cambpell with the tire iron that Henry had picked up planted firmly between Campbell's legs to lead him along, while David Campbell, his face grimacing in pain, walked in small increments, his pants puddled at his feet. Once at the property's only exit, Henry shoved David Campbell through the opening in the enclosure. David Campbell squealed and fell to his knees and now used his own hands as a bandage to bind up his manhood. Henry slammed the gate and locked himself inside the property, with the men outside. The men stood outside of Epoch One within the space between Epoch One and Epoch Two. Epoch Two was not yet complete and the opening in the wall of Epoch Two would not be secured with a gate until the wall was complete. Big Joe ran to his brother and helped him stand and make himself decent, then Big Joe tossed the sack of coins rashly over the gate trying to strike Henry in the head but missed liberally.

"Try to climb in here over my wall you cowards!" Henry taunted them, wielding the tire iron. "I'll destroy you one by one! Come! Climb my wall! I'll bash in all your heads! Come, you old cowards! Come, you dullards. What you come to talk to me about?" Henry shouted. He was panting and covered in sweat, and his head still bled from the blow from the rake.

Tom Mack turned behind him. Big Joe nodded, apparently to indicate there was time for discussion, and Mack said, "You goddamn spoke a whale-size fib about the water supply in your paper. We didn't invent no shortage, you hear?" Tom Mack was presumably referring to the article in the recent SOUNDER which asserted that the farmers had had plenty of water through the fall months. This alone, if true, would completely undermine the farmers' lawsuit, for success required a showing of immediate actual damage from a water shortage, not merely future speculative damages from a predicted shortage.

"Hold on," Henry replied angrily, still trying to gather himself from the beating he had just suffered, "Claire told me she interviewed you all, got the facts straight from you."

"Well, maybe city boy been snookered by the cute girl with them round apples," said Mack. "She did interview us, she did. See, we had plenty of water in the fall, because we don't need as much water in the fall as we do in the hot summer, you city slicker. But we was plenty short in the fall compared to our usual and customary supply of water, meaning with this blaring heat we're already short compared to the same time last summer, in terms of usual and customary, and by July we'll be growing dead crop. How do you like the sound of them apples?"

Several of the men chuckled at the recurring allusion to apples and Tom Mack's cunning way with words.

Years ago, Henry would have been embarrassed by this oversight. He would have offered to rectify the error in the SOUNDER, to republish the true facts, and to meet with the farmers' attorney to prepare an affidavit to clear the record. But who had been Henry's friend? Who had laid the welcome party for him with meats and cheeses and pastries when he had arrived in town? Who had sympathized with the plight of the educated urbanite forced to live in small-town Bluebird? And who had come to his defense when his son Charlie had been hurt by the broken window glass? Who had offered to shift their power from the status quo to the newcomer?

Henry looked across them blankly. He would do that which was required and no more. "If I were you, I'd stop asking questions and get my friend to the hospital before he loses his ballsack." Henry watched the men depart.

Refreshed with some water and a meat sandwich, Henry returned to his labors on Epoch Two. He kept an eye on the road for any visitors. Henry scolded himself for not having pressed Claire sufficiently about the water shortage to write an accurate story. During their conversation at Dickey's, he had assessed her as a smart, thoughtful girl. He was reluctant to believe that her feminine wiles had caused him to shortcut his normal work ethic, but maybe Tom Mack was right that Henry had been distracted by her beauty. It was after all Claire's first newspaper job, and Henry had had a hunch that her story might have suffered from a gap in logic. He probably should have inquired further before printing the story. The fault was his, it was true. In any event, where he had been violently attacked by Mack's gang, he felt no compulsion to correct the mistake. They could all go to hell.

***

The sun was still high in the sky and the sky around the sun was a cracked glare like shards of glass hidden in sand. The sound of an engine tore through the thin atmosphere. A motorcycle approached and stopped. Henry parked his wheelbarrow and locked himself inside the gate of Epoch One and awaited his visitor. It was Nathan Washington, father of Claire Washington, who had encouraged Claire to obtain exposure to journalism by working with Henry on the SOUNDER. Henry knew from his conversation with Claire that Claire was not terribly interested in journalism and that the real purpose of the internship was so that Henry would write Claire a supportive letter of recommendation when she applied to Washington University. The thinking was that a letter from a former faculty member would carry a lot of weight and help Claire be admitted or receive a scholarship.

Nathan passed through the opening in Epoch Two and stood at the locked gate of Epoch One, opposite Henry. Nathan was not particularly interesting as a physical specimen. He was medium height, slender boned with saggy chest and bottom, and wore baggy blue jeans with a tan golf shirt on top bearing a zoo animal logo of some kind over the left breast. His tennis shoes were of a nondescript style sold in a large bin at a department store. His forehead and stubble-covered face were especially wrinkled for his age, somewhat like a bulldog, making it difficult to discern his emotions.

"Hello, Henry," Nathan said in a nasally voice, "I was hoping we could discuss a certain matter, in order to achieve a greater understanding. I am a great negotiator, a fact which you are about to discover."

"Proceed."

"There has been a huge mistake in your newspaper, as to how plentiful water is in town for corn and other crops. You printed that the

farmers had plenty of water? You lied. The truth is the farmers are going to run out with this heat wave and with what Maddux is suction-
ing away illegally. You could have known the real facts of the situation,
were you not a fraud. When are you going to fix your massive mistake?"

"You talk to Tom Mack and his crew? You're late." Henry was tired
of visitors coming to his workshop today.

"I did talk to them. I am a great people person. I would say it's a
terrible oversight, for a newspaper editor, if you ask me. Hard to imagine such a massive lapse in judgment." Nathan's tone had grown more
serious.

"I don't know about that," replied Henry, "nothing that Claire and
I can't clear up next time we publish something. Mistakes happen."
Henry figured in a month or so, he would publish a retraction or cor-
rection.

"This has nothing at all to do with my daughter," shot back Nathan.

Henry said that the error was indeed related to Nathan's daughter.
He said that the mistake was ultimately Henry's, as he was her boss,
and he was the newspaper's editor, but that assisting in correcting the
error would be a good learning experience for Claire.

"Perhaps you have mistaken me for a reasonable person," said
Nathan in a staccato tone as if he had prepared for this moment but
was now struggling with stage fright in front of his audience. "Claire's
mother was a beautiful angel. She died when Claire was a baby. I promised my beautiful bride that I would take Claire unblemished through
life; I promised my wife that the suffering of the mother would be
offset by the ease of the child. My gorgeous wife was mine and I lost
her, and all that remains is my beautiful daughter and my promise to
keep. Since then I have done everything for Claire. She wears the latest
fashions. She eats the best steaks. She drinks only bottled water. Her
sheets are made of silk. She goes to St. Louis for treatments to her hair
and skin and nails and teeth and eyebrows. She has been tutored in
everything from Italian to cello. My only pleasure aside from providing
for her is television. Claire is a beautiful queen to me. And now my
beautiful daughter is a few days shy of adulthood, and I will visit the
cemetery in three days and report to my lovely wife's headstone that I
have taken Claire to adulthood without any harm befalling her."

Henry nodded dumbfounded at what he had heard relative to what
he had expected to hear. It was a reminder not to assume that a person

was or could be anything beyond the sum of his actions.

Nathan continued. "I will not have Claire dragged through the mud. Do you understand me?"

"If you are worried about your daughter's reputation, you made a poor choice in teaming her up with me. But you need me, you need my connection to Washington University, to support Claire's application. She told me she's not interested in journalism. In any event, I'm not writing her a good recommendation until this is over. I'll take the blame for the mistake. But I want Claire to help."

"Listen, you evil devil," hissed Nathan, who now stood on his toes and jabbed his fingers towards Dunstan to get his point across. "Claire is done working for you! You'll write her a glowing letter of recommendation."

"Unfortunately," Henry replied coldly, "I'm standing here behind this gate. It's locked. I have work to do. I told you what I will do. If you disagree with me, you can try to scale the rock wall but it is high. If you do make it over the wall and start to descend I will cave in your head with a tire iron."

"You will change your mind very soon," sneered Nathan, pushing his face against the iron bars of the gate. "Suppose I go to Haggerty, the great law enforcer Sheriff Amos Haggerty, and report to him that you have been groping my daughter? Suppose I tell you that I have already donated a massive sum of money to the sheriff's next election campaign. Suppose I have recorded a particular account of your behavior towards Claire, the words you have spoken, your methods of trickery, which Claire herself will attest to in writing and through interview with the police. Sheriff Haggerty already believes you are a nasty criminal. I know because I have spoken to him about you. I have great relations with law enforcement. I have asked him to be ready if I should call him and say that you have crossed the line with my daughter. Do you really want to go down that road?"

This was all false. There was no physical evidence of sexual assault, as indeed Henry had never touched Claire in all his life. There were no damning DNA, text message, or video surveillance, nor indeed could there be. All that was true was that he had sat across from her at Dickey's to talk about the newspaper, and that she had visited with him briefly on a couple of other occasions, also to discuss the SOUNDER. On the other hand, Henry had cracked the nose of the sheriff's son, and had no allies in town other than his wife and her brother Darren, neither of whom would turn to lawlessness to protect Henry. It would take months for any investigation to be complete and for Henry's name to be cleared, and in the meantime, he would lose precious time towards the building of Epoch Two and beyond, to say nothing of the hassle of dealing with the fools who ran the law enforcement bureaucracy or the possibility that he could be wrongly convicted.

"Well?" quizzed Nathan, seeing Henry puzzling over his options.

Henry slid his head forward at once and spat in Nathan's face. With Nathan startled, Henry suddenly reached through the gate and grabbed Nathan by the shoulder. Henry tried to pull Nathan in against the metal rails of the gate. But Nathan swatted Henry's arm away and backed up several feet, ready to escape if Henry threatened him further. Nathan now wiped his shoulder against his face to wipe away the spit. Nathan smiled with obvious delight.

"I am a tough and savvy negotiator, no? Shall I telephone Sheriff Haggerty," asked Nathan, smiling in apparent victory.

Henry's body relaxed finally. "What will you have me do?" he asked matter-of-factly, prepared to obey.

"In the next forty-eight hours, you will write my daughter the letter of reference she needs for Washington University. You will write that she is the most brilliant, elegant, and beautiful young woman you have ever met anywhere in this world. You will never speak to Claire again. You will go with Tom Mack to meet with the counselor Rob Beverly in Belleflower. You will explain to Beverly the tremendous mistake that you printed in the SOUNDER. You will inform Beverly that the farmers are indeed short on water. You will acknowledge the responsibility for the error as all yours. That's what I ask. You see, I am a reasonable man."

Henry extended his hand through the gate. Nathan approached. The two men shook hands. Henry felt no disgust towards this new enemy, only that Nathan had done what was in his power to do. Had their roles been reversed, Henry would have done the same.

***

Henry Dunstan, David Campbell, and Tom Mack were seated around a small circular table, each with a napkin and name brand bottled water in front of him, which had been provided by Sherrie, the front desk receptionist at Rob Beverly Law in Belleflower. David

Campbell had selected a bolo tie for the occasion. Tom Mack had tied his bushy hair in a rubber band. Henry Dunstan was clean shaven. The men, who had achieved between them an unsteady accord since the violence that had occurred at the Dunstan Hotel a few days ago, shifted awkwardly in their seats as the table was low and the chairs were crowded and it was difficult to get comfortable in this space. There was no air flow, and Tom Mack used his napkin to mop up sweat from his forehead. David Campbell, who was still in recovery from his surgically-repaired scrotal tear, spread his legs wide and used the bottled water to swallow a pill. Soon the room smelled of the warmth of men's bodies.

The door opened and attorney Rob Beverly stepped in. He carried three expandable legal files. He, too, was a full-sized man but sat himself gracefully without bumping his knees against the table. Henry observed that each man in the room was significantly taller and heavier than himself. A person's body could be used to impose violence upon another, Henry thought, but when it came to impositions of violence, words and money and weapons and other forms of leverage were just as useful as physical strength.

Rob Beverly enthusiastically greeted Tom Mack and David Campbell, and waited for Tom Mack to introduce the new guest, which Tom Mack now did.

Rob Beverly was pale with a long face and blonde hair that was more white than yellow. He had a gangly aspect to him, which was exaggerated by the tan suit he was wearing. He spoke crisply and exuded a great deal of confidence.

"Shall I update you on our civil matter?" Rob Beverly asked. Tom Mack nodded.

Mr. Beverly proceeded to update the men on their lawsuit against Maddux Brothers. He informed them that he had received several thousand documents from Maddux Brothers, but that he had yet to find any smoking guns in those papers, and likely never would.

"And why not?" asked Tom Mack.

"Let me give you an example," advised Rob Beverly. "We asked Maddux Brothers to disclose to us, through written narrative, how much water they utilize for their plant on average now compared to two summers ago."

"That would end this whole shootin 'match right there," urged David Campbell. "Case closed. *Cerrado*, as the Mexicans say."

"Let me read you their answer." Rob Beverly searched through his files and removed a manila folder with a legal document attached to it. *"Defendant objects to interrogatory number 11 on the grounds that it is overly broad, unduly burdensome, and unlikely to lead to the production of admissible evidence, etc. & etc. Ok, here it is. The defendant intends to retain an expert prior to the close of the expert discovery deadline cutoff to be deposed on this topic."*

"What the hell does that mean?" Campbell asked.

"It means, they will tell us later. In eighteen to twenty-four months, we will reach the expert discovery phase of the lawsuit, and they are notifying us here that they will retain an expert to speak to the water supply issues."

"What's wrong with that? So we have to wait to win the case? We can live with that."

"That is the very thing I wanted to discuss with you. At the outset of this case, we talked cost. Between you and the other plaintiffs, you paid me sixty thousand dollars up front, with the two of you paying more than your share."

Tom Mack nodded. David Campbell followed suit.

"And as we discussed from day one—and so much is reflected in the engagement letter, a copy of which I provided to each named plaintiff—I have asked my paralegal to work on as much as the project as possible, because her hourly rate is much lower than my own, and per our agreement, I reduced my hourly rate by twenty-five percent, knowing Maddux would likely wage a war of attrition with us. And yet, I will need more contributions from you as we get into the early deposition phases within the next while."

"I bet we can shake some trees and get everyone to ante up another five hundred dollars," said Tom Mack eagerly.

David Campbell agreed. "We'll hold another group meeting. *La cita.* Mack here has a way with words."

"Let me show you something," replied Rob Beverly, bringing the tone of the room back to one of pessimism. "These arrived yesterday." Beverly laid out a stack of papers on the table. Campbell and Mack thumbed through them gingerly.

"These are countersuits," said Rob Beverly slowly.

"Against us?" Tom Mack looked baffled. "That's the pot calling the kettle black."

"*Mierda!*" Campbell smashed his fist on the table. Henry became attentive for the first time since Beverly had begun talking about the case.

"Maddux Brothers denies stealing your water, and instead accuse you of the same—they argue that you are using more than your fair share! You, the farmers, are stealing their water, from their pharmaceutical plant! Moreover, they allege you have interfered with their sales, by speaking publicly about the case, to the detriment of their drug sales in this region, to the tune of at least twenty million dollars."

"That's a loaf of lumpy shit with corn," concluded Tom Mack, who was standing now.

"*Mierda*!" added David Campbell, repeating his earlier exclamation.

Rob Beverly opened the door behind him to allow air to circulate into the humid room. He called for Sherrie to bring them all a glass of water. In a moment, Rob Beverly himself stood up and went to the hallway, and apparently not locating this Sherrie, brought the drinks himself, which he served to the men.

"Of course it is. Of course it is *S.H.I.T.*," repeated Rob Beverly, who spelled out the curse word. "We are obligated to respond to these nonetheless. There's no real flush valve, to build on your analogy, in the court system. More paperwork, more of my time, more of my paralegal's time. More money from you. And this is just the beginning. They'll want to depose each of you—interview you with a court reporter present—more of my time if we submit. More of my time if we fight. Either way, more of my time—and more of your money."

"You are running out of power!" exclaimed Henry, reminding Tom Mack and David Campbell of the prediction he had registered at Mack's lemonade soiree at the outset of the litigation. "I knew it! What did I say about power? The rocks have been teaching me."

"And what have the rocks been teaching you?" asked Rob Beverly, irritated.

"That people in power use that power to the detriment of others and to the advancement of themselves, in every case, without exception. The story of the world is the story of power. The story of the world—is a tale not of should but can. What can you steal? What can you horde? What can you keep? Who must you hurt to steal and horde and keep?"

Beverly made a signal that he was ready to go on discussing the lawsuit. Henry continued his lecture.

"Layers of history all through Missouri prove my point. You know what I keep finding around my property? Indian flint. Little pieces of stone carved into arrowheads or spear points. Why do you suppose that's there? And where is the civilization that left those tools behind? You see a lot of Osage around here?"

"*Silencio!*" David Campbell shouted as he swatted at Henry, Campbell's open hand glancing off Henry's shoulder and striking Henry across the side of the head with force. Henry was immediately out of his seat and on top of Campbell, Henry's hand clutching Campbell's scrotum. Campbell moaned loudly like a cow. Tom Mack moved over behind Henry and hooked his arm around Henry's throat and squeezed the breath out of him until Henry crumpled to the floor.

Rob Beverly took command of the room. He yelled at all the men to be quiet, and that if they did not comply, he would not be able to represent any of them.

Each of the three pugilists returned to his chair to rehabilitate his injuries and compose himself. David Campbell had his eyes closed and teeth clenched. He pulled another pill from his pocket and quickly swallowed it with water. Tom Mack was drenched in sweat from his forehead to his temples to his chest and armpits and backs of his legs. He stretched his moist arms above his head. Henry sat there breathing steadily as if to test that the pulmonary mechanism remained intact. His black hair was wet and hung down below his eyes. The room reeked of glandular activity.

Rob Beverly indicated to the men to follow him and he led them to a larger meeting space where the air was cooler and not yet malodorous. Each man now sat with at least two chairs between himself and the next closest person.

When he had the attention of his guests again, Robert Beverly asked if they should continue their discussion. Then he answered his own question.

"Sixty thousand, we started with sixty thousand, and you say you can get me another ten. Ten is not enough. This is just the beginning for Maddux Brothers. We have sufficient resources now to finish the document exchange phase, withstand whatever court battles will come up there, perhaps commence depositions, continue to exchange demand letters, but then we will run out of resources again, and again, and again. They will battle us at every phase, because they can." Rob Beverly's voice drifted off as he looked out the window for inspiration. "I'll need ten thousand more dollars from you... at least twenty more times. At least. Do you understand me?"

Henry took advantage of the quiet moment to fulfill his promise to Nathan Washington and inform Beverly of the error in the SOUND-ER, that the article that had run recently about the farmers having plenty of water was inaccurate and based on his misunderstanding of the facts and that he was happy to print a retraction soon. Henry accepted full responsibility for the sloppy fact-gathering, the lazy writing, the non-existing editing, and then finally the foolish and fatal decision to print the story at all. He never so much as mentioned Claire Washington's name or the notion that he had relied on an assistant to any degree. Henry wanted to be sure that if Nathan asked Tom Mack, David Campbell, and Rob Beverly about Henry's apology that Nathan would judge Henry's performance to be without blemish. Henry wished to avoid being falsely accused of sexual assault by Nathan.

Tom Mack and David Campbell looked at Henry with surprise; they had apparently not known he was capable of any sort of apology.

"Fine, that will eliminate one little foray I'm sure," replied Rob Beverly dismissively, "but I am telling you, this is just the start. Just the beginning of the beginning. The very tip of the debut of the commencement of the beginning of the start. Do you understand what I am telling you?"

"The start of what?" queried Henry who all along had understood Maddux Brothers' tremendous financial advantages in defending the case but sensed that Rob Beverly was now speaking of something bigger than the lawsuit, something beyond what Henry had foreseen.

"That plant, it's just the beginning for them. Their lawyer tells me they like it over in Calypso. Now this may just be manipulation on their lawyer's part, but he informed me they have found a good crop of employees who drive in there from the little towns all around. They intend to expand their manufacturing here. Huge chunks of land in the hills east of Bluebird they are in the process of purchasing. Are you familiar with those parcels? Mostly empty now. Except for one large home made of glass and steel I hear. Even if we survive this case, there will be an appeal, and then another after that. I believe I was transparent about this from the start. This was never going to be easy, I told you as much. I told you we had a good chance of getting them to back off if we hit them hard. But they are in for the long haul and that was the risk we took."

"Those Bluebird hills are sacrosanct…" Henry muttered. *Maddux*

Brothers intends to build a new plant next to my workshop. Henry imagined the parking lot abutting right up next to his property, hundreds of cars parked there. Henry was not even sure that all of his rock wall was on his own property. Possibly part of his rock wall extended beyond the property line and would have to go. He saw in his mind his fortress crumbling.

"The Bluebird hills should be out of the reach of this silly game," Henry said. Henry's face evoked pain and anxiety: the first time he had shown any sign of weakness to his comrades. Henry felt a giant hole open inside of him.

Rob Beverly looked blankly at Henry and then at Mack and David Campbell.

"Our *amigo* here built that lonely steel and crystal palace in those eastern hills," said David Campbell, taking pleasure in Henry's misery.

"He is seeing that he himself is riding in the boat that a while ago he thought he watched from the safety of the shore," Tom Mack said grandly. "How does it feel now Henry to realize, based upon Beverly's news, that you are not simply a bystander but one of many people in a sinking ship?"

Mack and Campbell gloated over their rival, their arms folded passively. Thirty seconds passed.

Henry looked pleadingly at Rob Beverly and asked feebly, "What power do we have? Who do we know? How do we overturn this to our advantage, counselor? What are we missing?"

Rob Beverly sat there a moment silently. "I've already outlined the options. I need more money to move the case forward, and even then no guarantees, and even if we make headway in the lawsuit, there is no stopping Maddux Brothers from buying up other lands nearby."

Henry, beginning to recover, was unimpressed. "Talk to me as a man. As a man. As a man in nature, not as a lawyer. Ignore the law. What options do we have, within or without the law. Above or below it? Beyond it and beneath it? What can we do with power?"

Rob Beverly began to speak, but Henry put up a hand. Henry stood up and spoke frantically. He paced about, wiping a hand over his face. He seemed like someone who was about to harm himself. The other three men in the room kept their distance.

"Beverly. What if there were a filthy fatso with an STD, intent on raping your wife? Needle tracks. Smells like an outhouse. He's covered in grime. He's broken into your house and grabbed your wife. He's torn her clothes off. But you catch him right before he rapes her. What would you do next? Follow the law? File a police report and casually wait six months for the process to take its course? Or would you take the law into your own hands and beat out the bastard's brains with a wrench?"

Rob Beverly spoke to Henry sternly. "You are the most disgusting thing I have ever met. Get out." Beverly walked to the door to the conference room, opened it, and gestured for Henry to leave.

Henry leaned over the table and grabbed a few of the papers there. He intended to throw them across the room. But the top paper caught Henry's eye. The date on the letter was recent. It was a letter to Rob Beverly from the attorney for Maddux Brothers. The letter, written apparently as a courtesy, indicated that Maddux Brothers intended to purchase the lands in the Bluebird hills from a Dickey, the owner of Dickey's Diner. The closing on the sale of the land was anticipated for some time near the end of summer. Henry let the letter fall, and stormed out of the office.

Outside, as he gathered himself and scanned his mind for any possibility of escape from his predicament, Henry observed the bed of variegated blanket flowers already in bloom within the hardened earth surrounding the entrance to the law office. These with the unseasonal heat had been deceived into early blossoms and the scene looked somewhat like colored Easter eggs hidden in plain sight in a parking lot for a toddler egg hunt. Some of the flowers were as delicate pink-yellow pinwheels with a crimson center and others large grapefruit honeycombs and others oversized butter marigolds and others exploding pomegranates. Their clean fragrance reached his nostrils. He climbed onto his four-wheeler, backed it carefully into the flowerbed, and spun the tires until they had chewed up all life there, spreading a brown-green mulch with colored speckles across the sidewalk and against the base of the glass door.

CHAPTER TEN
SERVANT

[JUNE 13, 2016]

During the two months following the meeting in Belleflower with Tom Mack, David Campbell, and Rob Beverly, Henry frantically searched for a way to prevent Maddux Brothers from purchasing Dickey's land in the eastern Bluebird hills. Maddux Brothers had, according to what Henry overheard at the Amoco and the post office, offered Dickey five million dollars in exchange for Dickey's one hundred acres of land. This acreage of Dickey's abutted against the Dunstan land in the Bluebird hills, and from there covered an area primarily north and west of the Dunstan property. Henry had a little more than five million dollars in his various investment accounts, but neither he nor Melissa had any current source of income, and the most Henry would be willing to pay for Dickey's land would be two million dollars. Henry had until end of August to figure something out. If not, Dickey would sell to Maddux and that was that.

While continuing to build his second rock wall—Epoch Two—which ran outside of and parallel to the first rock wall—Henry probed his mind for an escape. It was intolerable that the land near his workshop, the land from which he derived clarity of purpose, would be converted into concrete walls, metal holding tanks, and office space. This land, Henry knew, had already lost its sovereignty and elemental wildness when it had been subdivided in the first place, assigned the misnomer *private property*, and passed down through the generations until Dickey had purchased it. *Private property—to steal something sovereign and infinite, dice it up into pieces, and convert it into a commodity.* And Henry himself had been a beneficiary of that absurd misnomer *private property*, without which he could never have obtained the parcel on which his own workshop sat. But for the violations against nature inflicted by others, Henry could never have had such effortless access to the rocks which he now sought to mimic—so much was clear to him.

Nevertheless, it was one thing for the land to have arbitrary invisible lines painted across it; it was a different matter for those invisible lines to grow into chain-link fences, asphalt parking lots, factory buildings, and perhaps even a goddamn sandwich shop adjacent to his workshop. At last, as Henry toiled day after day unable to discern an easy solution, he acknowledged the simple facts: he did not have enough money to outbid Maddux Brothers for the land, and he knew of no way to earn that much money in the short term. He instructed his mind to rest for a time.

Tirelessly he worked his body, taking little food or respite, trusting that completion of Epoch Two would reveal an answer to his dilemma. The second wall of rocks was no less substantial than the first, but this second wall was more unkempt; he lacked the energy to achieve evenness at all points along its height. Henry was moving larger boulders than before, in order to reduce the number of back-and-forth trips from his land to the rock quarry. This improved the speed of the drudgery but increased the pains in his wrists and forearms and lower back. His spine felt like a wrinkled-up dishrag. At times, if he stumbled at his work he was not strong enough to regain his footing and would crash into the dirt, barely able to get his hands underneath him to slow his fall. He took to sleeping at his workshop rather than returning home at night. Despite the sharp electrical pains in his body, sleep came easily. Night time passed like a meteor falling from the sky: once he lay himself down, a light electrical sensation shuddered through his cerebral cortex; then it was suddenly morning.

Without fanfare, Henry found himself one day placing the final stone atop the second wall. This stone was smooth and clay-colored and shaped like an enormous human head. He heaved it into place with the same motion as countless stones before it. And then it was done. He walked backwards thirty yards and looked at the completed Epoch Two. From this distance, the final head-shaped rock he had placed looked like his own head in profile. Standing there, looking upon his creation, he wondered if this is what the shadow-spirit of his vision had meant when she had delivered to him the *fate of rocks*—that a rock, resembling his own head, complete with a strong, wide brow, hook-shaped nose, and round jaw, would stand as sentry atop the second wall. No, this head-shaped rock did not seem like a satisfactory fulfillment of the soothsayer's prophecy, Henry thought.

As with the first rock enclosure that Henry had completed in winter, this second enclosure was taller than him in height and wider than him laying down. The two walls ran parallel to each other, with some five feet of dirt and weeds between them at the base. He had built a narrow opening into each structure, each opening aligned with the other, to allow him access to his workshop. Both such portals had been secured with high iron gates the posts of which were buried in cement. Each cement foundation supporting a post was four-feet deep. Each gate locked with a key, of which he had the only copy. He now had built, rock by rock, two considerable barriers around his workshop. He alone had done this. They were real and substantial and occupied space across multiple dimensions. He had exchanged the strength of his body for the strength of the formations. As he had decreased, they had increased. As if the result of earthquake or storm, each wall had been created by the displacement of materials, resulting from natural forces, from one point to another. They were, he thought, his Giza and his Stonehenge and his Terra Cotta Army. Future generations who visited Bluebird long after his death, Henry believed, would revere the vision and courage and lasting nature of his creation.

Standing there celebrating the completion of the second wall, Henry remembered his adjournment of cleansing and meditation inside the marble workshop in winter following completion of Epoch One, and felt ashamed. The old saying came to him that life could be lived only in a forward direction. Henry had no time for ceremony any more; Epoch Three would not wait; he began forming it immediately. Epoch Three would be a wall of stacked rocks, running parallel and outside of Epoch Two, and would be the same width and height as the other two walls.

Having emptied a few loads of rocks from the wheelbarrow to mark the beginning of the third wall, Henry's anxieties about the surrounding land heightened, and he decided to address them. Lacking any suitable plan for preventing Maddux Brothers from purchasing Dickey's acreage in the Bluebird foothills, Henry decided quite simply to visit Dickey and beg him not to sell. The intended sale was scheduled for the end of August, some seventy-five days ahead. Sleep-deprived, sore, disoriented, and fearful of losing the sanctuary of the hills to expansion by Maddux Brothers, Henry approached Dickey at his diner with wild thoughts beyond censorship, portraying a number of characters his mind had conjured.

"Dickey, sell your land to me, and we'll be brothers forever. You will be my milk and my honey in the wilderness. I'll pay you sweet homage forever, and the flower in thy cap shall never perish," Henry had said in a proper London accent, mixing Bible language with a flavor of Plantagenet chivalry.

Dickey looked at Henry bewildered. Henry continued, taking on an eastern European mobster voice and looking around spastically as if he were being followed.

"What do you need Dickey that I can you trade for? You have people causin' problems you need hurt? I'll do it; I'll cut down as many as you need, if you take your property in the hills off of the market. I got piano wires. Poison. Bone saws. You don't like to hurt people? You like pleasure. Okay. Girls then. All kinds. Big ones. Small ones. Little white Asian bodies with tan Florida beach girl tits. Black girl asses with Latino hips. I'll go over to St. Louis and bring you back a vanload. No girls? You married? Well, who don't need pills? I can get you anything, make you remember, make you forget, make you work hard, make you slow down."

"Now Henry," Dickey cautioned. "You need a hamburger, son? You're acting strange. I'm not so good either. I have a heart condition. My wife and I need that money for my procedures, and I doubt I'll work again when I'm through."

"You have a heart condition!" Henry exclaimed sarcastically. "I have something infinitely worse!" Henry shrieked dramatically like a teenage girl. "Oh no, a petit little teeny-weeny heart problem."

Dickey ignored Henry. "I have to think about my family. I hoped Nicki and Rickey would take over. But they're not Bluebird folk. They want to be up in Belleflower, where their lives are. So, I'm selling this place. And that was as far as I was going to go, but out of the blue a couple of suits from Maddux come over and offered me a landslide price for my land, all that land around your glass palace over there. I would have been happy to sell for much less, but they offered me five million. I bought those acres twenty years ago when land was cheap— hoped some day I'd build a house over there like you, or that maybe my kids would want to build on that land. But Maddux offered me the type of deal a wise person don't refuse."

"What do you suppose your kids will do with all your money?" Henry challenged, in his own voice, sinister. "How many Escalades do they need? One of every color? A gold one for driving their kids to basketball, a white one for lacrosse? Goddamn them. They'll spend all the money in a flash that it took you a lifetime to earn! They'll consume that money like goddamn hamburgers, and they'll be fat and plugged like you when it's through."

"Stop there, son, you've pushed it too far already." Dickey pointed his hamburger tongs at Henry and shook them.

"Who do you think runs Maddux Brothers?" Henry was standing and shouting now. "Let me give you a peek. Twelve fat rich men in a board room in Philadelphia. Sitting around a table nipping on pasta salads and iced cakeloaf. Their skin is soft. Their breath is sweet with sugar. Someone is up front moving through a presentation on the computer that no one is watching…"

Fat Dickey was fed up. Before Henry could finish speaking, Fat Dickey—all three hundred pounds of him—gripped Henry in a strangulating hug, squeezed the breath out of him, carried him out of the diner, tossed him to the ground, and told him to never come back.

***

The days following Henry's visit to Dickey's Diner were especially hot and dry. Every elemental strand of the atmosphere from the sun to the earth and in between became thinned and honed like a wire and made into a conductor of oppressive radiance. Animals of fur and animals of feather and animals of skin gasped into the airless sky for breath. The sun blazed inside dusty sepia houses and inside faded cars and upon nylon tractor seats and upon kids' outside toys. In the sideyard of a decrepit wood rambler, a sallow tabby cat skirted out from under a boxwood and jumped onto the metal ledge of the home's front window. The metal was searing hot; the cat leaped away and licked at its singed paws.

In the shade or out of the shade—it made no difference. Nor were doors or windows or decks or patios escapes. Sleep yielded restlessness but no rest. The dry wind seared, and when the wind ceased, the windless air scorched. When it rained—if it rained—for a moment here and there, radiance from the earth turned the moisture into a sticky mist that hung over the ground as an upside-down cloud. What few hardened and miniscule drops collided with the baked earth splashed off the inviolable surface and turned to steam before they could fall again. When the rain ceased, the mist scattered impatiently and all was as before.

And if all of Bluebird was hot, then the farmers of Bluebird were blistering hot. The water shortage impacted them directly. Their corn-fields were thirsty. Their lawsuit had gone stagnant, and there were no signs of change in Maddux Brothers' water usage. Attorney Rob Beverly had not been paid the additional legal fees he had requested of the farmers, and as a result, he ceased prosecuting the case until the farmers paid him. No one knew at this point that redoubtable circumstances would soon enough arise to create a conclusion to the dispute more abiding and legitimate than any judicial resolution could dream of being, in the way that fire is a more complete and valid purifier of filth than a thousand washrags.

In the meantime, the farmers took turns, as directed by Tom Mack, visiting the Maddux Brothers' plant and registering complaints with Jeffrey Sands, the Chief Operating Officer there. It was believed Sands would have sympathy for the farmers because of his connection to Bluebird. Sands had grown up in Bluebird, gone away to college, and then had worked for Maddux Brothers for many years back east. His appointment as the Chief Operating Officer of the Calypso plant had brought him back to Missouri.

A farmer, when it was his turn on the schedule, would drive east-ward from Bluebird, break northward off the highway to Belleflower, drive another twelve miles to Calypso where the Maddux Brothers plant was located, check-in as a guest, and request to meet with COO Sands. Sands was a serious late fiftyish fellow with white hair that he stuck to his head with salve. He had the wiry, tanned body and bearing of a man who spent a great deal of time golfing. Once with Sands, the guest would present the tragic story of how the pharmaceutical plant was stealing water from the river and drying out the corn, and how the farmers had already collectively identified certain fields they would sacrifice this growing season to save the remaining fields. Each farmer had agreed to reduce his crop and his income by a third rather than for each farmer to take what water he could get. This way each farm and family within the collective could plan and budget rather than some families surviving and others failing. And it was not easy for people already living on the edge to give up a third.

Hearing this, Sands, while stroking the lanyard holding his name badge complete with photograph and magnetic security strip, would express his deep regrets and promise to look into the question, which would take some time of course, since all important decisions emanated not from the office of the COO but from the office of the CEO—in headquarters, in Philadelphia, Pennsylvania. Sands was not insincere—he seemed to lack actual authority over the matter. Despite Sands' apparent good intentions, when the farmers realized that Maddux Brothers would not meaningfully respond to their complaints in a timely manner, they became hostile towards Sands, whereupon he ceased taking their visits. So the farmers took turns parking in front of the plant and cursing at Maddux Brothers' employees as they came and went. The farmers would block the entrances and exits to the parking lot with their farm trucks, forcing Maddux employees to park further away along the roads. When Maddux Brothers called upon Sheriff Amos Haggerty for help with this nuisance, the Sheriff rewarded the company's courtesies to Bluebird by delaying his return calls until evening, by which time the hay trucks had been moved and Sheriff Haggerty would claim the point was moot. Some Maddux Brothers employees, given the lack of police intervention, resorted to self-help by throwing rocks or sticks at the trucks, denting the vehicles or shattering their windows. In return, once these employees had entered the plant, the farmers would use their farm trucks to bash in the cars of the offenders. In this way, pressure mounted between the two sides, and no one would have been surprised if violence had erupted.

***

Several days after Henry's visit to Dickey's Diner, Dickey sat there at a white laminate table inside his burger stand, his face the color of eggplant, great globules of sweat standing upon his forehead and upon the creased fat on the back of his neck. He panted uncomfortably and his cheeks and eyes swelled. If the weather outside were hot, it was even hotter inside Dickey's restaurant.

Melissa Dunstan, the queen of Bluebird, entered the diner and sat across from Dickey. Melissa wore a new yoga outfit with her short hair pulled into a tiny ponytail on top, making her look younger than her age. Her thin fingertips shone with pearl-colored nail polish. She had heard that Fat Dickey's kids didn't want to run the diner and that Dickey had put the diner up for sale.

Melissa politely explained to Dickey that the Bluebird Society aimed to convert Bluebird into a fashionable spot in Missouri not unlike Williamsburg, Virginia or Sedona, Arizona or even Park City,

Utah, on a smaller scale of course. But the Society needed time and money to accomplish its goals, and if Dickey sold the diner to some out-of-town entity, Bluebird would lose control of an important part of its history.

This particular portion of the conversation all went pleasantly enough. But then Melissa made the mistake of telling Dickey, "You owe it to Bluebird to keep Dickey's Diner in the family, so to speak. We've never asked anything from you, and yet we have sent you customers for generations. You owe this to Bluebird. The Bluebird Society is trying to build something here. You can't let this diner go so easily."

Dickey exploded. He crashed his meaty hand on the top of the laminate table. His whole mass shuddered.

"Enough! I owe nothin'! To nobody! Henry was here several days ago, abusing me with similar lines, begging me not to sell my land in the hills. And now you come by to do the same. Your husband already gave me the pitch. No thanks."

Melissa apologized in a soft voice, handing Dickey a stack of napkins. "I'm sorry, Dickey. I didn't know anything about Henry's visit over here. I really didn't. The Bluebird Society has no interest in your land up there. Honest. You're right to be mad. It's we who are in your debt for the diner, and not the other way around. You gave us something of our own to look forward to, without always having to drive up to Belleflower. How many birthday parties have been celebrated here over the years? How many families have stopped here after soccer and football games?"

Dickey dabbed some sweat from his neck using the napkins. He appeared to be somewhat mollified.

"What makes you suppose that whosoever buys the diner from me won't keep it up?" Dickey asked.

"That's a good point," Melissa conceded. "but it's not the same if it gets bought out and turned into a Pete's Barbecue or some such. We can't build the reputation of Bluebird by sending tourists to Pete's for a squirt sandwich or whatever they sell over there. People want these amazing burgers and shakes! Just give me and Shirlene some time, see if we can raise the money or if someone from Bluebird rises up to buy it from you and keep it going as Dickey's Diner, as it should be."

"Okay, Melissa, I'll give you a spittin' chance. I've always liked your family. I know the Bluebird Society is up to good things. I'll give you and Shirlene and the Society some time. Besides, I'm about to get a payday for my land, so I can afford to be patient, for the right reasons. Six months delay, and then I sell the diner. Okay?"

"You're so kind!" Melissa stood up and hugged Dickey energetically. Their relative sizes were so disparate that she looked like a child hugging Santa Claus.

"If I may, now let me ask you something dear," Dickey said.

"What is it?"

"I don't know to say it around, so I'll just say it straight. Are you and Henry on the same page whatsoever? At all?"

Melissa stared at Dickey quizzically.

"Is your marriage upside down and backwards?"

Melissa's heart raced. Was it so obvious to everyone how disconnected she and Henry had been for so long?

"I already told you part of it. When Henry come in here the other day, he was fit to be tied, pleading with me not to sell my land over by his Hotel. He didn't say a word about the diner. He was acting downright crazy. Like he was all the roles in a mad play. Said I was giving in to privilege if I sold the land to Maddux. I've known him for a while and honest, I like him. Sees stuff not all can see. But I had to grab him and throw him out of here! And now you ask me not to sell my diner, but you could care less about the land in the hills. How can that be so that Henry is doomed by the sale of my land and you are all for it? And the diner is vital to you, but he don't care?"

Prior to this moment, Melissa had defended her husband publicly even if privately she had serious grievances about him, but with his selfish interests so at odds with her well-intentioned mission of rebuilding Bluebird, she chose to stop protecting him.

She told Dickey that her relationship with Henry was paper thin. She said that Henry was obsessed with his Hotel, that he was spending all his time there, and wouldn't even let her, Melissa, his wife, inside. She said that Henry didn't even try to fit in with the townspeople, that he intentionally alienated people with his newsletter. In short, she told Dickey to ignore anything that came from Henry's mouth.

Dickey seemed relieved at Melissa's words. Seeing some new arrivals taking their seats, he wiped the sweat from his palms on his apron and stood up suddenly to shake hands with Melissa. He smiled and said he needed to go to take care of the new customers. As Melissa slipped out the door, she watched Dickey ease into his role as host and gregariously welcome his guests.

***

Back at home, Melissa jumped out of the sedan as soon as it came to a stop. She fumbled with the house key as her mind battled itself. Would she truly act as recklessly as the ideas in her head were suggesting? Would she dare to put so much at risk?

Without consulting with Henry, Melissa had, nine months ago, moved thirty thousand dollars and then, in due course, three hundred thousand dollars of their joint savings into an electronic stock trading account, for the purpose of supporting the Bluebird Society's town rebuilding projects with gains on the investments. Melissa had promised God that if He would, over morning coffee, help her in the stock market by whispering ideas to her brain and illuminating her path, that she would, in return, devote everything to a good cause. God had indeed helped her, she believed. Not only had she made important contributions to the Society, but her investments had been so successful that she had used some of the profits, with God's ratification, to visit the spas and nail salons and hair parlors of Belleflower more often. She had not yet set aside enough money to buy the plum Cadillac CTS or black Escalade she had dreamed of, but such a purchase was at least now in sight.

Despite these successes in the stock market, raising enough money to pay for Dickey's Diner within six months was an undertaking of a wholly different scope. Dickey had proposed four hundred thousand dollars to buy the diner, although he might presumably negotiate downwards if someone from Bluebird would buy it and keep the diner operational under his name. Four hundred thousand dollars in six months! Even if Melissa could generate returns of fifteen percent on her investments, she would need to invest more than five million dollars to generate gains that quickly. Five million dollars at risk. The financial ruin of her family if the market crashed while the full five million were at play. But the alternative was infinitely crueler. No fame, nothing about Bluebird in any travel magazines or St. Louis papers. No radio interviews, no social media hits, no late night talk show appearances. No new stores in town. No move-ins. And it wasn't all about Melissa herself. No kids returning to Bluebird after college. No jobs. Bluebird increasingly forgotten with each generation until it would recede utterly into history.

Melissa was determined to raise the money for the Society to buy Dickey's Diner. Other practical considerations such as who would run the business or who would cook the food went unexamined. She could not afford any delay. Five million dollars! All she and Henry had. Twitching in her seat in front of the computer, with every neuron in her body firing, she logged into her and Henry's investment and bank accounts. With a mouse click she sold half a million dollars in a total stock market index and moved the proceeds to her trading platform. Then several hundred thousand dollars in an energy ETF. Sold. Common stock in a nursing home ownership group. Sold. Technology funds tied to interconnectivity products. Sold. Mixed-asset social choice accounts that scorned tobacco and fossil fuels. Sold. Dividend funds. Sold. And so on. She did this all decisively without reflection— by the time she had arrived home from Dickey's Diner she had already committed herself. No, she thought, she had committed herself well before that, the first time she had shifted her and Henry's money to this trading account without talking to Henry, and she had since then recommitted herself again when she had escalated from tens of thousands at risk to hundreds of thousands. This new level of engagement was not a new sin that required new guilt; it was a continuation of the status quo. If she were guilty of anything, it was of not talking to Henry when the whole design commenced. Now the work was just so many keystrokes to finish.

Her body twitched as she studied the numbers on her computer monitor. She cracked her ankles and knees and elbows and wrists and back and sternum and neck and all of her fingers and toes, swallowing deep breaths. Jolts of hot and cold current shot through her. She felt the need to pee. The computer screen indicated she now controlled 4,893,458 million dollars in her trading platform, and that less than two hundred thousand total remained in her and Henry's other accounts. She decided to leave the two hundred thousand dollars intact to ensure that any short-term expenditures by Henry would pass through the bank without a hitch.

She knelt and closed her eyes and tried to peer into the unthinkable beyond and read the future. She stayed there long enough that her knees ached.

As her brain slowed its cycling, a thought entered her mind that she received as divine revelation, for it was a new, unsullied idea that seemed to have arisen external to herself. She wondered how many people in the world knew, as she knew, that Maddux Brothers would soon be expanding their production to Bluebird. She doubted that the rumors about Maddux Brother's intended purchase of Bluebird land had traveled far. An official announcement of the new plant, domestically located no less, once sale of the land was final, would foretell strength, and almost certainly cause a short-term spike in the company's stock ticker MBRO. Too, she pondered how many knew as she did that the lawsuit against Maddux had ground to a complete halt. From what Melissa had gathered from speaking to Shirlene Mack and other ladies around town, the case was dead in its tracks. The farmers had stopped paying their attorney and he had ceased prosecuting the case. The case itself was trivial—a bunch of poor Bluebird farmers suing a gigantic company over water rights—but Maddux was tied up in a few similar cases in California and Oregon and a victory in Missouri would have precedential value elsewhere. And of course, the population was aging and demand for pills and injectables would only increase. Heaven knew how much money Melissa had spent on pills for her parents alone. And a lot of these pills were manufactured by Maddux Brothers. And from what her parents had told her, the new DuCorps drug at least seemed to be a cutting-edge drug and would probably be approved by the FDA. How many other baby boomers would need a blood pressure pill?

Yes, Melissa thought, there could be very few outside of the company itself who knew as much as she did about Maddux. Holding a long position in an individual corporation was contrary to her trading strategy that focused on intraday movements and dictated that she should never hold a position past market closing. Betting the whole five million dollars on one long position was insane. But in a volatile economy, good news could bring a lot of new investors to a bluechipper like Maddux Brothers. And with so much invested, she just needed a small bump. She believed that her new strategy made sense, especially given its divine source; when MBRO inevitably spiked she would sell her position and buy the diner on behalf of the Bluebird Society. It was settled.

The kids would be home soon. Maybe they would all have a frozen pizza tonight. She stood up. She smelled rank. Her anxious body exuded foul chemicals. She recalled the smell of Debbie Black, the Indian woman who had been stranded naked on the highway to Belleflower years ago. When Debbie had gotten into Melissa's father's car, Debbie had smelled acidic, like a leaky battery. Melissa's own scent now, it seemed, was similar. Melissa thought about the history of the Osage people that Debbie had narrated to Melissa and Melissa's father, and how the Osage tribe had been reduced and relocated by violence and disease. And how, despite this, Debbie had survived. Then Melissa considered what Henry had written in the SOUNDER about the history of humanity being a history of power, rather than a history of progress.

Sure, Henry was right to a point—there were forces all about beyond human control: violence, disease, natural disasters. The death of loved ones. But Henry's philosophy ignored human will as a factor. Debbie had suffered plenty, had just been brutalized when Melissa had first met her, but Debbie had been composed and polite nonetheless, focused on the future instead of being trapped in the past. Melissa thought that she, too, was a lot like Debbie. Melissa had lost a son, had an arrogant and absent husband, and yet despite these setbacks, Melissa was focused on saving Bluebird.

Maybe I'll meet Debbie again some day, and we can compare notes, and we'll see how much we have in common.

Melissa pulled off her wet clothes and threw them in the hamper. She went into the bathroom. She entered the shower to get clean. She shampooed and conditioned her hair, and washed herself with body wash and a loofah. She shaved her legs and her armpits. She stood there backwards under the warm water, her bony shoulders slumped in surrender, fervent beads from the showerhead pelting her skin and cascading down her body, water vapor forming in the humidity and heat, the water vapor cooling and thickening against the bathroom mirror until droplets formed there full enough to be lulled downwards by gravity and joined with other droplets into rivulets. The rivulets streamed downwards to the bottom of the glass until, finding no damn there, they rained down onto the white birdbath sink.

CHAPTER ELEVEN
GESTATION

[JUNE 27, 2016]

The firmament was Alice blue in color, the sun having chased all clouds and nearly all the tint from the sky. Today would be the warmest day in the history of Bluebird, but the record temperature was not the most unusual aspect of this inauspicious morning.

Henry Dunstan woke up in his own bed at home. Melissa was already awake. She was reading the WALL STREET JOURNAL on-line on the desktop computer in the master bedroom. Neither of them spoke a word. Henry showered and got himself ready for the day. After coffee, Henry exited the house and stood on his front porch, looking across the cooked land in an eastward direction towards the risen sun and then in a southward direction and then east again. His children now joined him outside. The children and Henry tossed around a blue and gold football. Henry was thinned and stooped and moved slowly, and his mind was elsewhere. Such were the acute pains and limitations on movement caused by the nerve spasms in his neck and back, that he had been forced to stop his work on the mountain for a time. He had purchased on credit as it were the strength of the fortress. The proffered credit had been the vitality of his own body. Now the account had come due.

At the juncture in time that his body had failed him, the third boundary surrounding the workshop—Epoch Three—was only one to two feet tall—a single layer of stones. The two completed walls—Epoch One and Epoch Two—protected his workshop and marked his natural habitat. Like the bed of a river is perfectly shaped to have and to hold the water that flows through it, so did Henry's stone boundaries describe and demarcate the lifeforce that had built and dwelt within them. Each rock that Henry had lifted and moved and placed had both spoken to him and eroded him. These rocks had altered his physical form, and he, too, had altered their form. Henry and the rocks were each the that without which nothing of the other.

Henry's head shifted suddenly when an idea came to mind, and without saying anything to Ginny or Charlie, he sauntered across the yard and lowered himself for a time in front of the cairn of stones. *Our Cherub, H.A.D.* He knelt there and rubbed his head as his children looked on. He didn't feel sad remembering his deceased son. He stood up carefully and made his way to the gate at the end of the driveway where he exited alone. The electronic fence sputtered for a time but eventually closed. Henry walked the gravel road westward under the culvert and over to Main. All about him he observed the thirst of Bluebird in the corn, the soil, the animals, and the people, none of whom saluted him nor he them. So intent had he been upon maneuvering to stop the sale of Dickey's land in the hills to Maddux—scheduled for the end of August, now about two months away—and upon construction of his rock walls, that he had forgotten about the larger and more tangible war being waged by Maddux Brothers against the farmers. That the farmers had already lost the war was evident in the thirsty land all around, even if the lawsuit were technically still active.

Main Street was already busy with the cars and foot traffic of those who wished to run their errands before the sun shone down even more severely. As Henry neared the post office, Shirlene Mack crossed the street in front of him, looked directly at him, then away, then back, and finally scurried over and gave him a warm greeting as she straightened her wig.

"Henry? You don't look well. What brings you to town?" She sized him up, her face expressing concern about his appearance. He wore jeans and work boots and a black t-shirt, all of which were clean, and his dark beard was trimmed neatly, but his clothes were two sizes too big, and when he rotated his head, it looked deliberate and forced as if he were biting down on a nail.

"Mail," he said.

Shirlene apparently felt that Henry deserved a little cheering up. "Henry, we women in the Bluebird Society sure appreciate all you and Melissa are doing for us. We have a real chance of doing something in this town the way you both are contributing. Why don't you come over with Melissa and the kids some evenin' and we can get you fed?"

Henry looked at Shirlene sideways and Shirlene paused for a moment as if remembering something. Then Shirlene quickly brushed aside the topic of contributions. "Never mind your donations and all that, I won't tell a soul, don't you worry. But you check with your little wife and let me or Tom know when you want to come by for dinner. I'll thicken you up yet with my fried porkchops and creamed corn."

Shirlene was quick to add, "Now don't be afraid of old Tom. I know you and he had your differences, but he's warmed to you."

Henry nodded and entered the post office.

A few minutes later, Henry walked over towards Campbell's Dry Goods with a few parcels of mail in hand. Sheriff Haggerty drove by in his police cruiser and waved to Henry. Suddenly, the sheriff pulled over against traffic and exited his vehicle.

"Well, well, if it isn't Mr. Property Rights," the sheriff said.

Sheriff Haggerty stood in Henry's way. Henry said nothing.

"Why you in town?" queried the sheriff, whose nose was a few inches from that of Henry. "You getting ready to shit out one of your newspapers? Looking for a kid to beat up? A young girl to squeeze?" Sheriff Haggerty snatched the envelopes from Henry's hand and looked over them, and finding nothing objectionable, let them fall.

Henry looked away and squinted into the distance.

Sheriff Haggerty stomped on Henry's left boot, then grabbed Henry by the shoulders and twisted him around. The sheriff patted Henry's ribs and hips and legs vigorously. Then, the sheriff spun Henry back around so the two men faced each other each again.

"What'ch you up to anyhow?" the sheriff asked again. The sheriff slid his fingers under the necklace he was wearing and held out the circular onyx pendant that hung there on a silver chain. "Your name Dunstan means black rock, don't it?"

Henry looked the sheriff in the eyes.

Sheriff Haggerty told Henry that he was more attentive than anyone in town recognized. He said that he kept his clothing, his hygiene, and his cruiser in an unkempt state in part to throw folks off, but more because he didn't give a damn about veneers. He said he had observed carefully the workmen and the trucks rolling through town over the years up to the hills to work on the Dunstan Hotel. He said he had written down names and phone numbers and made calls: Billy Irvin was a cement guy; Tadpole Brown did windows; Roberto Linares was a stone guy. The sheriff told Henry that without much pressure, for Linares had a warrant out for two unpaid moving violations, Linares had described to the sheriff the inside of Henry's workshop: the marble oval interior with two fireplaces; the giant altar and one end of glass; that Henry insisted that the surfaces be flawless; and the sense come evening that the whole situation resembled looking upon the night sky. Haggerty said he had probed Linares for an hour about the place, and Linares had told the sheriff there was no electricity and no toilet, that Henry pissed outside, and that when he pissed outside he always pissed in the same spot.

"How 'bout it?" laughed Sheriff Haggerty, still holding out the necklace to Henry. "I know you. I've got you figured."

Henry held out his hand. The sheriff unclasped the necklace and let it slide, stone first, into Henry's palm.

What had appeared circular was instead elliptical—the head of a large cat in profile. A jaguar or a tiger or a leopard. It was unclear. The onyx was encrusted with diamonds, the two materials creating the contrasts to paint the animal's features. The pendant was heavier than Henry anticipated, with a bumpy texture under his thumb.

"I know stones," Haggerty said. "I know you like 'em too. This necklace I got from bending the law my way. Those who love stones love the sense of permanence or at least a hope of permanence. That's why the lovers choose the diamond, of course, something hard and pure that will last maybe forever they hope. Stones are the main object to pass down through generations father to son, mother to daughter, and so on. They don't really wear down much do they? 'Course doesn't mean all won't die. But knowin' someone you love will have something leftover from you takes some of the sting out of it. I aim for my oldest to have this when I'm said and done."

Sheriff Haggerty told Henry he had worked a jewelry-store burglary decades ago, up in Columbia. The sheriff said the kid they caught was a drug addict with pulmonary issues with only one prior arrest and that the sheriff had told the storeowner that the jail wouldn't keep the kid for long on account that he'd be too hard and expensive to hold medically and the jail would let him out at the minimum or even furlough him if he needed hospitalization. The sheriff told the storeowner the kid would need money and would steal again. The storeowner offered the sheriff the pendant in exchange to make sure that did not happen again. So when the kid got out, the sheriff planted cocaine on him and the judge put the kid away for good with three strikes. The sheriff told Henry he had built his whole career out of making justice in uncommon ways.

Henry handed the necklace back to the sheriff and knelt down to pick up his mail. He stood up slowly, and the sheriff let him walk along. Suddenly the sheriff took out his baton and clubbed Henry's arm; the mail fell again. As Henry squatted, the sheriff leaned over him as if to help.

"Why did I strike you just now? My police record will say you snatched my necklace and I had to get it back." The sheriff pulled Henry to him so that he was speaking his hot breath right into Henry's ear. The sheriff's breath smelled again of sorghum moonshine.

"As long as you're in Bluebird, I'll always have eyes on you, god-damn property man. Four hundred citizen deputies in this town who don't like you any more than I do. Wherever you go, I'm watching." It occurred to Henry that someone had seen him walking through town and had called Sheriff Haggerty. He wondered who it was. Someone at the post office? Shirlene Mack? Not Shirlene, she had been happy to see him. Who then? Haggerty handed Henry the final parcel of mail from the ground and then walked back to the police cruiser.

Henry decided against entering the Dry Goods. Henry had come to town to upgrade to a new wheelbarrow. When he got feeling better, he'd go back to work on Epoch Three. But now was not a good time for this transaction. Joe Campbell would give him a hard time, and Henry was in no condition to fight back. He could avoid all this hassle and order one on Amazon. Come to think of it, he'd look online for a small trailer he could attach to his four-wheeler. That would allow him to keep working on Epoch Three some despite his pain.

Spying a welcome sycamore and its leafy protection on the other side of the road, Henry crossed over and half sat, half collapsed on the ground. He rubbed his bicep where the sheriff had clubbed him and rested his back for a while against the base of the tree until he dozed off. During this repose, his mind was a sheet of lightning white stillness.

"Mr. Dunstan? Mr. Dunstan?" A delicate voice reached through the haze of sleep and stirred him. "Mr. Dunstan? Are you okay Mr. Dunstan?"

Henry blinked languidly. His brow was feverish and his body stiff. He took a deep breath in through his nose. Eventually, he opened his eyes to see Claire Washington. Her full-sized body standing over him as he slumped there seemed to envelop and strengthen him. In that moment they were alone in the world. He examined her. She wore tight black running shorts with a small slit on each side. The black drawstring of the shorts poked out near the navel. Below a sports bra her stomach was sculpted rich cocoa butter. Her satin legs were bare and shoeless and glistened with sweat as if she had just been exercising in the heat. Her thighs and shoulders were stronger and more defined than he had imagined. She smelled oily and musky and earthy, like a woman; not like a girl. He was mesmerized. His body tingled with revitalization.

"Is everything okay, sir?" she asked, part serious, part coy. She seemed to take pleasure in the power she had over him. She squatted and leaned towards him, amplifying her cleavage.

He looked towards her helplessly as she maintained her gaze upon him. Her gleaming eyes seemed to see him, to understand him, to absorb him all in like a pond swallowing a pebble. Her body was ripe and nurturing and her voice soothing. She was right there, available, when he needed help, where he needed help. Her scent and her presence dominated him like a massive cloud overwhelming the empty sky. She had completely invaded his boundary, which he had not considered possible. Now that it had happened, he permitted it to happen. He studied her features, and she both noticed and encouraged this. A face older than its age. Resolute jaw and neck muscles. A faint shadow of a mustache above her lips. Her wavy hair was pulled off to one side and held there apparently by gravity alone. The bra strap on the uncovered shoulder was an inch or two out of place. She caught his eyes looking there and eventually adjusted herself with a smirk.

"Where did you come from?" he marveled.

"I live right there." She cocked her head to the side to signal the direction of her home.

"What happened to you? What brought about this change?"

She smiled. "I am still me."

When he had first met her and worked with her on the SOUND-ER, he had been strong and had perceived her to be naïve and innocent and immature and foolish. Now that he was weak, he perceived her to be womanly and strong and wise and experienced.

"You want some water?" She pointed to her and her father's place nearby. He glanced over. The Washington house wasn't twenty-five feet away. He could follow her inside for a drink and they could continue their exchange there, come what may.

Henry turned his head further; the front door of the house was open. Nathan Washington loomed there in the frame, looking back at Henry. Henry wondered if Nathan was the person who had noti-fied Sheriff Haggerty of Henry's presence in town. Nathan adjusted his testicles and thrust his hips forward in a crude way that Henry un-derstood as a warning that he needed to stay away from Claire. If not, Nathan would drum up some kind of false sexual assault allegations against Henry.

Henry straightened up his body and gathered himself. "No thanks. I'm not thirsty." He suddenly arose and dusted himself off. "I'm sorry about the mistake in the SOUNDER," Henry uttered, "I really am, and all the embarrassment that caused you and your father. I never should have done that. Please tell your father I told you I am deeply sorry."

Claire looked at Henry blankly. "What embarrassment, sir?"

"The article where the SOUNDER quoted the farmers as having plenty of water."

"I've been told that was a mistake, but no one has made a big deal out of it."

Henry now deduced that Nathan had never told his daughter of the visit with Henry and that Claire had nothing to do with Nathan's threats.

"I don't feel well. If you'll call me a doctor, I'll walk back home and meet him there."

"Sure thing, I'll call a doctor for you." She gaily offered to walk with him, but he feared what Nathan might do. Henry brushed past her slowly, and she patted him on the bicep for comfort. How did she know his bicep was sore? He was electrified by her touch and it seemed more than automatic or accidental. If he was not mistaken, she had not only patted but also caressed his bicep? Had her breast also brushed against him? He repeated, "I'll be at home. Doctor can meet me there. You stay here. Don't you come." He walked painstakingly back towards his corner of town, stopping every twenty yards or so to catch his breath.

***

Melissa had just seen Charlie and Ginny off with their Aunt Sa-brina to go swimming in Belleflower. Melissa seated herself at the com-puter to study the markets. The telephone bell erupted in a manner that seemed to portend great ill. She went to the kitchen and picked up the heavy receiver.

"Hello, Melissa. This is Nathan Washington. You remember me from high school days? I was one of the more prominent students at our school. Listen Melissa, I am disturbed by your husband's attention towards my daughter. She is a real beauty, and I look out for her like I promised my beautiful dead wife I would. Even though Claire is now an adult, my promises to Claire's mother to protect Claire will never end. You remember my gorgeous wife? Of course you do. Well, I made my deceased wife a wonderful promise. I swore on her deathbed no harm would ever come to Claire. Since then I have put Claire first."

"Go on," said Melissa, who was clenching her jaw and listening as best she could despite her panicked notions.

Nathan explained how he had just seen Henry with Claire outside of his home, that they were kissing under the sycamore tree, and that neither one of them knew they were being watched because Nathan had secretly observed them through a window. Nathan also informed Melissa that he had overheard Henry whisper to Claire to drop by his home later in the day when only he would be home and that he had given her the code to open the gate.

"Why is a married man inviting my beautiful daughter over to his home? His behavior is dangerous! I think you'll know best how to put a stop to this. He is even now walking home so I'll let you deal with him."

They finished their conversation, and Melissa thanked him.

As Melissa put down the handset, her pulse was exploding in her chest and temples, but she converted the desperate energy to plotting. To be sure, she would have preferred to do something else with her day, but Fate had delivered her an opportunity to capture and punish her husband. She would rather have had a faithful spouse, but if she could witness him in the act of adultery it would prove that her jealousy had been valid all along, and it would give her a clean, legitimate, explainable basis to divorce him and start anew. Ginny and Charlie had gone swimming with their aunt and wouldn't be back for several hours. Melissa wrote a large note for Henry that he would be sure to see when he arrived home soon—*Gone to Belleflower swimming with Sabrina and the kids. Be back tonight*—and drove off before he arrived home. Once she reached the main highway however, instead of driving east to Belleflower, she cut back west towards unincorporated Lampersville which provided ultimately a roundabout way to get back to the main part of

Bluebird, where she'd wait to spring the trap. It did not occur to Melissa to question Nathan's account—how it was that Henry and Claire were kissing on Main Street across from the post office without being noticed by anyone else, and how Nathan had somehow overheard them whispering even though he was inside the home and they were outside, and why Nathan hadn't intervened directly if he had indeed been so distraught to see his daughter kissing a much-older married man.

***

Henry lay on the couch in the front room at home awaiting the doctor's visit. He wore only his underwear. The intercom buzzed. Henry reached over to the electronic device on the end table and absently pushed the button several times to open the exterior gate so the doctor could enter. The gate had been malfunctioning lately. Sometimes it didn't open properly. Sometimes it didn't shut properly. He pushed the button a few more times.

A few moments later, the front door to the home opened.

"I'm sorry," Henry apologized. His eyes were closed. "I couldn't make it to the door. Thanks for coming Doctor. I'm not well."

"It's me," said Claire timidly. Henry recognized her voice at once.

"What about the doctor?" asked Henry.

"My Daddy and I called him more than an hour ago. He's not been by, sir? He should have been here by now. I came to make sure you and your wife didn't need any help running to up to Belleflower in case you needed any prescriptions filled."

"You said your Daddy was on the phone with you?"

"Yes. Doctor said he'd come right by."

"No, he's not been by," Henry groaned.

"I'm sure he'll be right over. Let's get you into your bed." Claire heaved him from the couch and let him lean on her as they went to the bedroom. To lay him down carefully she had to hold onto him tightly and press herself against him.

"Can you get me a cold washrag and some pills out of that bathroom? It's just to your left in the hall."

Claire returned and administered to Henry. He was nearly in a trance. She went to the kitchen and returned with a large homemade cookie which she fed him piece by piece. This restored him some, and he fell asleep for a few minutes.

When he awoke she was still there at the end of the bed. There was much silence between them but it was not uncomfortable. She looked at him as he looked her over. She was still in her running shorts and jog bra.

"You overdid it with your rock wall?"

"Walls," he said.

"Walls?"

"I'm on the third one now."

"Why?"

"It's what I do. It's what I want to do."

"I see," she said. "Is that why you told my Daddy you didn't want me helping on the SOUNDER? Because you were too busy with your work up there?"

"Come again?"

She repeated herself.

"I said no such thing to your father," said Henry, his tone serious. "You did a good job with your articles. That's the size of it."

She seemed both pleased and baffled by his praise. "My Daddy said you had pulled him aside and told him you were done with me."

"No. No. Your father told me not to talk to you again."

"I'm my own person," she said with spirit, quite pleased.

"I don't believe that. What have you ever done to challenge your father?"

"Well, I had a boyfriend he didn't approve of."

"You have a boyfriend?"

"Had. I had."

"How did that go?"

"He was a boy. He lived in a pack of eight to ten boys. Whatever they did, he did. What they wanted was what he wanted. He was, un-developed, I guess."

"And you are ready to settle down with someone serious?" Henry laughed.

"I want a strong man who knows what he wants." She monitored his response carefully; he was silent. She continued.

"You are strong. And you know what you want."

"What did you say?" He had heard her the first time but wanted to be sure. He was gaping at her cleavage.

"You know what you want."

"Before that."

"I want someone strong, who knows what he wants."

There was a question in her eyes, a shade he could not get to the bottom of, a suggestion that she needed to perform a deed for him, or him for her, and when this was done, her eyes could look more fixedly on the world. He looked back at her chest. There was so much life there in her body.

All of this she apparently noticed.

"You can look all you want," she said. He was seven feet away, his head on the pillow. He took it all in.

"You should go," he said.

***

Following her earlier phone call with Nathan, Melissa had driven to Lampersville so that Henry would not see her on his walk home from Main. She then returned to Bluebird on the back route. She parked her car fifty yards south of Nathan's house and waited for his signal. She had been there two hours when Nathan walked out into the street and made the thumbs up signal, meaning that Claire had left the house on foot forty-five minutes earlier, giving her ample time to walk over to the Dunstan residence, and presumably giving Henry ample time to seduce Claire. Melissa drove the sedan back to her home. The exterior gate was already open; it had been malfunctioning lately. She quietly parked the car west of the house—out of sight from the front window.

She tiptoed up the front porch and then burst through the front door. She stormed across the living room and into the master bedroom. Henry laid on the bed in underwear and Claire cowered in the corner in mini shorts and a bra.

In Melissa's imaginings, this was the moment when she threw the desk lamp to her left at her husband. But her imaginations had not taken account of how void she would feel before this lurid tableau. Void and empty, empty and vacant, vacant like a well, a well so deep that no matter the length of rope used the lowered bucket would return dry. Then a profound anguish began to fill the well.

"The queen of Bluebird," she murmured to no one. "The queen of Bluebird. With no king."

With Melissa's attention elsewhere, Claire guardedly backed out of the bedroom and towards the front door.

"The fool of Bluebird," Melissa screamed. "Whose husband made her so!"

Melissa's face was jagged with fear. Her face had been hard like this at the hospital after Albert's passing. A tremor of unprecedented empathy seemed to mollify Henry. He motioned for her to come and sit down next to him on the bed.

"Come," he said.

"Come, listen."

A third time he beckoned, "Come, listen, Melissa." He wanted to say something.

She stood there paralyzed, half of her wanting to take a seat next to her husband and accept whatever comfort he would offer—a big safe step back from the hostilities to avoid all-out war; the other half of her wanted to shed someone's blood. It was a fork in the road she would ruminate upon again and again in the future and wonder about the direction not taken.

Hearing the front door shut, Melissa awoke from her indecision, darted across the house and down the front porch, and caught up with Claire who was marching quickly now. Melissa viciously grabbed Claire's hair in both hands and dropped her weight, wrenching Claire down with her. "Look what I've got!" Melissa howled.

Both women were strong. They swung and scratched and clawed at each other and wrestled there on the asphalt driveway in the morning sun. They tore at each other's clothes. Neither could get the upper hand. They cursed and threatened. They spat and bit and kicked. Eventually, Henry appeared on the front porch and treaded across the driveway until he reached the melee. He grabbed Melissa's arms from behind and peeled her off of Claire.

Melissa swatted at Claire's face and tried to escape from her husband's grasp. Both women were frantic and kept at each other. Henry increased the grip on his wife. His hands were leathery and unmovable.

"Come inside!" Henry bellowed at Melissa and Claire. He had regained his strength momentarily and now scooped up Melissa and carried her inside as she wailed at him. Claire followed passively.

Once inside, Henry hurled Melissa onto the sofa and hollered at her. "You sit!"

He punched the wall above her head. When she tried to arise he shoved her down again and grabbed a lamp off a table and smashed it into the wall above her. He pointed to a chair on the other side of the room and drove Claire in that direction.

"Listen," he barked. "None of this leaves this room. None of it! Understood?"

He was engrossed in rage; both women nodded quickly.

"We are going to straighten this out," he continued at fewer decibels. "Right now. Right here. Before it gets out of hand. Before it involves parties outside this room. Before we reach a point of no return. Can we do that?" Claire and Melissa nodded again.

Melissa suddenly stood up and ran around the corner and into the bathroom, locking herself inside. Henry followed immediately behind.

"Come out here!" he thundered. "So we can settle this."

"When I come out, it'll be to tell everyone what I've seen and what a hell I've been in with you." She stopped short of threatening divorce, knowing that her deceit of investing nearly five million dollars in Maddux stock would be exposed if she went that far.

Henry attacked the door. Melissa shrieked from inside. The door splintered but did not give way. There was a loud bashing sound on the knob. The entire locking mechanism crumbled. Henry kicked the door open.

Melissa stood in the bathtub. She ripped the towel rack off the wall to defend herself. Henry lunged for her, and she collapsed beneath his grasp into the tub.

Before Henry could reach Melissa, a siren screeched outside the home and seconds later tires skidded to a halt. Henry ran out of the bathroom. Melissa stayed in the tub.

Melissa heard voices coming through the front door.

"Your goddamn hands in the air," shouted the Sheriff.

"You didn't think I would come for Claire?" a voice hollered. Melissa could tell this was Nathan Washington, to whom she had spoken by phone earlier. "I saw Melissa driving through down and knew you'd be over here trying to destroy my beautiful queen Claire!"

"Kneel," the sheriff's voice boomed.

From the bathroom Melissa could not see what was happening. She imagined that Sheriff Haggerty and Nathan Washington were surveying the situation. They no doubt noticed that Claire's clothing was torn and her body scratched and bleeding. They no doubt saw the scattered lamp parts about the sofa and the floor and the holes in the wall above the sofa. They likely figured it was the scene of a rape.

Melissa now heard the sheriff's voice ordering Nathan away from Henry. She then heard a deep cracking sound like wood splitting. She heard Henry cry out and then the sound of a body collapsing to the floor.

The commotion having receded, Melissa Mallory Dunstan emerged from the bathroom, still wielding the towel rack. The sheriff was hand-cuffing Henry. Both the sheriff and Nathan were surprised to see her, as if it presumably undermined the theory of the scene they had formed. She too was disheveled, scratched, and bloodied.

Melissa judged the setting: Nathan or the sheriff had cracked Henry's back with the police baton. But thus far, Claire had been acquitted of her crimes. Melissa made a showing of empathy towards Claire. Claire still sat in the chair alone as Nathan moved near Henry while the sheriff walked around the room searching for evidence.

"Are you okay, dear?" Melissa said softly, as she drew near Claire. Claire tensed up and almost called to her father, but Melissa relaxed her own body and moved more slowly still. "Does your Daddy call you the queen dear?"

Claire nodded.

"How sweet. Have you ever been a real queen?" asked Melissa deviously.

"I was Homecoming Queen my senior year."

"Were you now?" responded Melissa. "Did you know I was Home-coming Queen, too, when I was in high school? Did you know that people around here still call me the queen of Bluebird?"

Claire shook her head.

"How do you think it feels to be a queen and find your king fuck-ing some stupid girl who thinks herself a queen?"

"Nothing happened," Claire screamed.

Now a few feet away from Claire, Melissa whipped the towel bar at Claire and Claire brought her hands up in defense. The bar made a crunching sound across Claire's forearms. Melissa continued to swing the towel bar at Claire's arms, gashing them further. Melissa yelled, "I am queen."

"Stop!" Sheriff Haggerty shouted. Melissa let the towel bar fall. The sheriff had finally taken control. When Nathan ignored the warn-ing and moved towards Melissa, the gun exploded. Blood shot from the hole in the back of Nathan's thigh as he fell to the ground. Sheriff Haggerty turned the revolver towards Melissa, and she backed away from Claire.

Order had at last been restored. Henry was immobilized face down on the ground, handcuffed, with a fractured backbone. Nathan writhed all about with his hand applied to his leg wound. Claire's torn arms dangled at her sides, and she wailed in agony. Melissa moved about freely despite her emotional wounds. Only the sheriff was intact. Sheriff Haggerty radioed for three separate ambulances to come down from Belleflower, and he kept an eye on things until all three patients had been safely stowed away. Melissa gathered some of Henry's things—his keys, wallet, cellphone, cellphone charger, and a change of clothes—and threw them into a duffle bag and placed them on the ambulance with him. Then she hurried over to the shed, returned with Henry's backpack, and placed that in the ambulance with Henry as well.

The sheriff and Melissa stood there on the porch of the Dunstan residence, each with a thick film of sweat along the brow. One by one the ambulances exited the property, and turned northward to join the highway to Belleflower. The sun, more than halfway towards its most direct point of the day, shone down like a spotlight on the scene. The sheriff walked over to his car, opened the car, and returned. He handed Melissa a pen and a blank report on a clipboard.

"Fill this out," he said. "Your name and address go here on the top." Then pointing to a dozen or so blank lines he added, "And here, write down exactly what happened." Melissa's body sank as her legs gave way from the strains of the day. When she came to, she turned upwards helplessly towards the sheriff who stared down blankly, a cigarette in his mouth. When she extended her arm for assistance, he pretended he didn't see her, and loafed down the porch stairs to no apparent end.

CHAPTER TWELVE
EYE OF THE STORM

[AUGUST 1, 2016]

"Pastor Darren."

Henry Dunstan whispered this hoarsely as he drew open the outermost iron gate of his citadel in the hills. Henry stood behind the gate, his back against a solid wall of rocks, and looked up at the cloud-covered sky. The temperature had been unseasonably pleasant as of late and it seemed to be an eye in the heatstorm that could not hold. Pastor Darren had left a note here yesterday that he'd be back the following day to call upon Henry. The note had been placed in a large manila envelope and tied around the iron gate of Epoch Two with a string. Henry had seen it when he had exited the workshop to survey his property.

Henry now opened the gate to its maximum to show the Pastor that he was welcome; Pastor Darren surrendered whatever apprehensions he might have had and entered. Henry closed and locked the portal behind them, and they now stood within the interior of the two barriers of rock Henry had built, each of which rose to a height several feet above the men's heads. Here on both sides of the men in the gap between the two walls, scrap lumber with exposed nails, scrap metal with sharp edges, cement bricks, old tires, and garbage had been piled several feet deep. Henry's purpose in filling the space between the walls with refuse was to encumber an intruder who had penetrated the outer wall and was set on attaining the inner wall. Henry now unlocked by key the gate to Epoch One, Pastor Darren and Henry walked a few paces across the property, and Henry showed his brother-in-law into the grand workshop.

Pastor Darren surveyed the workshop in apparent awe. He touched his hand to the marble walls. He gazed up at the mirrored ceiling. The place was spotless and glistening and smelled of ammonia. The empty fireplaces located along the longer southern and northern sides were large enough for Darren to step into, which he did. Now Darren looked out the large windows at the west end of the room, whistling the call of some bird.

"Thdrrr, thdrr, drr. Thdrrr, thdrr, drr. Thdrrr, thdrr, drr."

"That sounds real," Henry murmured with admiration.

Darren warbled the same bird song again as he retucked his tangerine dress shirt.

"Thdrrr, thdrr, drr. Thdrrr, thdrr, drr. Thdrrr, thdrr, drr."

Darren pointed outside. Henry gingerly approached the window. A male bluebird sat perched atop the interior rock wall to the rear of the property. The bluebird did not appear to be concerned that he had invaded Henry's fortress and now stood atop the Flamingo Fire, his intense royal blue plumage punctuating the flames below. The bluebird ascended, fluttered about in a loop, and landed again in the same spot as before.

"That's where I piss," Henry said, pointing to the area of the wall below the bird. "See how those stones there come together to look like a flamingo juggling fire? I have taken naps there in between that spot on the wall and that wild bush there."

"I can mimic a lot of birds," Darren said. "Cardinal. Blue jay. Oriole. Finch. Amazing all of God's creations. Truly. I had a VHS tape as a kid that I watched over and over to learn each bird's sound. Those were the days. Nothing but time. Melissa and I found all kinds of flint arrow points outside, flint tools, and such. I have a decent collection at home. Fascinating how we have our houses and farms here and in the soil underneath are bones and artifacts of the people before us. You wonder what if anything from our time will interest archaeologists in the future. Can you imagine sifting through all the trivia on the Internet to try to sort out what was really important to people in our time?"

Henry smiled at the thought of a future archaeologist looking through trillions of social media postings from the modern day and wondering what the hell people had been thinking.

"Come to think of it, did Melissa tell you about the time she and I came upon a porcupine around here somewhere? It had to have been maybe right where your workshop is. If not, then not far from here at all. Not as far away as that spot where you get your rocks. When the porcupine saw us, it ran away and hid in a small hole. We followed it. We jabbed our sticks down into the hole over and over. Eventually we realized we had killed it."

"Why did you kill it?" Henry asked.

"The sticks weren't really sticks, they were long branches we had pulled from a tree. We could poke the porcupine without seeing what we were doing. I guess we killed him just because we could." Darren's voice sounded as if he felt guilty for what he had done.

"You spared him the trouble of living," Henry muttered.

Darren seemed taken aback by this and stepped over to the immense sleigh-like altar in the center of the chamber and leaned his full weight against it. The altar didn't budge at all.

Henry smiled, "Ten ton."

"What for?"

There was a long silence before Henry spoke. He deliberated whether to reveal to his brother-in-law the supernatural inspiration behind the interior of the workshop. Henry had never spoken to anyone about the altar, the marble surface, the egg-shaped room, or any of it. From time to time, he wondered if the vision in which the interior of the workshop had been revealed to him had really occurred, or if he had fabricated the whole thing. There was, after all, no tangible evidence of the long-ago event. He had read many studies of how unreliable memory was. And the vision had occurred decades ago, when Henry was eighteen.

Maybe I'm not remembering something that happened in the physical world, I'm remembering some earlier memory that I planted in my mind for a different reason. Perhaps when I was at the university I wrote a story about a man who attended a carnival and met a giant soothsayer there—that would explain how I remember the story so vividly. Of course, if that were true, wouldn't I be able to remember the process itself of having written the story?

Henry thought that by speaking aloud the words of the vision, and hearing the words vibrate within his own ears, he would be able to discern if the story were true.

"I had a dream just after I became an adult—an awake dream. I went to this big fair in St. Louis." Henry shut his eyes, as if he were making out old film footage on the insides of his eyelids. "I am driving by, on the way to wash my car, silver with tan interior, and I see all these lights, all these people. No one person, no one light—that electricity, that blur of people, that projection of lights. My car window is down and I can hear that amusement park sound—motors grinding and flywheels spinning and teenage girls' undulating screams. I'm not planning on stopping, but this car pulls out right in front of me to make a left-hand turn. Silver Mercury Topaz. Same as mine. There's too much traffic so he can't merge and just stops there right in front of me, perpendicular. The driver is masculine and weary with a big strong head, thick black eyebrows, penetrating stare, like a mob boss in the corner of his restaurant reading everyone's faces to see who will betray him next—I'm looking in the mirror it seems at another version of myself. And he's looking back at me, too—he's thinking the same thing about me in reverse as I am about him? By the time he clears out I decide to park and go inside. The carnival smells of popcorn and animal dung and cotton candy. Now I feel funny inside witnessing the World's Largest Alligator and Sheep Rides and Prize-Winning Chickens and hairy women in tube tops and kids screaming and kiosks selling specially formulated ring cleaner. What do I care? Was I born upon the wrong planet? Were all the people of my tribe slaughtered when I was young? I wander around, looking everyone in the eyes, searching for something familiar. And I'm asking myself, *Why did I enter?* Now I buy a Coke in a bottle and sit there at the outdoor food court. I drink it slowly through a straw like a girl for something to do. There's a smell of corndogs, hamburgers, churros. No one comes close to me. I am waiting for an interaction or a sign. But it's as if I am stationary on the platform and everyone else is on the departing train and I can't cross over into their world. So I turn down by the hot tubs and the Dutch oven cookery to make my exit. I walk by two huge men in flannel shirts. They are squatting down over a Dutch oven coal fire and still, squatting down, they are gigantic. I'll just slip past them back to my car."

Henry was surprised at the amount of detail he could recall. It was as if the whole thing had happened yesterday. He had seen inside the Dutch oven pot. It had contained some type of flaky cobbler or cake. He remembered thinking that the food the men made must have tasted good, because both men were carrying a hundred extra pounds, at least, in their mid-sections.

"Then, from the side, while I'm trying to leave, this strong hand grabs my forearm. Right here above the elbow. Right here. It really hurt. It's a giant woman, and she's pinching my arm. She has hulking shoulders and a man-sized head and she's covered in capes and jewelry. Her fingers on me are long and strong and she kneads my arm now and draws me into a tent I have not noticed before where I sit down when she orders it so. She never says she's a fortune teller or a witch or a sorceress. She doesn't have to—from the moment she touches my arm I feel she will show me a revelation. And she does. She shows me myself; she shows me the future… something like this." Henry extended his hand to communicate that he had envisioned the entire workshop. Henry opened his eyes and returned to the present. Henry was standing, leaning back against the enormous marble altar for support, and Darren stood about ten feet away. Darren's tangerine dress shirt had come completely untucked. Darren motioned for Henry to continue.

"In the vision, the soothsayer lady sent in her spirit self to visit me. I held this long bright curved sabre with ancient grip in my hands. The sword had a wide cutting surface—the Chinese Baquashendao as I later learned, although I had never seen one before my vision. I was alone with my sword, nude, and everything around me was hard and pure and clean and strong. I felt true and comfortable there. Without a care. Or beyond caring. Like I was the rock and the rock was me. So that the size of my own self had expanded and become the size of the entire room of marble. I was still myself, unique in identity, but I was also indistinguishable and indivisible from the stone around me, so that if someone were to kill me, I would not become extinct but would live on through the stone. The soothsayer came into the vision in spirit, to give me my fortune, but I wanted to create my own fate, so I swung the sword through her midsection free and clear—chopped her in half. That stopped her. I was powerful in that place. Nothing could hurt me. I was sure of that. For more than twenty years after that event, I lost my way with education and family and community and commerce and such, but I am at last trekking back to that true place of sanctuary within the mad carnival. I was going to make this place into a writer's paradise. Nice furniture. Wood floor. When Albert died, I switched gears. Undid, redid the interior. You know, she came to me again, right here, last winter, that huge woman did, she came to me in a vision, and she told me my fate was the *fate of rocks*."

Henry walked over and put his mouth next to Darren's ear and spoke in a whisper. "Darren, I tell this to you as a man and a brother; I've told this to no one else—I want to resonate like this marble without highs or lows. I want to become no more and no less than inanimate. Like stone, like Indian flint—I would become authentic and insentient—beyond subjectivity—beyond connotation. Then I would be immortal as there would be no meaning to be washed away and no life spirit inside of me to dry up."

Pastor Darren looked at Henry as if Henry had recounted something totally ordinary, instructions for changing the time on the digital dashboard clock in an automobile when daylight savings time ended, perhaps.

A telephone rang. An alien sound. Each man looked at the other. Henry patted his pockets and found the source. His cellphone. When he had recovered from his back surgery well enough to move around his hospital room and use the bathroom on his own, he had found his cellphone and his cellphone charger among his affairs. Melissa must have sent them on the ambulance with him. Prior to that time, he had gone without his cellphone for more than a year, but the cellphone had come in handy lately. He held up a finger to Darren and answered.

"Walter George here."

A male voice was on the other end of the line. "Yes, this is Jeffrey Sands. I believe you left me a voicemail?"

"Appreciate the return call Mr. Sands. Mind if I call you Jeff?"

"That'd be fine."

"Listen Jeff, the St. Louis Post-Dispatch wants to do a story on Maddux Brothers. I'm a new business writer up here. Most of my career has been in Columbus until recently. You're the COO over there? Vanderbilt, then MIT?"

"That's right. I spent most of my career at Maddux Brothers headquarters in Philadelphia before being transferred to Calypso."

"I figured as much from reading your CV. Now, my editor is interested in your expansion into Bluebird. When do you close on the land over there, end of August, right?"

"Day after Labor Day."

"The fellow you're buying from, they tell me he's the same fellow who runs the diner near Bluebird? Good fellow?"

"I wouldn't be able to get into all the specifics with you. You understand I'm sure. I could talk more when it's a done deal."

"Of course, of course, that goes without saying. Anyone can walk away from the deal. All the conditions have to be satisfied first. Day after Labor Day you say?"

"Un-huh. That's the target. Subject to all the conditions being satisfied."

"I'm still piecing some things together but are you going to be available in a month or so? I'd like to travel down your way and see your plant and interview you."

"Last week of August maybe?"

"Yes, just prior to the big closing."

"Sandy can coordinate the date and time."

"Exactly my thoughts as well. Don't want to count the chickens before they hatch. I'll call Sandy back with details and to confirm. Thanks very much. I'll talk to you soon."

"We'll talk to you then."

Henry put his phone away and looked around absently and then back at his brother-in-law who stared at Henry curiously.

"That was a lie. Of course, you wouldn't have to be a pastor to know that. Your name ain't Walter George." Darren seemed to want Henry to explain himself. But Henry said nothing.

"How do you see this all turning?" Darren asked, after a minute of silence. Darren spoke in a careful tone, as if to draw Henry out. "You and my sister, you are different planets with different orbits. There's a gravity that keeps you apart. You haven't seen each other once since when—the craziness at your house? And that's only the tip of the iceberg with you two I'm guessing. How does this all end so that things can get back to normal?" It was clear to Henry that Darren had coaxed a lot of information out of his parishioners over the years. He had a sincere, tolerant tone.

"Normal isn't interesting. If normal is your goal, you have a boring soul." Noticing his own rhyme, Henry added, "I said that."

"How about sane? How do we get back to sane?"

"That was never attractive to me," Henry said in a dismissive tone.

"You'll do as you please?" Darren's voice had a hint of irritation to it now.

"No more than any bird. Jesus said that."

"The human is on a higher trajectory, don't you think?"

"Have you visited a graveyard? Birds eat worms there while man sleeps."

"Do you believe in an afterlife?" It seemed to Henry as if Darren were trying to steer the conversation towards more familiar ground.

Henry raised his eyebrow warily as Darren went on.

"Death isn't the finish line. There the dead will rise and all our questions will be answered and all the tears will be wiped away with the Lord's gossamer handkerchief; we'll clap and we'll sing and we'll shout and we'll praise Him. We'll wallop each other on the backs with joy. With joy! A joy as exquisite and tangible as violence. But you, by isolating yourself in your stone egg, you have removed yourself from the building blocks of God's plan—love, community, church, husbands and wives, parents and children, brothers and sisters, grandparents, helping and serving, sharing your talents and receiving likewise from others."

Henry interrupted before Darren could finish. "All of that… is a different play in some other theatre in some other town. New staging, new director, new characters, new lines, new plot, new playbill. That's not the show we're in. Not at all."

The good Pastor looked at his brother-in-law quizzically.

"Why do Christians read the New Testament?" Henry asked.

"*My Father's house has many rooms… I am going there to prepare a place for you. Where I am going, you cannot follow now, but you will follow later.* Folks read the Gospel to get back to God."

"Of course," replied Henry. "The Good News—you *may* die, but you *will* live again through Jesus. You *may* die, but don't worry, there's something better ahead. You *might* die. You *might* suffer. You *will* live again. You *will* see Jesus."

"Just so," Darren agreed this far.

"You have it backwards," Henry said. "You have placed the question mark in the wrong spot."

Henry extended his index and middle fingers while radiating his wrist to show that Darren had switched things around.

"It's the reverse. Death is the exclamation point, and the afterlife is the question mark. You *may* live again—there's no telling, no one can know—but first you *will* die."

Henry spoke delicately now. "You will die. I will die. The first truth of every morning—today is a special day—it is the day of my extinction. If not today, tomorrow, and so on. And the same at night—tonight is a special night—for tonight I become extinct. And if not tonight, then tomorrow night, and so on. Death is first and death is last. There is only death and without death there is nothing. It's the medium. The contrast." Henry slapped his right palm against the marble altar and then lifted his hand slowly away, and slapped his palm against the marble again. This he did to demonstrate that the wall was death and that everything leading up to the wall was life, and that without the solid finality of the wall, the whole movement of the hand would be without meaning.

Now Henry stood fully and walked in a circle with big, deliberate footsteps. He stood before Darren again.

"Look at my feet. We are here. Feet planted right here. You hear my foot stomping on the marble? This earth is our only stage, and our play is a tragedy. Everyone dies in this play. Everyone. The porcupine. Albert. Me. You. Everyone. The lines we speak are our only lines, and the sun and the moon and the stars are the only lighting. No, no, you say, there might be another play later in some other theatre. In that other play, there is peace, there is joy. The people dwell in the presence of divinity. Very well that may be, but at best, it's unknowable. We know our show is a tragedy—the playbill says so. Knowing how the play ends, we must nonetheless carry out our scenes with dignity to the last iota. It is not for us to speak the words of another play. We have our instructions."

"You are forgetting something," countered Pastor Darren, who did not appear moved by Henry's words. Darren rubbed his hands together, as if signaling they had reached the crux of the conversation. "The two plays you speak of, they are intertwined. What happens in this theatre predicts what happens in the other. The next play is not yet written, and the lines there depend on what we do here. Life has a purpose. Accept Jesus, acknowledge your fallen state, confess your sins, and live with God again some day. The Good News is not generic. It's for you, too. Your life has a purpose! Take advantage brother!"

"You are not facing this life with honesty!" Henry spoke forcefully now. "You have deferred life. You have substituted this experience for the dream of another."

Henry wandered over towards the door where his backpack and duffel bag were located. He leaned over his backpack, rooted around for a time, and returned with part of a Hershey chocolate bar that he had broken off.

"Here, here, eat this. Try it. Taste it. I give you a taste of chocolate. What does this taste like? Now, instead of tasting the flavor the richness the boldness the bitterness, you say, you say—the chocolate has a purpose, that this purpose is to help you, through contrast, to taste something superior later. Or to help you be grateful for how delicious food can be. To give you calories for energy so that you can work or preach or take care of your family. To give you energy to do God's work. To make children smile. You say the chocolate exists *in order to… in order to* achieve something else. Chocolate is chocolate. It has no purpose. It's not for later. It's not for kids. It's not for energy. It's not for gratitude. It's chocolate. It tastes like chocolate. It smells like chocolate. That's what it is! That's all it ever will be. What does it taste like for hell's sakes?"

"Tastes good," Darren muttered with a tone of surrender.

"Exactly," Henry shouted. "It tastes damn good."

Henry limped over to the window. The pain in his back was flaring up again. Darren followed him there. The two men stood side by side. The bluebird Henry and Darren had seen earlier hovered all about, unrestrained. It flittered here and there, now inside Henry's property, now outside of it, as if it were making a point about the futility of his rock walls. A brown spot in the sky drew closer and closer, now descending rapidly and evening out with spread wings. The brown spot was a hawk, and it measured its trajectory like a war plane. The bluebird ascended at the last moment but the hawk adjusted itself easily along multiple planes and extended its legs and dug its talons into the bluebird's flesh, and the men could not hear the squawk of the bluebird for they were inside a thick glass window, but the hawk continued its flight and both birds were now out of sight.

"The point of life is life!" Henry continued with new emphasis. Darren and Henry continued to look out the window. "That's it. To be alive. This earth—ancient; sovereign; autonomous… it has nothing to do with us. It exists for no object external to itself. All life on it is free. All life is self-explanatory, self-justified, and exists for no reason exterior to its own self-propulsion."

"But you're not happy, brother," Darren interrupted eagerly, putting his arm around Henry's shoulder. "I am. I got joy. Got joy? Get it? If you ask me, I'll say yes, without hesitation. My joy is a brick wall that I can see and touch. You are weighed down and forlorn, lost and wandering. I can read it on your face. Yesterday at the gas station, the gas man asked me why I was smiling. *Because I have joy in my heart,* I said, *Jesus washes me clean and gives me joy supreme.* This is real, Henry. I'm not brainwashed. Set all the rest aside, all your mental tricks. All else equal, wouldn't you want to be happy if you could? God wants you to be happy brother, that's what I would tell you more than anything. And God wants Melissa to be happy, too." Darren removed his arm from Henry's shoulder.

Henry did not agree with Pastor Darren's views. At the same time, Henry did not believe Darren was lying, at least not intentionally. There were plenty of liars and frauds, but Pastor Darren was not among those. It was true that Darren seemed happy, or at least that he portrayed a certain objective version of what many people would call happy. Maybe it was possible that there was some other world after this one, some other life. Henry spoke more quietly now.

"Maybe… maybe there is a God, maybe, in some other show in some other theater. But this show here, the one we're in—He doesn't have any lines. I've read the script a million times. I haven't seen Him around the set or in the playbill. No sign of Him here."

"You talk tough," Darren guffawed suddenly, "but I know you better than you think."

"So you say," Henry said.

"All the money you and Melissa are donating to these town renovations—Shirlene Mack tells me how generous you are. She swore me to secrecy. Oops. Secret's out. Schoolhouse total rebuild with air conditioning even and a nice bathroom. So that tourists are comfortable there. And so on. It's good of you. You're not half as gloomy as you say…"

"What else did Shirlene tell you?" Henry interrupted, as if he already knew the answers, although this news was a surprise to him. He had no knowledge of any donations to any town rebuilding project. He recalled bumping into Shirlene near the post office a while back and that she had thanked him for his generosity but in all that had followed that day with Claire and Melissa and Nathan and Sheriff Haggerty he had not considered Shirlene's news at all.

"Of course she told me about the plans to rebuild the old post office, too, and my church, and you hope, too, to buy up Dickey's old diner?"

"You mean Dickey's land?" Henry corrected his brother-in-law. "I'd like to buy his land, and stop Maddux Brothers from encroaching, but I haven't the money to match Maddux. I have to find another way."

"It wasn't Dickey's land; I'm confident it was the diner." Darren suddenly looked uncertain and turned to Henry, "why am I telling you this? Of course, you know what you and Melissa are paying for?"

"Of course," Henry answered quickly, "I just wanted to hear Shirlene's account."

"See, I do know you better than most," chuckled Darren knowingly. "Not only are you giving, but despite your requests to be anonymous, you like to hear your praises sung."

Henry kept his questions and confusion to himself. Perhaps an opportunity would arise when he could bring Melissa to confession, should he see her again, and find out what Darren meant by all this.

"This has all really energized Melissa," continued Darren. "I know things are broken between you two—but my sister really has a sense of mission in this town as of late and it's rubbing off. When you are ready to come back to Bluebird, you'll see how different it is now that your philanthropy is known. There's a few holdouts still—the sheriff still has his doubts about you. Come back to us, brother. Take your time, get better, eat something for heaven's sake—your eye orbits look like sapphire—heal, think it through. But at the end of that, you come back to us. You'll see the open arms you never got when you first moved here."

Pastor Darren shifted his weight from foot to foot, as if awaiting a crucial admission from his brother-in-law, some acknowledgement from Henry that he would attempt reconciliation. This was the purpose of the Pastor's visit, after all, Henry assumed. A ponderous wall of air—the stagnant remnant breath of their argumentation—separated them. When it was clear neither would deign to cross over the gap, Darren uttered, "well, my brother," as if to recapitulate their dialogue but his voice trailed off, and he turned and moved deliberately towards the workshop's door which Henry opened for him. Outside, Henry wordlessly escorted Darren through the portals in Epoch One and Epoch Two, until Darren again stood beyond the locked citadel with Henry secured inside. Henry was thankful to be on his side of the partition, free of his kin, and to stand under the welkin alone.

CHAPTER THIRTEEN
TIME

One morning in Bluebird a few weeks after Pastor Darren's visit to Henry's workshop, a new stack of Henry's SOUNDER newsletters were piled outside the post office on Main. The post office had not yet opened for the day. Sheriff Haggerty, seeing the stack of papers, loaded them into his cruiser before anyone else could read them. He drove to the police station in Belleflower, removed the stack of newsletters from his car, and tossed them into the dumpster in the parking lot. As the newsletters sailed through the air, a small, green, piece of paper fell away from the stack and twirled about until it hit the ground. The Sheriff picked it up—it was a one-hundred-dollar bill. *So that's how Henry got the post office to distribute unauthorized material. Looks like free hotcakes and coffee for my breakfast for the next few weeks.*

BLUEBIRD SOUNDER
Newsletter of Historic Bluebird

WHERE ARE WE?

A cylinder, ninety-three billion light years in diameter, teeming with shimmering luminosities—the Observable Universe—those galaxies visible from Earth with the aid of powerful telescopes with apertures the size of a tractor. From within this impossibly vast celestial drum, and not without difficulty, a single point of light is identified—the Local Superclusters, a concentration of one hundred thousand galaxies of fire, each galaxy filled with billions or millions of stars along with gas, dust, and other matter, each star itself an ancient explosion of incomprehensible heat. Within the Local Superclusters a point of light is located—the Virgo Supercluster, itself a swarm of galaxies, each containing billions or millions of stars, and so on. The exercise is repeated multiple times—a single point of light within the Virgo Supercluster is the Local Galactic Group, a congregation of some fifty galaxies; within which is the Milky Way; within which is the Interstellar Neighborhood; within which is the Solar System, within which is Earth. The Earth, in cross-section, a spirited bowl of seven layers, some solid metal, some glowing orange molten rock, some in between. The tiny layer of crust on the edge of the bowl is the domain of humans, under constant torment for five billion years from water and wind, to say nothing of the violent heat bubbling beneath. Once the land was a single continental structure surrounded by waters, but it has been ripped apart by volatile heat and the shifting of tectonic plates. One such tectonic plate called North American Craton bears a continental burden; above which—other rocks, wrenched and twisted, above which—layers of ancient glacial till and sediment from river flow. Somewhere north of 36 degrees north 30 minutes latitude and between 91 and 94 degrees west longitude. Bluebird, Missouri, United States of America.

WHAT TIME IS IT?

Near the commencement of the fourteenth Maya b'ak'tun, a cycle of 144,000 days, long count 13.0.3.13.14, which reckons time since the end of the gods and the creation of the world as it now is. Tzolk'in date 6 Ix on the sacred Maya calendar; Ix in glyph form represented by the face of the jaguar and its spots. Fire Monkey year, fifth day of the eighth month, 4714, in the Chinese agricultural calendar, a calendar for farmers in which the beginning of each month coincides with the arrival of a new moon. September 5, 2016, some two millennia since Jesus in the Christian method; or, the beginning of the seventh millennium since God's creation of the world. Thirteen billion, seven hundred seventy-million and one solar years from the genesis of the universe. Today.

CHAPTER FOURTEEN
FRUIT

[SEPTEMBER 5, 2016]

The sky was an ash tint, and it was heavy like a lid on a dish, abolishing any chance of escape.

Henry, gaunt as a ghost, fell to his knees upon the callous earth and uprooted a dry blade of grass for nourishment. He had been up late the night before writing the SOUNDER and had arisen early today to deliver a stack of newsletters to the post office before its opening. His enervated neck, legs, and arms burned. This pain emanated from several compressed vertebrae, which pinched diverse nerves and radiated jolts of electricity throughout his flesh. The late summer air was thick, and he gulped to take in as much as he needed. He rolled from his kneeling posture onto his side and found a momentary respite from his agony when his skin touched the soil beneath. The land was his mentor and he was its pupil and the lessons were nearly complete.

What is the meaning of the hours I have spent here on my property in the hills of Bluebird except to say that they were significant to me? Significant to me. The only judge whose decrees matter. I have knowingly exchanged my finite days for the fulfillment of the carnival fortuneteller's vision from long ago. I could have traded my time and my energy for something else, but I didn't. This is what I have chosen. And all the choices of all the people who have ever lived, together constitute the Age of Man. If the history of the universe is an infinite line as long as the universe itself, the Age of Man is an imperceptible scratch on that line. How vain for me to have wanted to leave a mark.

When the bank opened tomorrow after the holiday, Fat Dickey would close on the sale of his land in the Bluebird hills to Maddux Brothers. Once this transaction was complete, Maddux Brothers would send heavy construction equipment into Bluebird to widen the road to the hills. There, in the hills, the construction equipment would raze vegetation and excavate spaces for the new plant and its many outbuildings, parking lots, and supporting network of pipes and cables. There would be traffic, noise, and people as well as new smells and quite possibly even a credit union or goddamn sandwich station near Henry's property. In short, Henry's work and his glory would be undone. All this played through Henry's mind as his body rested there upon the earth.

It was required of Henry, pursuant to orders issued to himself by himself, to employ the last remnant of his strength to that end for which it had been given to him in the first instance. And that end, he believed, was not foreordained. Rather, his strength was to be expended or not expended according to his own will, to the extent that the direction of his will could be separated from the shaping of that will by the external pressures of the natural experience.

Sleep came over him like a tide rising over a shoal. His body shuddered and convulsed upon the ground, as if his brain were sending out bolts of energy to prevent the appendages from achieving a state of final relaxation.

After a few minutes, he awakened sodden with sweat and willed himself to arise to the fullest height his bent frame would allow. His face in profile was triangular with jaw pressed forward like a dead president on a coin. From his pocket his cellphone knelled the wistful tune of Fur Elise. This tune was one his wife had downloaded on his device at some point years ago as a ring tone after an argument about their marriage lacking romance. Henry wondered why she had chosen this day to attempt to speak to him for the first time since the fight in which his back had been broken by Nathan Washington. Henry reached into his pocket and shut off the sound. He checked the time on his phone.

He needed to be on his way for his interview with Jeffrey Sands, Chief Operating Officer of Maddux Brothers. Through calls from his cellphone, Henry had held himself out to Sands as Walter George, a business reporter from St. Louis, who was doing a piece on the proposed Maddux expansion into Bluebird. Sands and Henry had agreed to meet today, on Labor Day, when the pharmaceutical plant would be closed and Sands would not be prone to interruption. In another world, Henry thought, he would have cleaned himself up for this meeting, but this was not another world. This was the only world. Since the hospitalization for his back fracture some two months ago, Henry's hygiene regimen had been limited to trips to the Amoco in town every few days, where he shaved and toweled himself off in the bathroom while giving his phone a charge. Then, he would stock up on water, food, toilet paper, and other necessaries and return to his workshop. Three evenings ago, Henry had visited the supermarket in Belleflower to buy new underwear and t-shirts and a canister of lighter fluid. He had been eating only a few hundred calories of food per day, the amount needed to keep him from fainting. He had set up a latrine area at the rear of his property, inside the wall, adjacent to the Flamingo Fire. The latrine was a large flat boulder. He would sit on it, with his weight borne on the middle of the backs of his thighs, his backside protruding beyond the rock. Dung and toilet paper littered the ground behind the latrine.

Henry rode his motorcycle north across the dry prairie. There was not a road here but, despite the difficulty in the terrain, he wanted to avoid riding down into Bluebird. He made his way across the earth. Each bump sent waves of pain through his forearms and lower back. He persisted. He navigated poorly a little rift in the earth and was shot over the front of the motorcycle, his knees ramming the handlebars as his body flew forward. He straightened himself up, pushed the motorcycle for a while, and then remounted. He arrived at the highway, drove east for a short while, and then turned northward towards Calypso where the Maddux Brothers plant was located. Arriving close to the plant, he pulled his motorbike well off the road beneath a couple of sycamores. He verified the contents of his backpack. Then he placed the backpack over one shoulder and limped the distance to the main entrance of Maddux Brothers. Several vehicles were scattered in the front of the parking lot, which did not concern Henry for a plant like this was always staffed in one way or another. It was unlikely anyone but Sands was present in the administrative wing today.

As arranged, Sands met Henry just outside the front of the plant where, Henry gathered, the C-suiters probably toiled. Sands wore grey two-pleat slacks, a heavily starched open-collar yellow dress shirt, a tweed sport coat, and a high-gloss dress belt with matching cordovan tassel loafers. Henry guessed that the leather belt and shoes were made of the real cordovan leather from Spain, the kind taken from the soft spot on a horse's rump. Sands seemed appalled at Henry's appearance and opened his mouth as if to say so. Henry was dressed in loose dirty jeans that were ripped on one knee, black boots, and a filthy black t-shirt. His hair was speckled with gray streaks and dirt. Henry was breathing heavily, slumped, and beaded in perspiration. Before Sands could speak his mind, Henry put him at ease.

"Mr. Sands. Walter George, St. Louis Dispatch. I apologize for my appearance. My sedan broke down about five miles back, and I jogged the rest of the way here. Didn't want to hold you up at all."

This explanation, while incomplete as it did not account for Henry's casual clothing or rugged facade, seemed to satisfy Sands. The two men walked towards a glass door. Sands held his name badge in front of a square plastic panel. The door released. Sands escorted Henry into the building.

The COO's office was cluttered and warm, like an old general store. Rich wood flooring and shelving were accented with dim under-cabinetry lighting. The space was replete with hunting prizes including skins of a variety of big cats, bears, bison, and even monkeys. The skins were lain about the wood floor in lieu of rugs. Heads of beasts protruded from the long wall opposite the windows. The windows were shielded by thick, dark, wood louvers. Moving about the room, the men had to be careful not to bump into the stuffed animal heads, nor the myriad of figurines, carvings, puppets, masks, teaspoons, clocks, lamps, and other curios on display after their retrieval, Henry deduced, from all parts of the globe. Sands invited Henry to sit. Henry did so, placing his backpack at his feet. Sands stepped out of his office briefly and returned with two glasses of iced cola. Henry motioned to his cell phone and requested permission to record their session. Sands agreed. Henry fingered through a series of machinations on his phone, ostensibly to test the audio recording. Henry feigned dismay at the playback and asked Sands if they could shut the office door to eliminate white noise from the hallway. Sands agreed, stood, and shut the door. Sands now returned to his seat opposite Henry.

"Where do we begin?" asked Sands with a polite grin, his lips thin and bluish like those of a corpse.

The room was silent except for the ticking of clocks. The blown cool air inside had ceased. Henry reached into his backpack and his eyes flashed. When he brought out his hand, he wielded the five-inch flint knife he had found in the boulder field earlier in the year, in January. The knife was a dark mahogany color with hints of a rust color throughout. The knife, Henry believed, had been used by a member of the Osage Indian tribe for hunting and skinning mammals. Henry had sharpened the blade of the knife with his tool sharpener in his shed at home. He held the knife with his index and middle fingers on the handle, his thumb extended and pressed against the back of the knife. Seeing the knife, Sands shouted *No!*

Henry leapt across the desk in an instant and wrapped his left arm around Sands' throat with his right hand holding the flint knife tucked under Sands' chin. With such a small handle and the need to press his thumb on the back of the knife for leverage, the blade of the knife was necessarily pointed away from Sands' neck. Sands wriggled about so Henry angled the knife and pushed the sharp tip of the knife in to Sands' neck just enough to cut the skin. This drew a small amount of blood. The COO relaxed and Henry leaned all his weight forward to wrestle Sands from the office chair onto the floor. Now Henry manhandled Sands and dragged him away from the desk area until Henry could reach his backpack. He removed a roll of duct tape while pressing the point of the knife against the back of Sands' neck. Henry's body was weak and sore, but his hands and arms were still strong from his labors.

When Henry released the pressure upon his captive to manage the roll of tape with both hands, Sands slipped his knees under him and tried to stand. Henry grabbed Sands with both hands by the shirt and jacket collars and wrenched him down violently against the shape of his body so that Sands' left knee tucked underneath himself awkwardly while the right leg extended forward. Sands howled. Henry surmised that Sands' left knee ligaments had ripped apart. Henry seized one of the soda glasses from the desk and shattered it across Sands' forehead, knocking him out and opening up a bloody gash above one eye and projecting cola and ice across the room.

When Sands awoke, he was wearing only his striped briefs. Henry had strapped Sands with duct tape to the desk chair. Sands' wrists were taped together behind him, and his legs from his ankles to his knees were taped together underneath the chair. Henry thought Sands' lean body looked vulnerable undressed from the regalia of his position, although in Henry's estimation, the distinct tan lines along Sands' biceps and ankles probably came from golfing and were their own form of a different sort of regalia. Sands moaned, but the sound was dulled by the duct tape across his lips. The bridge of the COO's nose was crusted with blood from the gash in his forehead. Henry had piled Sands' clothes in one corner, submerged Sands' cellphone in the second glass of soda, and slashed Sands' landline with the flint knife. The computer monitor was on directly in front of Sands, its cerulean screen reflecting vaguely Sands' image.

Seeing Sands awaken, Henry stood and approached from behind, then cut the tape tying the COO's hands to the chair. Henry smacked the back of Sands' head with the palm of his left hand.

"Log yourself in," Henry said, and Sands obeyed by pecking at the keyboard. Henry now put the flint knife in the back pocket of his jeans. Henry hauled Sands to the far corner of the room, and pushed Sands and the chair to which Sands was taped onto their sides. Henry again taped Sands' wrists together with duct tape. The COO groaned and writhed.

Henry knelt before the computer, opened the Internet connection, and proceeded to move about there all the while taking notes by hand using paper and pen on the desk.

After approximately thirty minutes, Henry returned to the email function and composed a message.

TO: DFujisaki@fda.gov

FROM: Jeffrey.Sands@madduxbros.com

RE: WHISTLEBLOWER ACTION

Dear Commissioner Fujisaki,

I am Chief Operating Officer of Maddux Brothers, Inc.'s pharmaceutical plant in Calypso, Missouri. Maddux Brothers is in phase II FDA clinical trials for the drug DuCorps, with hundreds of high-blood pressure patients spread over multiple centers. This drug is manufactured here in our Calypso, Missouri plant. I write to alert you to unethical and fraudulent conduct by myself and other company officers.

I have been in meetings with key leaders of the company where we have discussed how to conceal harmful side effects suffered by research subjects who have been prescribed DuCorps as an Investigational New Drug. I have participated directly in bribing scientists with lavish vacations and gifts to influence their findings. I have overseen confidential settlements with the injured research subjects and their families. I have uncovered a plot by several of my colleagues to destroy material evidence related to these studies.

In addition, Maddux Brothers has set its eyes on expanding its operations from Calypso, Missouri into the nearby town of Bluebird, Missouri. To this end, I have personally overseen unlawful diversion of the water supply by Maddux Brothers away from farms in Bluebird to put the farms out of business to reduce property values for company purchase.

I cannot in good conscience continue my unethical and criminal behavior. What I have done cannot be undone. I pray for mercy, knowing I will need it shortly.

Jeffrey Sands, COO

Henry had no facts to support such an email. Henry had no information to suggest unethical conduct by the company in its development of the drug DuCorps, nor had any evidence been unearthed to prove that the company's use of water was unlawful. Henry's intention in sending the email was to stir up enough confusion in the market to temporarily affect the stock price. Perhaps this crisis would cause Maddux Brothers to postpone their purchase of the land in the Bluebird hills, giving Henry enough time to consider a different solution. Henry moved the arrow over the Send icon and clicked the mouse. He then opened the Sent Items folder in the email system and forwarded this same electronic message to the five deputy commissioners of the Food and Drug Administration, with copies to the WALL STREET JOURNAL, the NEW YORK TIMES, the ST. LOUIS POST-DISPATCH, the ST. LOUIS AMERICAN, and the U.S. Attorney's Office for the Eastern District of Missouri.

Satisfied that the email communications had been successfully dispatched, Henry reached under Sands' desk and ripped the computer tower from the wall. Henry then walked over to his backpack and removed a canister of lighter fluid he had purchased a few evenings ago at the grocery store in Belleflower. He doused lighter fluid about the desk and computer tower liberally. He walked the length of the space systematically and administered the fluid to each animal skin strewn about the room, here to two African leopards, here to an American bison, here to a yellow baboon, there to a black bear. He thought of a priest sprinkling holy water and how all that was touched was blessed, but in Henry's case, all that was touched would burn first and hottest. He sprinkled the wood shelves and the clocks and the lamps and the beast heads upon the walls. The largest of the dead monsters was the mounted head of a Western moose which jutted out some four feet; its eyes were open and could seemingly see in every direction despite its head being fixed and even in the face of its preservation in this un-natural and laughable manner its gaze appeared to be curious rather than judgmental. A bead of oil dripped from the moose's beard. Henry knocked the figurines and puppets and other curios from their resting places, and they toppled over and scattered.

Henry stood over Sands now who remained bound to the office chair which had been tipped on its side. Henry had not noticed before, but Sands and the chair to which Sands was bound laid atop the thick and soft skin of a Siberian tiger apparently, based upon the thickness of the fur, killed in winter. This made for an unusual scene—the waifish beige man in only briefs taped to a square black leather office chair and this bundle, tipped on its side, resting atop the tawny tiger fur with pale and black stripes. Henry studied the scene for a moment. He withdrew the flint knife from the back pocket of his jeans. He cut the tape that tied Sands to the chair and cut the tape that bound Sands' wrists and ankles together, and he stood there away from Sands while Sands cautiously removed the remnants of tape from his mouth, hands, ankles, and torso. Sands waited there on the tiger skin gathering his breath; he looked about as if judging his chances of escape with one useless leg. Henry tightened his hold on the knife.

"You are free," Henry said with a wry smile. Henry leaned over and pulled up the office chair so that the chair again rested on its feet. He sat in the chair, three feet away from Sands.

"You won't hurt me," Sands coughed, finding his voice, "you know I'm innocent. I don't know why you're here."

Henry did not respond. He wanted to see what Sands would say without any prompting from Henry.

Sands shortly obliged Henry. "I'm guessing you are not Walter George after all. Maybe you think you were hurt by one of our drugs; maybe you were hurt. Someone in your family was hurt? It's no one's fault. It's as much your fault as mine. Whatever you are upset about, blame yourself."

Henry blinked and lowered his head, as if hurt by Sands' words. He wanted to give Sands the impression that Sands could talk his way out of the predicament.

Sands continued, his voice louder. "You paid for this. Maybe you think you didn't but you did. When you watch TV, you are paying for our ads. You go to the doctor, you are buying our drugs. Supply and demand. If no demand, then no supply. Point that knife back at yourself."

"I don't care about your drugs. I don't need help with my hard-on. Do you need help with your hard-on?" Henry looked in the direction of Sands' crotch.

"What's your beef then? The water? You're one of those Bluebird farmers? Your corn is drying up? Were you part of that lawsuit? That's it." Sands squinted his eyes as if he had Henry figured. Henry thought perhaps this squinting of the eyes was a technique Sands used to intimidate his peers at work.

"Crops are thirsty. Poor people are getting poorer. People are living on the edge." Henry said this without emotion.

"I have a written legal opinion from outside counsel that Maddux took no more than its share of the water. I'll show it to you. It's in my desk. You know I grew up in Bluebird? I really did all I could to advocate for those farmers with leadership group in Philadelphia."

This man thinks that the word legal has any significance whatsoever, thought Henry.

"Legal is a sleight of hand. You're stealing from me. Tomorrow your company will buy up land in the Bluebird hills. Your new plant will ruin my situation. It won't be quiet anymore. I won't be alone there. You'll convert the land to a parking lot."

"Mr. Dickey put his property up for sale. Fair and square. It's our right to buy it. Outbid us if you want the land. That's how the law works. The law protects your property, too. Level playing field. Unless you prefer to live like a savage. Bring your lawsuit, appear before the zoning board."

"Let me speak to you in the only language that makes sense," Henry responded. "*Rights* is another word for *wants*. That's all. Violence is your instrument, not rights. It is violence you wield to obtain and to keep the land. Your power comes from money, political access, reputation. Maddux has more power than the farmers, so Maddux will do what it wants with the water. Maddux supposes it has more power than I do, so Maddux supposes it will do what it wants with the land, too. But I still have a final remnant of power to expend, and I'll stop your thievery if I can."

Sands had a disgusted look on his face. "You are the thief. You have resorted to savagery. I live by property rights. I follow the law. This enables peace, predictability, and prosperity. Look which one of us is holding the knife."

"I admit I am a thief. Everything I have I keep through power. This knife, I stole from the land, not because it was right, but because it was what I desired. Will you confess your sins also?"

"I shall do so no such thing. Everything I have I have a right to."

"Your property isn't yours. Your golf clubs. Your car. Your tie and coat."

"I earned them. I work hard. I take risks. They are mine."

"They could just as well belong to a Jack or a Job or a Kara or a Kim."

"My property is my reward. I took great risks. No one would take risks if they couldn't accrue wealth."

"I have seen birds and children take great risks."

"My things are mine. Mine!"

Henry's mind for a time had ceased its functions of observation and censure. His mind was clear and hard like an empty vault. Sands slowly inched forward on his knees and made a fist and punched at Henry's wrist to try to cause Henry to release the flint knife. Henry jerked his arm out of the way before Sands could land a blow.

An inevitable rupture occurred in the tectonic plates upholding the two men, and the volcanic temperatures underneath surged forth. Henry reacted to the orange-white heat he felt pulsing through him and he pounced from his seat knees first on the COO and flattened him. The COO arched his back to throw off his oppressor. As Henry rolled to the ground, he grabbed Sands' white hair in his left hand and slashed the point of the knife across Sands' throat with his other hand and there was no hurry or resistance now; Sands' jugular was slit. Sands pressed his fingers against his own throat. Henry mounted Sands casually; the COO stared blankly as crimson lifeblood spilled out. Henry used his knees to pin Sands' arms to his sides and punctured Sands' throat with a corkscrew movement of the flint knife. This yielded more blood and a thick gurgling sound. Henry twisted his wet red hand all about with the blade until a jagged flap of tissue unfolded at Sands' throat, and Sands' body turned forever stiff. Henry put the knife in his rear jeans' pocket, took up the canister of lighter fluid again, removed the lid, and dumped the remainder of the liquid onto Sands and the tiger skin that made his bed.

The office smelled of petroleum and exotic proteins. Henry stepped over by the office door and removed a matchbook from his front pants pocket. He lit a match and dropped it into the office and the fire caught and spread easily across the pattern Henry had created. The fire began to lick up the animal skins and papers and books and binders and legal pads and sticky notes and office furniture and flooring and masks and carvings and figurines and Sands himself. Sands' hair vanished in an instant, and the fire, for a moment, formed around his body like a flaming sarcophagus. Sands' golden skin tightened and sweated and then melted. Henry watched the fire for a while. An eager cuckoo bird emerged on schedule from its delicately carved housing and began to count the hours in its manner but combusted before it could finish. A fifteen-piece set of baby blue snow queen matryoshka dolls, signed by the artist, looked on in a state of pleasant resignation. A piece of lace cloth, hung in a glass frame, grew distorted from the heat. A decorated plate on a plate stand turned black. Two Inuit dolls standing in a corner warped. The immobilized heads of beasts mounted to the wall withstood their plight courageously for a time as flames licked their beards and necks before engulfing their proud heads entirely and spitting out gray ash. The flames crackled and hissed and the air tasted of roasting flesh and hair and the air conditioning reasserted itself and this infusion of oxygen drove forth the flames.

***

Henry operated out of instinct, beyond the reach of reason, the impulses translated into action without oversight.

An office adjacent to that of the now exsanguinated COO yielded a bounty of wooden chairs, books, and documents that Henry threw into the hallway to feed the fire. He darted about from office to office knocking boxes and bookshelves to the floor as the flames stretched and spread. The copy room provided several boxes of unopened paper that Henry placed in the hallway. The fire roared exponentially now, and it consumed carpet and sheetrock and ceiling tiles; it began to growl like wind and roll and churn like a cloud as it blew thick gray smoke in front of it. Henry ran and escaped from the front doors of the pharmaceutical plant. A fire alarm screeched throughout the interior and exterior of the plant. Several employees of Maddux Brothers had evacuated the building and fled from the parking lot in their vehicles.

Amidst the pandemonium, no one seemed to notice Henry limping away from the scene with his hands stained in blood. He hurried as best he could by foot the quarter-mile along the paved street back to his motorcycle. He rode his motorcycle towards his workshop the reverse of the way he had come earlier today. Stiff winds reared up, as if to stop him from retreating. It was difficult for him to see with dust blowing, and he fell backwards off of his motorcycle when he unwittingly rode over a bush, causing the front wheel of the motorcycle to rear up. He abandoned the motorcycle and walked the remainder of the way.

He arrived at his fortress. Using his keys, he opened the portals in the two completed rock walls, locking each gate behind him. He entered his workshop. Once inside, he removed his clothing. He crawled on top of the marble altar, and he twisted his neck about to the one position that caused him the least pain. The marble seemed to absorb him the way a mattress or blanket would. He nestled himself there like a cat making up its bed.

CHAPTER FIFTEEN
OUTPOURING

[SEPTEMBER 5, 2016]

That same Labor Day afternoon, clouds congregated overhead in the Bluebird sky; clouds balled up like a mob forming to dole out a deviant version of justice in response to some faraway and self-fulfilling and possibly true rumor. The clouds swelled and rolled in every direction north and south and east and west, and they thickened grey and brown and cast great anvils of shade upon the prairie below. This brew of trouble above now released its watery ire and spears fell down towards the earth through the gloomy atmosphere. Bluebirdians had prayed all summer for moisture, but in nature's cruel way, when she finally gave them what they desired, she gave them too much of it. If it rained as hard and as long as the television meteorologists had predicted, this close to harvest, the consequences would be grave. Excess moisture would propagate fungi and disease upon the crops and wash the nutrients away from the soil. Soggy fields would prevent the old combines from doing their work of harvesting.

Through the storm's precursory winds, Melissa Dunstan had started up the way from Main in Bluebird to the Dunstan Hotel, first in dirt and dust clouds, but now with the rains, she marched in sticky grime. Soon she trekked through mud, and rivulets formed at the sides of the dirt road to carry off the excess water. The rains poured on in engorged globules that pattered upon the vegetation in a reckless percussiveness. Melissa moved deliberately, for in spots the muck on the road had turned to slime, so that she had to slide her feet along as if on ice to keep from slipping. She wore a new pair of hiking boots that kept her feet dry and helped her keep her balance, as well as a new lightweight waterproof jacket with hood. With these articles of clothing, she was not uncomfortable in the storm. In her right hand, she carried an old .22 single-shot bolt-action rifle of her father's in a tan canvas zippered case that she used for now, butt down, as a walking staff. In her jacket pocket, she carried the shells for the rifle in a small, clear, plastic bag.

Melissa had not seen Henry since the day she had caught him with Claire, the little whore standing there in the master bedroom in her tight shorts and push-'em-up bra, with Henry on the bed in his underwear. Melissa believed that had she arrived home a minute earlier she would have caught them in each other's arms as she had always pictured she would. Henry's betrayal had been more than two months ago. Melissa regretted not having thrown the compact banker's lamp at her husband as would have been faithful to her fantasy. But Melissa had not, after all, discovered them in bed together, and there had been a seed of doubt in her mind about what Henry and Claire might have done together and whether they had crossed a certain threshold. And so, she had not thrown the lamp at her husband.

Following this violent episode at home involving her husband, Claire, Claire's father, and the sheriff, Melissa had hatched no particular plan to see or not to see Henry at the hospital, the workshop, or otherwise. The preceding two plus months had, to her, not been so unlike the months prior when Henry was building his walls at all hours and rarely came home. She assumed that he would return home at some point, as before, and perhaps they would then as a couple address what had transpired between them in the intervening weeks. In any event, she, the Queen of Bluebird, was on schedule to fulfill the ambitions she had proposed for herself and for Bluebird.

As Melissa had predicted, based upon her conversations with Shirlene Mack, Joe Campbell, and others in town with knowledge of the farmers' lawsuit against Maddux Brothers, the court had, two weeks before Labor Day, dismissed the lawsuit, without prejudice, at the request of the plaintiff-farmers who had run dry on funding. According to newspapers, even though the plaintiff-farmers could technically refile the lawsuit at a later time, this court dismissal was seen, by the national legal community, as a precedent for other similar legal cases against Maddux Brothers pending in other jurisdictions. As such, the market had rewarded Maddux Brothers by driving up the price per share of Maddux stock some five percent. For Melissa, who had invested five million dollars in Maddux Brothers' shares, this five-percent increase represented two hundred fifty thousand dollars. Three more percentage points of increase in the price of Maddux Brothers' shares was all she needed—three more percentage points and she could sell her position at a gain of four hundred thousand dollars. She would then turn the cash over to the Bluebird Society for the purchase of Dickey's Diner. The other part of her plan was to divorce Henry. In the divorce, their assets would be split fifty-fifty she assumed. With two-and-a-half million dollars of her own, she could live in Bluebird in peace and prosperity with her children, and she could continue to raise money through her day-trading for other town rebuilding efforts. Henry would presumably move back to St. Louis and leave her alone.

At least this had been Melissa's plan before her vision the night prior.

Perhaps because the day ahead would be Labor Day when the stock market would be closed, Sunday had been as comfortable a day as Melissa could remember. She had grilled shrimp and corn on the cob for the kids and served this with a lime slaw, Tex-Mex rice, buttery rolls, and huge portions of chocolate pecan pie with ice cream. After dinner, Melissa, Ginny, and Charlie just sat there in the front room, sedated and full, without the TV on for once, chatting about things of no consequence. They laughed and enjoyed being together. Time seemingly stood still, and there was no burden to existing and no anticipation that the tranquility would end. When she slipped into bed that night, Melissa's happy heart radiated abundance all about her. When she fell asleep, she was transported by and by to a place of light within another dimension of space and time that could not be measured in height or width or depth. This was an interior dimension, like a hole or vacuum, some infinity of space and time existing in opposition to the finite limitations of those resources in the material world.

Within this vacuum of light were differing gradations of light, so that Melissa could still see, as it were, and distinguish one form from another. Within this unburdened atmosphere, her body moved effortlessly up a vast spiral staircase of stone, step by step, towards something ahead, something apparently set aside or chosen for her. She sensed Albert had a role in bringing her to this place. The staircase was wide and enclosed and the walls around the staircase were made of stone too. Because of the spiral nature of the structure she could see only a few yards in front of her, yet she continued upwards. The steps were smooth with wear, and the handrail was a burnished bronze; it was obvious that the way was not unique to her but one of an ancient and everlasting pilgrimage as old as the souls of women and men and children.

At the top of the staircase, she found herself in an open cobblestone courtyard framed by manicured dogwood, azalea, and holly that gave in all directions onto a ceaseless garden kept in the French manner where, stepping down into it, she heard the burbling of a fountain beyond her vision. She moved towards this fountain. She was given to understand that the garden contained a limitless concourse of persons but that the garden was nonetheless immense enough that each searcher could have her own privacy. Melissa maneuvered around hedges and statues and under rows of pleached hornbeams lined up as sentinels, when finally she came to the fountain she had heard. A little boy was there rinsing his face in the water that pooled beneath a bronze of a muscular winged creature in chains. The boy turned and looked at Melissa. This boy was Melissa's lost son, little Albert, who was no longer a toddler, but now the age of an elementary school boy. Mother and child ran together with fervor. She embraced him, and she picked him up and squeezed him and twirled him around; he called her name, *Mommy, Mommy, Mommy* and she called his name *Albert, Albert, Albert*. The tears fell from her cheeks and watered the boy's hair, and with each teardrop, he transmogrified progressively into an old Indian grinding stone. In the vision, she was not sad or surprised by this change in Albert, but she understood it in the receptive and non-judgmental manner that is customarily possessed by participants in supernatural events. She cradled the rock and twirled it around and kissed it and held it close to her bosom; her tears dried up, and the rock changed back into a little boy. This time, however, the boy's face was that of her husband, Henry, as a child. Melissa held this boy and loved him and twirled him about and kissed him upon the cheek and the forehead and she called his name *Henry, Henry, Henry*, and the boy smiled back at her. She set him on the ground. He ran to the fountain, jumped inside the pool of clear water, and disappeared. Next, the chains on the statue fell away and the bronze angel stretched as if awaking from a sleep of a thousand years and then flew upwards and away.

Awake in her bed afterwards and still in rapture, Melissa had understood the vision as God's call to action. She knew the vision or dream was of deity—it had untangled her mind in a way that could not be true of any power but divine power—it had spoken to some part deep inside of her beyond the reach of consciousness.

Her interpretation of the vision was that her love would save Henry. In the vision, Henry had first been a stone, and with her love, he had turned into a boy, and then jumped into the fountain and disappeared. She believed that her love was a warmth that could penetrate stone, and if love could penetrate stone, it could surely penetrate her husband, no matter how distant he had been.

In response to the vision, therefore, Melissa plodded towards her husband's workshop through puddles that made light tympanic notes when stepped in. She attained the plateau within the hills and walked a bit further until she reached Henry's workshop. Still, the rains came down. The workshop was completely encircled by two walls of piled stones, and there were also the very beginnings of a third wall of piled stones. The tall gate built into the outermost completed rock wall was locked. This did not surprise her. She unsheathed the rifle, removed a .22 cartridge shell from the small bag in her jacket pocket, and opened the breech of the rifle. She placed a round inside, closed the bolt, released the safety, and used her sleeved forearm to push back her hood. She took aim, and she could see through the outer gate to the inner gate, and beyond the inner gate, the workshop's door. She pushed the rifle against her shoulder, took a breath and held it, and fired. The gun cracked, followed immediately by a high piercing sound, and she believed she had hit the upper-right-hand corner of the door; this was her intention.

She waited a bit, but no one came. She repeated the exercise, waited a little longer, and fired again. After ten or twelve rounds, the front door swung open suddenly from within. There stood Henry nude, frail, and bent with both arms curved above his head in surrender, each arm burgundy from forearm to wrist to fingers. She threw the rifle into the mud, and she called his name three times, *Henry, Henry, Henry*. Henry looked confused and went back inside for a moment, then returned and staggered forth through the downpour. Melissa called his name to urge him onwards. He ambled his way barefoot to the inner gate which he unlocked with the key. Then, he unlocked and opened the outer gate. He stood before her now, his stubbled face black and silver, and his dark hair shiny and flat with rainwater. The eyes of husband and wife met like those of two wild creatures in a forest.

Raindrops shelled them both. Henry's arms were streaked now burgundy and clear like those of a vigneron. Melissa seized his wrists and exclaimed, "You've worked yourself to the bone," and she rubbed her hands along the tops of his hands and his wrists and his forearms and slowly she washed the blood from his skin. She pulled his closest arm over her shoulder behind her neck, reached her hand about his waist to hold him steady, and with her bearing up Henry, they hobbled side by side into the workshop.

Henry collapsed into the marble altar, and she assisted him up and followed him there, which required some acrobatics. She held him to her like a sick infant. She was strong and motivated by divine intervention; he was weak, and he would not resist. He pushed his face into the cradle of her neck and the remainder of his body was slack. She held him there folded in half. She kissed his wet hair, wiped her sleeve across his face, and looked upon his sunken chest with pity. After a time, she began to hum to him the same songs she had sung to the children— low, quiet, and true. She rocked him and the movement was innate to both like grass rippling in the wind. She was nurse and priestess and mother and wife. When he struggled to speak, she pressed her hand over his lips.

"Now now," she said gently.

He fell asleep fitfully, awoke and tried again to speak. She forbad it again. The altar was wet and hard and dirty, and she took no respite, and she nursed him. Through the window to the west, the firmament changed from storm cloud to pale blue, and still she held him. Pale blue sky turned to grapefruit-orange and dying beams of light shone into the ovular room. If she concentrated, she could follow a light beam like a movie theatre projection from its genesis at the window to its splaying across the marble and dissipating and disappearing. Pink sky changed to dusky brown and then charcoal, and the night absorbed the day and the stars rose and called attention to themselves through everlasting shimmerings; she looked upon them with wonder and reverence and her husband slept there in her arms, and the night wore on and she was ever faithful.

Next morning, she awakened and could not feel him there, and she lifted up her head and Henry was there standing with his back to the window. He hobbled over to her.

He opened his mouth and breathed out a lament like a soprano saxophone seeping forth its plea across a music hall.

"Everything has led to this. To the end of my story."

"Now now," she said sitting up, "hush."

"This is my final scene. I know it."

"Ssshhhh. Ginny and Charlie need you. It's time to come home."

"There's no audience. No newspaper review. No curtain call. No validation. No exquisite justification."

"Ginny has a new flute number you'll love. Charlie talks more than ever. The other day he said *damn it* when he dropped something. I couldn't stop laughing."

"Not even an echo."

"I need you. I haven't always known that lately."

"I knew when the show was over they'd turn the house lights on and the place would be empty. A sliver of me hoped to be wrong."

"I had a dream night before last. It changed everything."

"A whole theater with but one person inside."

"Full of compassion and love and healing."

"What is the meaning of an unwitnessed life?"

"Binding us together without fear or bitterness."

"When there is no who to remember, was there ever a what?"

"Somehow I had missed the clearest part."

"Where does the light go when it goes out?"

"That's why she had an impact on you. That's why Claire got to you. She was available. She was, simply, there."

"The most gorgeous human song—never heard. A peasant mother in wet rags, humming to her little corpse. Saints and demons stopped up their ears with wax it was so sorrowful."

"I am here. I will make myself tangible to you. You won't need to turn to her anymore."

"The hottest fires, the brightest starbursts, the wildest beasts, the ripest fruits, never seen nor recorded nor studied."

"I am saying I understand, but don't do it again."

"I am seeing in sepia."

"Did you hear me?" She began to wonder if they were in the same conversation.

"Yes," he said.

"I'll make you bacon and pancakes."

"Yes, that's it, everything in brown and tan. The present as antiquity."

"Fresh squeezed orange juice."

"They'll be here soon to take me. It shall be exceedingly unpleasant. I underestimated the value of my liberty."

"That's all over. They won't hurt you anymore."

"It won't take long for them to find me."

"I've made peace with the townsfolk."

"There must be cameras everywhere."

"It must have felt like that for you as an outsider."

"I'll die in my cell."

"We'll fix up the old place. We'll make the whole town better. We'll get a coffee shop with Internet and some of the things you like. You'll see. I'm on the precipice. And today Dickey sells his land to Maddux Brothers. Everyone's going to see what a strong company they really are."

"Do you hear that drum?"

"Ssssshhh."

He leaned against the altar.

"It's getting closer. It's low and deep."

"Listen to my voice. Concentrate on it."

"They're going to ask me about the dead body. What a sight that must have been."

"That was years ago he died. Stop talking. I'll get you home."

"I bet you want to know if I feel bad for what I did?"

"I know how you feel."

"I don't feel a thing. It was inevitable."

"It was my fault."

"For every action an equal and opposite reaction."

"I said it was my fault."

"He moved about freely until Nature showed her power. And then he was no more."

"I don't follow."

"He sowed the wind and reaped the whirlwind."

"Are you goddamn out of your mind? He was a little boy."

"How long will this whole stupid process take, to end this, start to finish?"

"Were you talking about Albert back there?"

Melissa's question somehow got through to Henry. He stared at his wife blankly. "I've been talking about Jeffrey Sands, COO. As in the death of. By Nature's hand."

"Oh." She gathered herself and found her core of peace again, a bit baffled from her husband's apparent confusion, but relieved Henry was not suggesting that Albert deserved to die. She assumed he was again railing at Maddux Brothers for their role in the water shortage in town.

She picked up their conversation again. "It's short. All downhill. I'll help you."

"I'll plead guilty to get it over with."

"Albert drowned because of me. Don't make me say it again."

"No need to pay to fight the obvious."

"No more fighting. I've made sure of that. I've figured it out."

"There's no proof of life."

"We'll build up the town together."

"I'll be like Albert."

"He was a good boy."

"Beyond reach. As if I never was."

"It wasn't your fault."

"I built that rock boundary out there for proof. But who can guess how long it will stand."

"I was day-trading when he drowned. I still am. I should have told you. I wasn't napping. I was in the house hunched over the computer. I made up the rest. There, I've said it all."

"How long will it last?"

"Just a while longer."

"Fifty years?"

"Heavens no. I'll stop soon. I'm already halfway there after the dismissal of the lawsuit. Dickey is probably at the bank right now signing the papers. Once investors know they're expanding, the stock will march up some more."

"How long do walls last?"

"I can't imagine it will take more than a month or two."

"Whatever I did it was always going to be futile. Wall or no wall."

"You had to be a rock to protect yourself. That's over."

"One way or another. Every road the same."

"We learn from our mistakes."

"They'll leave this place alone for a while at least. I can come here in my own mind."

"I've saved Bluebird. I'm going to buy the diner."

"There is nothing to hold on to."

"There will be. The diner, then the school house. The Dry Goods. The post office. Each in turn. Come home and look at my plum Cadillac CTS. Charlie helped me pick it out."

"There was never anything to hold on to."

"There will be."

She got down from the altar and went to him, and she unbuttoned her shirt and put his hands on her breasts over her bra. He closed his eyes. All was quiet for a time but their breathing. Suddenly Henry stepped away from her to the window.

This time she heard the sound, too. It was a heavy grinding sound, stopping and starting, chambered air building and releasing. Outside a red excavator was crawling across the land towards the western edge of the Hotel property. The excavator rolled gently up and down over the bumps in the land; it looked gangly and unnatural against the landscape. As best Melissa could tell, it was Sheriff Haggerty at the controls, in full uniform, wearing a round cowboy style outdoor police hat.

The Sheriff had responded to the fire at the pharmaceutical plant yesterday. His team had already started reviewing the surveillance videos, in which they had observed grainy footage of Jeffrey Sands greeting Henry outside of the plant's administrative wing. There were hours and hours of footage from numerous cameras to dig through, but the video they had seen didn't prove anything but that Henry had been there. And of course, they had seen the emails from Sands' account to the FDA, but those were up to the feds to sort out. The sheriff, sure of his instincts, had sought but been denied a warrant for Henry's arrest. When this failed, he kept his detectives at work at the scene in Calypso while he rented the old excavator and brought it down to Bluebird on a flatbed and then navigated it up the dirt road to the Hotel.

Melissa and Henry watched through the window. Haggerty brought the excavator parallel to the outside wall of stones running east to west along the southern border of the property. He was situated precisely at a point where if he dug all the way through to the interior of the wall the Flamingo Fire would be destroyed. It was as if Haggerty knew exactly where Henry had slept and pissed so many times, as if he knew the one spot on the wall that Henry cherished most. Haggerty swiveled the machine ninety degrees and wildly swung the bucket against the outermost wall. This knocked rocks every which way. Now, Haggerty lowered the bucket, gathered rock and earth, rotated the bucket one hundred eighty degrees, and dumped the load.

Seeing this destruction from the window, Henry's eyes turned wild, and he ran across the oval room still naked.

"Don't you go out there," Melissa ordered, cutting off his exit. She was strong and composed. "I won't let my dream slip away."

"I won't stand by and watch my work undone," he hollered.

She stood in his way still and he tried to push her aside but couldn't.

"If you want to help, get out of here," Henry said.

Melissa's vision from two nights prior gave her confidence that everything would somehow work out between her and Henry. Objectively, she knew that if she returned home, he could act irrationally and get himself hurt again. On the other hand, the vision; this foretold peace for her and Henry. And Henry was giving her permission to leave. In addition, she was curious to get home and check her trading account on the computer to see if the sale of Dickey's land to Maddux Brothers had become public and already made an impact on her investment. She didn't need much movement, just a slight jump in price. Three percent more and she'd sell all her shares and have enough money for the diner.

Melissa did not know that, because of Sands' death, the sale of the Dickey's land to Maddux Brothers had not closed. Further, she did not know that, in response to the fire at the pharmaceutical plant, and in response to the emails sent from Sands' account to the FDA and the newspapers, that investors assumed that the fire must have been started by someone inside the company trying to hide research misconduct. Given the appearance of research fraud and injury to patients, Maddux Brothers' share price had crashed from a price of forty dollars per share to a price below eight dollars per share already, and Melissa's five-million-dollar investment in Maddux Brothers was now worth only one million dollars. Henry had fabricated the contents of the Sands email to the FDA. Henry had no factual basis for asserting that Maddux Brothers had committed research fraud nor that they had violated the water rights of the farmers. Under normal circumstances, once Maddux Brothers could respond to the allegations and assure the market that the fire was started by a criminal, and the email to the FDA was fraudulent, the share price would return to the status quo.

As Melissa debated whether to go home or to stay with her husband, she recalled the vision again and was quickly awash in its expectant thrust, in a sense of inevitability in what she had foreseen. She now spoke calmly to Henry.

"I'll be back with Darren and Mack. They'll take your side. They'll persuade Haggerty to leave. And we'll hire someone to rebuild your wall. Give me twenty-five, thirty minutes before you do anything stupid. I'll round up the kids. They'll be happy to see you. Promise to wait."

She envisioned a great barbeque with meat and corn and rolls and cakes on the First Baptist grounds. Melissa would announce to all gathered that she had raised enough to buy the diner. Melissa would be hailed as the Queen of Bluebird and Henry, dressed to the nines, would be hailed as the King of Bluebird. It would be an evening of demar-cation—dusk for stale old Bluebird and dawn for a new glamorous Bluebird.

"Okay," Henry said, agreeing to stay put until Melissa returned. Now, he opened the workshop door and accompanied Melissa through the two portals in the rock walls. Once outside of the fortress, Melissa jogged down the prairie towards home.

As soon as Melissa was out of sight, Henry, too, exited his fortress. He remained stark naked. He quickly located and picked up in each hand a stone the size of a baseball. He limped around the outside of his property towards where Haggerty was working the excavator. Henry stayed close to the wall, out of Haggerty's line of sight. Henry crept closer until he was fifteen yards away from Haggerty. Haggerty was pointed away from Henry at a sixty-degree angle, digging away at the outermost rock wall with the machine. Henry just stood there, waiting for Haggerty to rotate the excavator a bit to his right, so that Henry would have a better target for his stones. When Haggerty turned the excavator to nearly a zero degree angle, Henry launched the first stone. To Henry's surprise, this first throw was on target and the stone, the size of a baseball, hit Haggerty in the jaw. Haggerty slumped to his left and appeared to fall from his seat. Henry dropped the stone in his left hand and raced around the excavator to where Haggerty had fallen to the ground. Haggerty lay there on the earth still moist from the rains, kneading his jaw absently-mindedly, his mind apparently dulled by the stone and by his fall. Henry leaned over, removed Haggerty's ser-vice revolver, and threw it away from the scene. Using his heel, Henry kicked Haggerty in the ribs once, twice, three times. Haggerty coughed and rolled towards Henry to shield himself with his arms. Haggerty's onyx pendant hung down sideways above his shirt. Henry grabbed the necklace, tore it from Haggerty's neck, and threw it to the ground. Now, Henry squatted and gathered a large, heavy boulder with both hands, and held it against his naked belly. He leaned back and hoisted the stone up further to shoulder level with an intention of dropping the boulder onto the sheriff's head. Henry pressed the rock up above his head and stumbled towards the sheriff.

Henry did not see Detective Michael Deguchi approaching behind him. Deguchi, at Haggerty's instruction, had secluded himself in a clump of brush some ways off, and had crept close to the scene unno-ticed. When Henry raised the stone above his head, Deguchi closed in and whipped his police baton with full force across the back of Henry's skull, splitting it open and spraying out blood and brain matter. Henry's body and the stone he had been holding toppled to the ground casually there in the mud and the grass. Henry was dead.

"Waited long enough," Haggerty muttered to his comrade as both officers wiped tissue and blood from their faces.

"The closest cover is that clump of brush a back there," Deguchi said. "Man, did you call that or what?"

"I am familiar with the ongoings of men. They act in a way they believe unique but which in fact forms a pattern." Sheriff Haggerty stated this with an air of pride. The two justice officers radioed for an ambulance and an investigative team.

Both men were tired now as the adrenaline surge gave way to fatigue and malaise over the termination of a man and the knowledge that for the next weeks they'd both be tied up in a use-of-lethal-force review to say nothing of investigating the fire and apparent homicide of Sands at the pharmaceutical plant the day prior. Deguchi lay himself supine upon the damp earth, and Haggerty did the same. They looked above upon the mixed heavens, royal and azure directly overhead fading to aqua and turquoise along the edges where distance had drawn away the bolder colors, large cotton clouds threatened by the grey shadows circulating in their midst.

Deguchi said he had never been at a scene such as this and asked if the investigative team would need to clean the blood and the brains from the ground at the end of the day.

Haggerty said it would rain again very soon, and there would be no need for clean up. He said that the grey shadows above were made of that same primordial mist that had been intact and unchanged since the beginning of the planet, circulating from sky to soil countless times over and over, over and through the course of all life, through and throughout every form of animal and plant and geographical receptacle and inch of atmosphere, that indestructible and uncreatable and necessary substance that after billions of years still was pure and clean and untainted by the acts of its hosts, so that when it next rained later that evening, though it be the same droplets of water as had fallen on brontosaurus and Lucy and Adam and Qin Shihuang and Mother Mary and Shakespeare and Madame Curie and Stalin and on a tiger carcass on the savannah and upon a crowded salmon hatchery and upon the Crow Creek remains or upon a ghetto of dogs and grime or a medical waste sanitation facility or a rice farm fertilized by human feces, still it would come down full and clear and unsoiled and fresh, washing and washing and washing away habits and memories and deeds wherever it fell, a watery veil of forgetfulness, the last rains the same as the first, the first rains the same as the last, such that the new day to come after the coming storm would be as clean as the first daydawn the world had ever known.

EPILOGUE

Henry's death did not shake Melissa. The state of peace and direction she had found in the heavenly dream two nights before Henry's death stayed with her. Somehow things were going to work out. She thought often of Debbie Black, naked and stranded on a highway, unashamed, simply looking for a ride into town. The need to forget the past and move forward.

Melissa decided to entomb Henry in his workshop. There, he would remain in his most natural state. She paid for his body to be embalmed, and then had his body placed, face up, upon the altar in the workshop. She had the corpse of her son Albert exhumed from its burial plot in the corner of the yard in Bluebird, cleaned up, and placed on the altar alongside his father. Steel bars were mounted over the workshop windows and the workshop's front door was replaced by a slab of marble. In this way, the workshop was made into a tomb for Henry Albert Dunstan, father, and Henry Albert Dunstan, son. The letters *H.A.D.* were twice carved into the slab of marble guarding the door to the tomb.

H.A.D.

H.A.D.

Although Henry had fabricated the contents of the September 5, 2016 email sent from Jeffrey Sands' computer account to Commissioner Fujisaki at the United States Food and Drug Administration, the WALL STREET JOURNAL, and various other newspapers, the email and the fire at the Maddux Brothers plant in Calypso, Missouri were more than sufficient to attract the attention of the FDA. The September 5, 2016 email claimed that key officials within Maddux Brothers had concealed harmful side effects of an Investigational New Drug called DuCorps, which was a drug aimed at treating high blood pressure. The email further claimed that Maddux Brothers officials had bribed scientists to influence the research findings related to DuCorps. The timing of the fire at the Calypso, Missouri plant suggested to the FDA the possibility that an insider had intentionally started the fire to destroy evidence of fraud.

Over the coming months, the FDA investigated the research findings related to DuCorps, interviewed scientists associated with the manufacture of DuCorps, and determined that the company's claims regarding DuCorps were scientifically valid. All across the country, people with high blood pressure, people like Melissa's parents, kept taking the drug.

Following the death of her husband, Melissa learned from Sheriff Haggerty that Henry had started the fire at the Calypso pharmaceutical plant and had murdered Jeffrey Sands. Believing, based on her conversations with Sheriff Haggerty, that the FDA investigation would conclude that the September 5, 2016 email had no factual basis, Melissa held on to her shares of Maddux Brothers, waiting for them to rebound from their price of eight dollars per share to something closer to the forty dollars per share at which she had purchased these shares. However, during the course of its investigation, the FDA uncovered evidence of research misconduct in the manufacture and marketing of two different, unrelated Maddux Brothers drugs. This information, when made public by the FDA, caused a frenzied sell-off in the stock market. Melissa immediately attempted to sell her complete position in Maddux Brothers. However, in the frenzied sell-off, large-volume institutional traders were allowed to execute their trades first. By the time Melissa could sell her position, her shares sold for four dollars fifty cents per share. Her five-million dollar investment in Maddux Brothers was now worth only five hundred sixty thousand dollars. She had lost more than four million four hundred thousand dollars in total on her investment in Maddux Brothers.

Maddux Brothers thereafter closed the Calypso, Missouri plant as a cost-cutting measure. With the pharmaceutical plant closed, the water levels in Bluebird in early spring of 2017 returned to normal. No evidence ever surfaced as to whether Maddux Brothers had used more than its share of water, but the farmers found their proof in the fortuitous correlation between the drug company's departure and the renewal of the water source. Maddux Brothers would never finalize its purchase of the land in the eastern Bluebird hills from Fat Dickey. With Maddux Brothers out of the picture, Fat Dickey could not find a buyer interested in purchasing his land in the hills. Dickey therefore passed title of the land to his children.

Following the collapse of the Maddux Brothers stock price, neither Melissa nor the Bluebird Society could afford to purchase Dickey's

Diner, so Dickey sold his business to a Randall Welke, a fellow from Belleflower who proposed to keep the diner and its name, Dickey's Diner, intact. This arrangement was, of course, more agreeable to Melissa and the Society than they could have reasonably expected, given the circumstances. The diner was not under the control of a family in Bluebird, but at least the name and menu were not changed.

Shortly after the sale of his diner, Dickey was hospitalized in Belleflower for his heart condition. Doctors informed Dickey and his wife that his heart was failing. He was transferred to a large hospital in St. Louis and implanted with an LVAD, or Left Ventricular Assist Device. Following an extensive hospitalization in St. Louis, Dickey was released home. The out-of-pocket medical expenses exhausted the proceeds from Dickey's sale of the diner, rendering it impossible for Dickey to provide the intended financial support to his children. Dickey and his wife remained in their home in Lampersville and lived off their social security checks.

Although the investment with Maddux Brothers had proven a financial catastrophe, Melissa still had several hundred thousand dollars in the bank. Further, she owned outright the old family home in Bluebird. Melissa had enough money to stay in Bluebird and raise her kids there if she budgeted her affairs carefully.

Six months after Henry's death, in March of 2017, Melissa received a phone call from an Amy Lin with PEOPLE magazine. The story of Henry's murder of Jeffrey Sands, Chief Operating Officer of Maddux Brothers, the fire at the pharmaceutical plant, and Henry's and Albert's entombment in the workshop in the hills had come to the attention of the magazine. It was a dark story, but still potentially a good human interest story if framed correctly, Ms. Lin said. Ms. Lin requested to travel to Bluebird to interview Melissa about the events leading up to Henry's death, to find out how Melissa was coping, and to take photographs of the town. Melissa welcomed this visit.

Two months later, in May of 2017, a one-page story regarding Henry, his workshop, and Bluebird, Missouri, ran in PEOPLE magazine. The story minimized the violence Henry had committed and focused on how Melissa had entombed Henry and Albert in the workshop as a final act of love. She could have sold the property in the hills for money, but instead, because of Henry's attachment to the land, she had entombed him there along with their son. In the story, Melissa referred to Debbie Black as a sort of mythical icon for always moving forward.

The photograph attached to the story was a black-and-white overhead helicopter shot of the workshop. The workshop was surrounded by its two completed walls of stone. The unfinished third wall of stone was barely visible. From far above, the property looked like a simple square within two concentric circles. The article, written by Amy Lin, quoted a symbologist who interpreted the square inside two concentric circles to mean that Henry had communicated, through these structures, that he was a tangible, mortal being attempting to make an impact on the everlasting circle of life. The article was clear not to condone Henry's violent methods, but did note that the cornfields of Bluebird had been inadvertently saved by Henry's actions. The article further noted that Melissa, Ginny, and Charlie were intent on remaining in Bluebird and that Melissa and the Bluebird Society were still doing what they could to renovate the town.

The article in PEOPLE magazine generated interest in Bluebird as a tourist destination. By July of 2017, there were ten to fifteen new visitors per week in Bluebird. They would park in town along Main Street, hike up the dirt road to the hills, look at Henry's workshop and its rock boundaries, and take pictures. Back in town, these tourists would buy sodas and snacks from Joe Campbell's shop or the Amoco, or they would stop at Dickey's Diner for lunch. A few visitors with flat tires or other minor car troubles called on the services of David Campbell.

The number of new weekly visitors to Bluebird doubled from fifteen to thirty by August of 2017. Shirlene Mack made a point of talking to as many of these visitors as she could. Without exception, the visitors had seen or heard of the PEOPLE magazine article about Henry and Bluebird, and felt compelled to visit, although none could articulate exactly why. One couple said they had seen the magazine article, happened to be in St. Louis for a wedding, and decided to drive over. When Shirlene asked them why, they said they didn't know, but maybe it was because life seemed so vague, and here in Henry Dunstan's example was someone who had left something tangible behind. Shirlene Mack, Melissa, and the other ladies in the Bluebird Society decided to organize brief walking tours of town, for five dollars a person or ten dollars for a carload. The tour consisted of a visit to the site of the original schoolhouse, then to Campbell's Dry Goods, and then a walk up to the workshop.

One day in August of 2017, Melissa walked a tour group from Main up to the Bluebird hills to see the workshop. Melissa wore sandals, a gray skirt, and a white tanktop. The group, Melissa learned, was from Dallas, and was in St. Louis for some type of health food convention. They had taken a day off from the conference, rented a van, and driven over to Bluebird as a group of ten.

Several people in the group were out of shape, and the walk was a slow, laborious one. Melissa walked at the head of the group. They eventually reached the plateau from which the workshop and its walls were visible. They all stood there for a while.

"Who built this?" one of the tourists asked out loud to no one in particular.

"Someone who understood that a rock will always outlive a man," a second tourist replied.

"He must have had a heavy weight about him," a third tourist said.

"I have a heaviness in my chest just beholding his work," the first tourist added.

"It's like an enormous piece of flint," the second tourist said, in reverence.

"No, the whole thing is a gravestone," said the third tourist.

Melissa walked a few feet away from the group. Her tanktop was soaked through with sweat. This was her second walk up the hills today. She had quoted the tour group ten dollars for a car load, but they had arrived in a van. She decided she would charge them twenty dollars for the tour. Next summer the Bluebird Society would start a website and sell t-shirts and mugs and bumper stickers. These would say things such as *Bluebird, Missouri* or *Because Rocks*. Melissa had already inquired with PEOPLE magazine about licensing the photograph taken from above of the workshop and its surrounding walls. She believed they would get some kind of deal done. Maybe the Society would even rent out a couple of ATVs so that tourists could drive up the hills instead of walking. Five, ten, twenty dollars at a time, she and the Society would collect the money needed to rebuild Bluebird. Five, ten, twenty years from now, Bluebird would be stronger than it now was, and there'd be more jobs and more shops in town, and her kids, when they finished college and got married, would come back and raise their own families in Bluebird.

OTHER ANAPHORA LITERARY PRESS TITLES

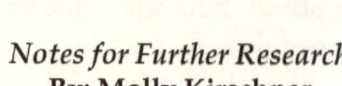

The History of British and American Author-Publishers
By: Anna Faktorovich

Notes for Further Research
By: Molly Kirschner

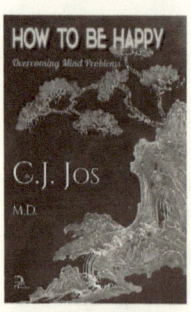

The Encyclopedic Philosophy of Michel Serres
By: Keith Moser

The Visit
By: Michael G. Casey

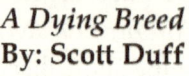

How to Be Happy
By: C. J. Jos

A Dying Breed
By: Scott Duff

Love in the Cretaceous
By: Howard W. Robertson

The Second of Seven
By: Jeremie Guy

www.ingramcontent.com/pod-product-compliance
Lightning Source LLC
Chambersburg PA
CBHW031956010726
47493CB00007B/2218